KV-513-367

'You have humiliated me, Colonel,' he said
quietly. 'You have caused me to lose the trust
of the people for whom I have worked for many
years. You have brought about the death of one
of our most valued agents: Fraulein Eklund, for
whom the younger Von Regen felt a special
affection. Now his father, the count, is on his
way here to see for himself that you will no
longer be a problem. It humiliates me even
further that he feels required to do this.'
'You better tell your count all you've got is one
man,' I grunted. 'The others will keep going.
They don't need me.'

# Brass Diamonds

**BERENT SANDBERG**

SPHERE BOOKS LIMITED
30-32 Gray's Inn Road, London WC1X 8JL

First published in Great Britain by
Sphere Books Ltd 1983
Copyright © 1981 by Peter Lars Sandberg and Berent &
Woods, Inc.
Published by arrangement with the New American Library,
Inc., New York, N.Y.

TRADE
MARK

This book is sold subject to the condition that
it shall not, by way of trade or otherwise, be lent,
re-sold, hired out or otherwise circulated without
the publisher's prior consent in any form of
binding or cover other than that in which it is
published and without a similar condition
including this condition being imposed on the
subsequent purchaser.

Set in Linotron Times

Printed and bound in Great Britain by
Collins, Glasgow

To Nancy and Mary Bess

# 1

My first thought when I heard the door open was that someone had the wrong room key. I was staying at the Wiesbaden Bachelor Officers' Quarters, where mistakes like that could happen whenever you got a non-German desk clerk on the late shift. The room was dark. It smelled of booze and sex, Rhine wine and Rhine-maiden sweat. The girl lying beside me was naked and asleep. I'd been using her breast as a pillow. It was a fine full breast, and though I couldn't remember the girl's name, or how we'd met, or what we'd done after I'd slipped her into the BOQ, it annoyed me someone was about to see her this way.

I raised my head and squinted towards the door. Two men were standing there, outlined against the soft yellow light of the hall.

'You've got the wrong room,' I said. 'Shut the door when you leave.'

I had expected whoever had barged in like this to be US military: a major or colonel who, as soon as he saw the room was occupied, would start to back out, mumbling his apologies, trying not to stare at the girl, staring all the while.

But the two men I saw in the door didn't look military or US, and there was nothing apologetic about them.

They came in. Before I could say anything more, one of them pressed the light button, flooding the room with two hundred watts. I blinked and swore. The men were similar in height, each just under six feet. Both wore green Bavarian hats, the kind with little häer feathers

tucked in the band; both had on green suits and striped ties. There the resemblance between them ended. The one who had turned on the light was narrow. His partner was wide. For a half-moment they stood gazing at me, as if in fact they had made a mistake. Then the narrow guy nodded and said, 'Ja, Ja, this is the one,' and the wide guy turned to close the door.

I felt the blood pump through my neck, and a building sense of rage. I smelled of rut and sweat, had a three-day start on a beard, was carrying twenty pounds over my best weight. My lungs ached from cigarette smoke; there was a whiskey thump in my head. In my better days, I might have tried to negotiate. Those days were gone.

I exploded off the bed, trailing as I did the top sheet that had covered me and all of the girl below her breast. The wide guy had just gotten the door shut when I hit him kidney-high, full press with my shoulder. I heard the wind go out of him and the splintering sound of the upper door panel as he went through. I rolled to my right, certain the narrow guy would be on me in an instant. The girl sat bolt upright in bed. The whites of her eyes were showing and she was mouthing soft gulping screams with her hands pressed flat to the sides of her head.

'Call the desk!' I shouted. 'Get somebody up here!'

I started for the narrow guy. He wasn't six feet away and I was so ginned up I didn't realize at first that he had a gun.

'*Halt!*' he said, as I lunged towards him.

The gun was a small-calibre nickel-plated automatic. He held it with both hands, muzzle pointed at the level of my nose. By the time I managed to skid to a stop, I was close enough to smell the solvent he used the last time he cleaned the barrel.

'Okay,' I croaked. 'Okay. You win.'

His voice was unemotional. He told me to back to the wall and stand there with my hands flat on my head. I did that. He gestured at the girl with his gun and told her

2

to keep still. She did that, stopping in the middle of a scream, her eyes still wide, her hands still pressed to the sides of her head.

The wide guy was struggling to pull his head and shoulders back through the door. I could hear him grunting and cursing, and when he finally freed himself his hat was flat and there were plywood splinters sticking like quills from the lapels of his suit. He located me and came for me, lumbering across the room. I looked past him at the narrow guy, feeling just about as naked as I had ever felt in my life.

'Karl!' the narrow guy said. '*Nein!*' But Karl wasn't listening. His face was blood-red and meaty. His eyes were the size of dimes. When he reached me, he planted himself and hit me twice in the gut, one left, one right, and as I doubled over he brought his knee up hard into my groin. I cried out and went down.

The floor was cold. I lay on my side, holding myself, knees drawn tight to my chest, gritting my teeth to keep from sobbing like a baby. The girl was watching me from the bed. She was still sitting upright, had pulled the bottom sheet up around her shoulders. Karl had gone to stand beside the bed, just behind her. She looked terrified. When the narrow guy said something in German, Karl reached around and clamped his hand across her mouth. She began to struggle. The sheet fell away.

'*Fräulein, bitte*,' the narrow guy said. 'It is useless for you to try to resist. We have no wish to harm you.'

He put the automatic on the bedside table, unrolled a leather pouch he had taken from the vest pocket of his suit. I tried to get up, but I couldn't. He had a piece of surgical tubing, a small rubber-capped bottle, and a disposable syringe. The girl's breast lay heavily along her arm. He moved it away, tied the arm off between her elbow and shoulder.

'You will sleep for a while. That is all,' he said. His

voice was impersonal. 'Try to relax. We don't want the needle to break.'

He gave her the injection. She began to go limp even before he had finished. I was on my knees, trembling, ready to vomit. The anger-adrenaline surge, the familiar copper taste in my mouth, had gone sour. The narrow guy put his kit away, picked up his gun, and looked at me.

'It is fortunate for all of us, Colonel Eberhart,' he said, 'that the rest of the rooms on this floor are unoccupied. We were told at the desk that you had had a great deal to drink and were in no condition to cause trouble.'

'I didn't cause any trouble,' I croaked. There was a sofa along the wall behind me. He gestured towards it, told me to sit. When I still had trouble getting up, Karl came over and gave me a hand. He had a grip like a bolt cutter. The narrow guy produced a large folding wallet from the other vest pocket of his suit. He thumbed out a paper and handed it to me.

'You will read this,' he said.

'Sure,' I told him. But I was dizzy, and very bubbly in the gut, so I put the paper next to me on the sofa and reached for a green bottle of tafelwein that was open on the end table. Karl took a step towards me, but I shook my head. There wasn't any fight left in me. All I wanted was a drink. He backed off and I took the bottle and gulped down some of the wine.

'I'd like my shorts,' I said, trying to gain some control. 'They're on the floor by the foot of the bed. My cigarettes should be there too.'

Karl went and brought them back. I hauled on the shorts, stuck the last of my Raleigh filters between my teeth. The narrow guy flashed his lighter, a Siemens electric. I didn't want to, but I let him light me up. The two quarter-size scars on my back were flaming. I could feel them. They always did that whenever I felt anger or fear or humiliation.

'How about covering the girl,' I said.

The narrow guy snatched the top sheet from the floor, floated it once over her, snapped it into place. His eyes were the same green color as his suit, and they only flickered once as the sheet settled. He wasn't paid to letch, and he was proving it.

I picked up the paper he had given me. It was a telex: thin stock, carbon-backed, first copy. I read the machine print.

LIEUTENANT COLONEL MATTHEW B. EBER-
 HART, USAF (RETIRED)
AMERICAN ARMS BOQ, ROOM 239
FRANKFURTER STRASSE 17
WIESBADEN, WEST GERMANY
21-NOVEMBER-75
COME TO WHITE OAKS AT ONCE. THERE IS
 HOPE FOR YOUR SON.
COYLE

# 2

I read the message twice, slowly, word for word. By the time I had finished reading it a second time, my hands were trembling. There was only one subject on earth that could bring me to White Oaks, and it was typical of the man who had sent me this cable to know what it was and to use it. I looked up. The narrow guy was watching me.

'So you work for Coyle,' I said.

'That is correct, Colonel. My name is Dieter Hoefel – Deutsche Coyle GmbH.' He pronounced the letters: *Gay Em Bay Hah*. They were the German equivalent of 'Incorporated' or 'Limited.'

'There's a phone in this room,' I said. 'I've been staying here for six months. You could have called.'

'Our orders were to deliver the message personally.'

'In the middle of the night?'

'We were told the matter was urgent.'

I shook my head. 'My son's been in a deep coma at Walter Reed Hospital for over a year,' I said. 'His prognosis for recovery is practically zero.'

'Surely there are new medical discoveries happening every day,' Dieter Hoefel said. He sounded conciliatory. 'Here in Germany, for example . . .'

'No,' I said. 'One of my son's nurses is a close personal friend. If there was anything like that, she'd have the information to me within an hour of hearing about it. Ditto any change in my son's condition.'

Dieter shrugged. 'We have our orders, Colonel,' he said.

6

'To strong-arm that girl and dope her up?'

'The situation for us in Wiesbaden is not as dependable as it used to be. We've lost certain connections. Were she to attract the attention of the police before we left the city, the situation could become difficult.'

'I could attract just one hell of a lot of attention between here and your car,' I said. 'Now that I know who you work for, I don't think you're going to use that gun.'

Dieter Hoefel nodded gravely. 'We have an extra syringe, Colonel,' he said. 'We would hope that among gentlemen there would be no need to use it.'

I finished what was left of the wine. It was too warm and sweet. The bottle felt sticky in my hand. Big Karl watched me, looking as if it would suit him fine to see the needle go up my arm. Dieter checked his watch.

'You have one hour fifteen only to your flight,' he said. 'There is time to shower and dress. You can shave in the car. Please hurry, Colonel.'

Twenty minutes later, we were on our way out of the BOQ. I had gotten into a sports jacket, slacks, turtleneck, had thrown my kit into my bag along with a change of clothes, carried my trench coat over my arm. Coyle's boys had already signed me out and paid my bill. I wondered how much the desk clerk had made on that deal. He had agreed to go up when he got off duty and take care of the few personal belongings I had left in the room. I guessed it was going to surprise him some when he saw what had happened to the door and found the girl, sleeping like a child.

We went out the double set of swinging doors and along the walk to the parking lot. The night was still dark at this late hour, and our breaths fogged in front of us as we made our way across the well-trampled snow. There was a low overcast. Terrible flying weather, I thought. Instruments only.

The Coyle limousine was a Mercedes 600 Landaulet with German BN plates, indicating it was out of Bonn, 118 kilometres north up the Rhine. The car was glossy black where it wasn't slush-spattered, and it carried three antennae on the trunk.

Dieter and I got into the rear seat. I got in slowly. I hurt. Big Karl wedged himself behind the wheel. He raised the glass partition between the front and rear seats, engaged the automatic locks on the rear doors. Then, just as the Rathaus morning bells began to ring, he fired up the big six-liter engine and we were off. We moved southeast towards Berliner Strasse and the Erbenheim entrance to the number 66 Autobahn. Our destination would be the international airport outside Frankfurt. I sighed, wanting a cigarette, remembering I was all out. Dieter seemed to sense my discomfort. He pointed to a dark walnut cabinet that had been built into a desk area in front of us.

'Pull this down, so, Colonel,' he said.

I pulled it down, so, and there everything was: two telephones; a television set with a ten-inch screen; computer terminal; stainless-steel washbasin, mini-refrigerator, drink service, gooseneck lamp, Dictaphone; neat little pigeonholes with useful items for the office and bar. Everything Mr R. J. Coyle would want to impress his clients and connections in this particular part of the world. I found a pack of Dunhills, shook one out, and lit up.

Coyle had come from old-line money in northern Virginia. He had served under my father in the OSS during the Second World War. My father had been killed on a mission after he, Coyle, and my future father-in-law, Campbell Cooke, had parachuted into the Alps in 1944.

Coyle had gone into the war rich and had managed somehow to come out even richer. He was Mr International Megabucks now in import-export, was involved

with everything from fighter aircraft to Oriental art. From what I had heard in recent years, he seldom left White Oaks anymore – his estate in Virginia that was so big it had its own zip code.

Campbell Cooke was Boston Brahmin with a pedigree that went back to the *Mayflower*. Not much money in the family, but a lot of the kind of rock-ribbed integrity I had always admired. Campbell had served with distinction during the war, and when it was over had gone on to make his career with the CIA. I had married his daughter, Diana, and though she was gone now, I still saw Campbell from time to time. He had no use for the skid I'd been on since I'd retired from the Air Force, and he had told me so more than once.

As for Coyle, I hadn't seen him in sixteen years – not since I had married Diana and our reception had been held at White Oaks (Coyle's gift to us, and one that I could have done without). I had never liked him, his methods, the sort of people he employed, the way – unlike most of us – he always seemed to get whatever he wanted.

'You seem distracted, Colonel,' Dieter Hoefel said. 'Would you like a brandy?'

'Yes,' I said. He poured me one. We were accelerating up 66 past Flugplatz Wiesbaden. Through the early-morning fog I could see rows of US Army M-113's parked along a runway I'd used many years ago. Then, before Headquarters USAF/Europe moved to Ramstein and the Fourth Armored Brigade came to clutter up the place with their tracked vehicles, I'd been a young lieutenant fresh out of the fighter school at Nellis.

In love with my country, wildly in love with my fighters. I'd flown the last of the sport models, the F-86 Sabrejet, out of Spangdahlem. We had dogfights with the Canucks in the thin air over the continent, gunnery practice in the Libyan desert, tense alert at Fursty. We

were all of us filled with ourselves, and I could have gone on like that forever. Bright-eyed and bushy-tailed.

Eyes dim now, tail tattered. From the 86s I'd gone on to the F-100, then to the big F-4, the Phantom. The years of practice over Europe and Africa turned to years of combat over the Delta, the Trail, up North – my enthusiasm for the cause waning steadily from the moment I began to realize we were being programmed to lose.

Then the assignment in Cambodia that all but ended my life.

The lights of the oncoming traffic loomed and flared through an atmosphere that was gritty and ghost-grey.

I put my brandy on the desk in front of me, found the Norelco, and began to shave.

'Your beard changes your appearance, Colonel,' Dieter said.

'Coyle sent you a picture, I suppose.'

'We had one on file with your dossier at our headquarters in Bonn. Your features are angular, almost Prussian. The beard softens them. Also you are wearing your hair longer. There was a moment back there when I was certain we had the wrong room.'

He reached into his jacket pocket, handed me a photo. It was the one used in my promotion folder. There I was, in Class A's with ribbons. Angular face looking here as if I were bucking for full colonel. Hair a lot shorter then, and lighter from the Asian sun. They always photograph you from the left angle so all the hero stuff shows. In this picture the flash from that side also brought out the two-inch scar on my left cheekbone. It looked as if it had been earned in combat, and I suppose in a way it had. I had gotten it when I was eight years old, growing up in Montana. Another kid and I were horsing around in the junkyard outside Wolf Point. He sailed a licence plate my way. The wind caught it and slammed it smack against my face.

That had happened in 1944, the year my father was killed in the war. I remember him as a taciturn engineer with a degree from the Montana School of Mines and a speciality in demolitions. By the time I graduated from high school, my mother had died of cancer, brought on I think at least in part by her grief over the loss of him. I enlisted in the Air Force at eighteen.

'I didn't know Coyle had been keeping tabs on me,' I said, as I handed back the photo.

'Would you care to see the file?'

'Yes,' I said. 'I would.'

I put the razor away, picked up the brandy. I was curious to see what kind of information about my life Coyle and his people had seen fit to store in the memory bank of their Central European computer in Bonn. Dieter dialed his code into the terminal. It took less than a minute for the data request to start showing up on the television screen.

| OFFICER CAREER BRIEF | EBERHART MATTHEW B. | AFSN470286484 |
|---|---|---|

| COMPONENT USAF/REG | DATE PREPARED 75 NOV 21 | REASON GENERATED INQUIRY CLASSIFIED |
|---|---|---|

STATION OF ASSIGNMENT
   RETIRED

SPECIAL EXPERIENCE IDENTITY
   COUNTERINSURGENCY OPERATIONS
   UNCONVENTIONAL WARFARE
   LANGUAGE FRENCH     FAMILIARITY FAR EASTERN
   DIPLOMAT COMBAT ZONE

TEST PILOT NATO FIGHTERS
PARACHUTIST SPECIAL FORCES


TOTAL FLYING TIME
  4784


TOTAL COMBAT FLYING TIME

| 752 HOURS | JET | F-100 | F-4 | |
|-----------|------|-------|------|------|
| 303 HOURS | PROP | U-10 | T-28 | C-47 |


TECHNICAL SCHOOLS
  JUNGLE    SEA    DESERT    SURVIVAL
  DEFENSE LANGUAGE INSTITUTE

PROFESSIONAL SCHOOLS
  SOS    ACSC    DIS

AERONAUTICAL RATING
  COMMAND PILOT


AWARDS AND DECORATIONS
  I X SILVER STAR    2 X DISTINGUISHED FLYING CROSS
  I X BRONZE         2 X PURPLE HEART         26 X AIR
     STAR                                        MEDAL
  I X VIETNAMESE CROSS OF GALLANTRY   I X LEGION
                                         OF MERIT
  I X CAMBODIAN DIVISIONAL MEDAL


CURRENT DEPENDANTS DATA
  ADULT
     WIFE DIANA (NEE) COOKE        KILLED IN ACTION
  CHILDREN
     I MALE    BRIAN    DISABLED    WOUNDED IN
                                        ACTION

'Shut it off,' I said.

'Of course,' Dieter Hoefel said.

We had turned off the number 66 Autobahn and were rolling east on E5. I finished the brandy, poured myself another. Dieter watched me through his green eyes.

'Is everything satisfactory, Colonel?' he asked.

'Sure,' I said. 'Everything's swell.'

# 3

Karl and Dieter walked me through passport control at Frankfurt Main. The people who mattered there seemed to know them. Big Karl was careful to keep a couple of steps behind me. Dieter walked by my side. He had left his dope kit in the car and appeared almost relaxed now that his responsibility for me was about to end.

We walked up the long, wide ramp to the international lounge, which resembled a large, very plush American shopping mall. Here departing travellers could buy the finest products tax-free. As with all international shops, the markup matched the tax savings. There were posters in several of the shop windows urging the German voter to come out for Helmut Schmidt in the upcoming election for chancellor. Dieter said that with Brandt's resignation the year before due to the spy scandal, the '76 election was going to be rough for any but the cleanest of candidates.

'I stopped caring about politics a long time ago,' I said. He smiled as he handed me my first-class ticket.

'You may take your suitcase directly on board; it has been arranged with the authorities,' he said. 'You will be met at Dulles by one of our drivers. *Auf Wiedersehen*, Colonel.'

'Your gun's showing,' I said. He smiled, as if his modesty prevented him from letting me know he was permitted to carry it. He adjusted his suit coat. I looked at big Karl.

'You need a new hat,' I said. 'I'll bring you one when I come back.'

14

'Please, Colonel,' Dieter Hoefel said.

'My balls still ache,' I said.

'Neither was it so nice what you did to poor Karl,' Dieter said. 'Now, be a good boy. They're holding the flight.'

The plane was a Lufthansa 747. As soon as I boarded I arranged with the first-class purser to downgrade myself to cabin class. The purser, a young German named Georg (*Gay-org*, as the crew called him), was not happy about my wanting to do this.

'The flight has been for you delayed fifteen minutes already, Colonel,' he said. 'You will take your assigned seat and wait until after takeoff to go aft.'

'No, sorry,' I said. 'I'll be going aft now. Put my bag in one of your storage compartments. I'll be strapped in in plenty of time before we roll.'

Gayorg told me this was highly irregular, and I suppose it was. But unless I'm doing the actual flying I always make it a point to sit as far aft as I can: away from the fuel in the wings and near the best avenues of escape should anything go wrong during takeoff or landing.

Besides that, the armrests fold up back there and the long seat rows make a fine bed. You can't do that in first class.

The plane began to taxi as I walked aft. I guessed it was about two-thirds full – well over a hundred in cabin class. Several of them looked at me as I passed, making it clear by their expressions they did not appreciate this rough-looking lout in a turtleneck who had apparently delayed their flight.

*Take it up with Mr R. J. Coyle*, I wanted to say. *He's your man.*

I took a seat aisle-side, last row starboard, and buckled myself in. Except for me, the row was empty. By long habit, I fixed in my mind the wing and aft exit doors and the turn direction of the handles so if I had to I could work one upside down in smoke and dark.

15

Then I heard the swelling scream of the engines and felt the gentle G-forces as the captain did all required to meet Newton's law and Bernoulli's principle. We got airborne without any help from me at all. He took off westerly from Frankfurt and eased into a right turn. I could see the Rhine and Main rivers converge; Wiesbaden, set east of the Rhine and west of the Taunus mountains, fast disappearing as we entered the cloud cover.

We hadn't finished our climb to cruising altitude before I began to doze. I remember hoping as I felt myself start to go that the bomb that killed Diana and all but destroyed Brian would not go off in my dreams, that I wouldn't wake suddenly with a scream in my throat and the other passengers all peering back and Gayorg and his merry band rushing down the aisle with restraining devises and sedatives.

After two combat flying tours in Vietnam, I had been assigned in August of '72 as air attaché to our embassy in Cambodia. In spite of the war raging around Phnom Penh, the Defense Intelligence Agency classified the city as safe for dependants. I was told the final decision as to whether or not I should ask Diana and Brian to join me there would have to be mine.

Swamped with the details of my new job, I put that decision off for almost a year, while my wife and son urged me in letters from Washington to let them come over. Finally, in the summer of '73, I agreed. Other families had already arrived. And I found I had missed mine more than I had ever believed I could.

They flew commercial to Bangkok, then transferred to an Air Cambodge Caravel for the flight to Phnom Penh. When I met them at the airport, they looked as fine to me as I had ever seen them: Diana radiant in tan slacks and blouse; Brian very much the world traveller in his green Dacron slacks and short-sleeved sport shirt; each

'Please, Colonel,' Dieter Hoefel said.

'My balls still ache,' I said.

'Neither was it so nice what you did to poor Karl,' Dieter said. 'Now, be a good boy. They're holding the flight.'

The plane was a Lufthansa 747. As soon as I boarded I arranged with the first-class purser to downgrade myself to cabin class. The purser, a young German named Georg (*Gay-org*, as the crew called him), was not happy about my wanting to do this.

'The flight has been for you delayed fifteen minutes already, Colonel,' he said. 'You will take your assigned seat and wait until after takeoff to go aft.'

'No, sorry,' I said. 'I'll be going aft now. Put my bag in one of your storage compartments. I'll be strapped in in plenty of time before we roll.'

Gayorg told me this was highly irregular, and I suppose it was. But unless I'm doing the actual flying I always make it a point to sit as far aft as I can: away from the fuel in the wings and near the best avenues of escape should anything go wrong during takeoff or landing.

Besides that, the armrests fold up back there and the long seat rows make a fine bed. You can't do that in first class.

The plane began to taxi as I walked aft. I guessed it was about two-thirds full – well over a hundred in cabin class. Several of them looked at me as I passed, making it clear by their expressions they did not appreciate this rough-looking lout in a turtleneck who had apparently delayed their flight.

*Take it up with Mr R. J. Coyle*, I wanted to say. *He's your man.*

I took a seat aisle-side, last row starboard, and buckled myself in. Except for me, the row was empty. By long habit, I fixed in my mind the wing and aft exit doors and the turn direction of the handles so if I had to I could work one upside down in smoke and dark.

Then I heard the swelling scream of the engines and felt the gentle G-forces as the captain did all required to meet Newton's law and Bernoulli's principle. We got airborne without any help from me at all. He took off westerly from Frankfurt and eased into a right turn. I could see the Rhine and Main rivers converge; Wiesbaden, set east of the Rhine and west of the Taunus mountains, fast disappearing as we entered the cloud cover.

We hadn't finished our climb to cruising altitude before I began to doze. I remember hoping as I felt myself start to go that the bomb that killed Diana and all but destroyed Brian would not go off in my dreams, that I wouldn't wake suddenly with a scream in my throat and the other passengers all peering back and Gayorg and his merry band rushing down the aisle with restraining devises and sedatives.

After two combat flying tours in Vietnam, I had been assigned in August of '72 as air attaché to our embassy in Cambodia. In spite of the war raging around Phnom Penh, the Defense Intelligence Agency classified the city as safe for dependants. I was told the final decision as to whether or not I should ask Diana and Brian to join me there would have to be mine.

Swamped with the details of my new job, I put that decision off for almost a year, while my wife and son urged me in letters from Washington to let them come over. Finally, in the summer of '73, I agreed. Other families had already arrived. And I found I had missed mine more than I had ever believed I could.

They flew commercial to Bangkok, then transferred to an Air Cambodge Caravel for the flight to Phnom Penh. When I met them at the airport, they looked as fine to me as I had ever seen them: Diana radiant in tan slacks and blouse; Brian very much the world traveller in his green Dacron slacks and short-sleeved sport shirt; each

with a couple of suitcases and an over-the-shoulder bag.

It took the usual twenty-four hours for them to get over their jet lag; then we were off to a gala reception held in their honour by the senior Army attaché.

They settled easily into the house where I had been living. The servants liked Diana, and she liked them. Brian began attending the French Lycée in Phnom Penh. He was a better-than-average student who, by early '74, had distinguished himself by winning the highest honours of his class.

Then one bright morning in March, a Cambodian fighter pilot named Tru decided to defect to the Khmer Rouge. He took off from Pochentong in a T-28 prop job with two MK-82 500-pounders aboard, and on his way out of the city he made two passes at the palace of the Cambodian premier. Killing the premier would assure Tru a fine welcome in the North. It was the kind of harebrained stunt none of us had anticipated.

Tru's first bomb fell long. His second fell short. The short bomb exploded a yard and a half from my house. Diana and Brian were home. I was at the embassy, four blocks away. I heard the bomb go off. I've been hearing it go off ever since.

Coyle knew all this, of course. I had received from him at the time a handwritten note of sympathy which I had never bothered to answer. I had gone on to finish my tour in Cambodia, then had retired my commission. The rest had been a history of drunken nights and hungover days and women whose names I couldn't remember or maybe had forgotten to ask.

COME TO WHITE OAKS AT ONCE. THERE IS HOPE FOR YOUR SON. From the moment I first read Coyle's message, I had a hunch he was in trouble. I had no idea if my hunch was correct, but the idea intrigued me. COME TO WHITE OAKS AT ONCE. That was the thrust of the message. Coyle wanted to see me in person, and badly

enough to authorize the use of automatic pistols and hypodermic syringes (and a promise of hope for my son) to see to it that I arrived.

Though he had a flair for the dramatic, Coyle loathed publicity. Personal items about him seldom appeared in the news. There had been a kidnap attempt a couple of years back; since then nothing that I knew. A month or so ago one of his enterprises in Uganda – a large coffee plantation – had been sealed off by Amin. Some of Coyle's key people had been visiting at the time and, so far at least, had not been allowed to leave. I could easily imagine that Coyle was furious about this, that he had perhaps decided to put together a mercenary group to go in and bring his people out. For that kind of operation he would need a pilot.

But all this was speculation. I really had nothing to go on. Just my hunch, and Dieter Hoefel's comment to me that whatever this matter was, it had become urgent.

I don't know how long I had been asleep when I sprang suddenly awake to the touch of the stewardess's hand on my shoulder. She looked worried, spoke softly.

'Colonel Eberhart?' she said. 'Please forgive me . . .'

'What's wrong?' I said.

'The captain wishes to have a word with you. Would you follow me, please?'

The lights were dim in cabin class. Many of the passengers were asleep. Most of the ones who weren't were tuned in to the in-flight movie. They had their stereo headsets on and paid no attention to us as we went by. There was no turbulence, no indication we were doing anything other than cruising peacefully above thirty thousand feet.

Then we entered the first-class section and I caught the odour of cordite and burnt flesh.

It was an odour so familiar to me that for a moment I thought I had been transplanted through some warp of

time and space back to the killing grounds of the Far East.

The atmosphere in the first-class section was subdued. All of the passengers had turned in their seats to look down the aisle to where the Lufthansa captain and a doctor were attending to a third man, who lay on his back. The third man was groaning. He looked to be middle-aged, was stout, balding, wore wire-rimmed spectacles and a business suit. The right sleeve of his suit coat and right cuff of his shirt were charred halfway to his elbow. Part of the heel of his hand was gone. The stewardess looked away.

'What happened?' I asked.

'I don't know,' she said. 'He had just ordered an after-breakfast drink. I was bringing it to him, and all of a sudden there was a *poof* of flame like an explosion without much sound . . .'

'Where was he sitting?'

'Right there.'

I took a look at the seat she had indicated. The right armrest was badly scorched. There was a black smear running up the food tray on the opposite seat back. The ashtray had melted into a crusty green lump. I took a sniff, but I didn't have to. The odour was unmistakable.

'What can you tell us about this, Colonel?' the Lufthansa captain said. He was a darkly handsome man in a white shirt and tie, black pants, an officer's cap set precisely on his head. He spoke quietly.

'I'd say somebody put a ration of black powder in the ashtray,' I replied. 'It wasn't packed tightly enough to explode, but the coal of a cigarette would have been all it would take to set it off like a flare.'

'Are you acquainted with the gentleman?'

'No. I've never seen him before.'

'His name is Bennett. First name Myron. He's from Chicago, returning now from a three-week business trip

in Europe. He is employed as a salesman by Agro-Chem Corporation. His passport and credentials seem to be in order.'

'Does he know why someone would want to do this to him?'

'He believes it was an accident. He upgraded from cabin class shortly after takeoff. The purser gave him the seat that originally had been assigned to you.'

I looked at the scorched armrest and at Myron Bennett, who lay in the aisle not far from the place where I stood. The doctor had put a wet bandage on the hand and was giving him a sedative. Most of the first-class passengers had turned away, now the excitement was over. I felt the hair rise on the back of my neck. From the upstairs lounge I could hear the tinkle of a piano and a clinking of glass.

'I'm on board as a guest of Deutsche Coyle,' I said.

'Of course,' the captain said. 'I am aware of that.'

'If that ashtray was booby-trapped for me,' I said, 'I haven't got a clue as to who did it or why.'

'Almost certainly whoever did do it is still on the aeroplane, wouldn't you agree?' the captain asked.

'Yes,' I said.

'We have 169 passengers on the manifest. Twenty-one first-class. 148 cabin-class.' He shrugged. 'Unless you were to recognize someone . . .'

'There's no one in here,' I said. 'I've already looked. I'll check the lounge before I go back. Can you vouch for your crew?'

'Without question.'

'Are you going to make an unscheduled landing to get him to a hospital?'

'No. Mr Bennett says he prefers to continue on.'

'Have you radioed Dulles?'

'Not yet.'

'I'd appreciate your keeping my name off your report.'

'Of course.'

The captain took off his cap, ran a hand through his hair, put the cap back on. Then he looked down at Myron Bennett and sighed. 'It's a trick of fate, you know?' he said. 'Herr Bennett tells us that he gave up cigarettes a month ago. Since then he has allowed himself one cigar only after each meal.'

'Maybe he'll give those up now,' I said.

'I can see, Colonel,' the captain said, 'that you are a man of compassion.'

The captain returned to the flight deck. I had a Scotch-rocks in the upper lounge. There were a half-dozen people playing backgammon and skat at the café tables, a half-dozen more sitting around the piano bar. Most of them were far enough into their in-flight drinking to be high-spirited, and as far as I could tell, none of them paid me any attention or even seemed aware something had happened downstairs. The piano player, a rumpled-looking man with a rounded chin and protruding belly, was playing '*O du lieber Augustin*' over and over as if it was, perhaps, the only tune he knew. He kept hitting a sour bass note, which caused the people in the lounge to laugh. I studied each face long enough to be sure I had not seen it before, then returned to my seat in cabin class, checked my ashtray, and settled in.

I knew the captain might be right in his assumption that the booby trap had been rigged for me, but I was not quite as ready as he had been to accept Myron Bennett for the man he appeared. The fact that his passport was in order and he carried the credentials of a legitimate salesman could add up to nothing more than run-of-the-mill cover for a clandestine operator.

Whoever had dropped the powder was certainly professional enough to do it after Myron had upgraded to first class. All he would have needed was a few

seconds on his way up the aisle, with Myron off to the head or maybe even dozing in his seat.

I began to favour this theory, because it was comfortable and because I couldn't think of one reason why somebody would want to torch the hand of a beat-up fighter jock, even if he were travelling compliments of R. J. Coyle. As far as I was concerned at the moment, the odds looked pretty fair that it was Mr Bennett and not me who had an enemy on board.

So, Eberhart, I thought. Keep your eyes open, check your six-o'clock position, and enjoy the flight.

The stewardess brought me the food and drink service I had missed during my nap. I ate heartily, with scarcely a thought that the breakfast sausage might be laced with cyanide. Whoever had Bennett's contract (or mine) had been told to disable, not kill.

Once I had finished and the service had been cleared, I peeled my stereo headset out of its sealed bag and put it on.

I like most kinds of music, and whenever I have a choice, I'll go with whatever suits my mood. The in-flight classical track was featuring Puccini's *La Bohème*. I dialed in, checked my ashtray again, lit a cigarette.

Of my 147 fellow passengers in cabin class, not one looked or acted in any way that struck me as suspicious. They drank their drinks, peeled their oranges, walked up and down the aisles, talked to each other, and slept. The movie had ended; most of the headsets had been put away. I wondered if the few that remained were tuned to the opera. It was, always had been, a favourite of mine. Mimi's aria at the end of act one had been known to bring a lump to my throat.

This time, however, it brought me something else.

The performance was in Italian, one of Toscanini's that had been recorded in the mid-'40's. Licia Albanese was the soprano who had Mimi's role. She had just

22

begun to sing '*Si. Mi chiamano Mimì*' when the opera suddenly went dead and I heard a male voice speak sharply in French:

'*Attention! Colonel Eberhart. N'allez pas à White Oaks sous peine de mort. Attention! Colonel Eberhart . . .*'

I yanked the headset off, made my way up the aisle. Three stewardesses were gossiping beside one of the galleys.

'Who's been using your intercom?' I asked. They looked at me as if I were crazy. I pointed to the console on the wall beside us. It was set up like a wall telephone: standard receiver; toggle switches; labels indicating each of the available channels and hookups.

'Is there some problem?' the senior stewardess asked.

'I just got a message through my headset,' I said. 'I'd give a lot to know who sent it.'

'You must be mistaken,' she said. 'No one is permitted to use the public-address system except for the crew.'

'Have you been standing here long?'

'Ten minutes.'

'There are other consoles like this, aren't there?'

'Yes. Three others.'

'I'd like to have a look at them.'

She touched her finger to the side of her head, looked at her fellow workers.

'Yeah, I know,' I said. 'But the minute you humour me, I go away.'

She showed me the other consoles. One was in view of the first. The other two were similarly placed on the opposite side of the big centre galley.

'That's funny,' she said when we came to the last.

'What?' I said.

'All the switches are supposed to be down when the console is not in use.'

There were six switches in all. They were labelled

23

Flight Deck, Purser, Engineer, Ground, Cabin Speaker, Headset. The Headset switch was up.

'We have some people who are feeling very good in the first-class lounge,' the stewardess said. 'I think maybe one of them played a joke on you.'

'Bet you're right,' I said.

'Is there anything else I can do for you?' she asked.

'Do you like opera?' I said.

'No,' she said. 'The opera is to me like a knife in my ear.'

I smiled. On my way back to my seat I passed a guy who was holding his headset in his hand, pointing at it and talking to his wife. He was French, and he sounded excited.

'*N'allez pas à White Oaks sous peine de mort!*' he said, repeating the message he too had heard.

Do not go to White Oaks.

Or you will die.

# 4

Campbell Cooke told me once I was one of the few people he knew who actually enjoyed being caught between a rock and a hard place. I guess there is some truth to that. When life becomes routine, I get bored. When I get bored, I drink too much and go to fat and don't like myself very much. That has always been true. It was true before I lost Diana, and even more true since.

But I wasn't exactly enjoying myself as I watched two orderlies load Myron Bennett on to a stretcher at Dulles. According to the doctor who had treated him on board, he would face months of painful skin grafting and would probably never have full use of his right hand again. All because he had had the bad luck to sit in my seat and light a cigar.

I stood alongside the stretcher, holding my bag, wanting to tell Myron it was a rotten world sometimes, where the innocent suffered and the guilty went unpunished and the cavalry didn't always arrive on time.

But Myron looked as if he already knew these things. Just before they put him into the ambulance, he glanced up at me. His eyes were dull, his skin wet and pale. He shook his head. 'My old lady's going to kill me for this,' he said.

'I'll give her a call, if you like,' I said.

'They already called her. She's going to murder me.'

'Take care of yourself, Myron,' I said.

I made my way to the terminal and went through customs, so preoccupied with the warning I had received

on the plane that it was several minutes before I became aware of the extraordinary presence standing patiently by my side.

He was a man just over five feet tall with shoulders almost as broad as he was high, and broken-knuckled hands that seemed to reach the floor. He wore a leather coat belted tightly around his narrow waist and a leather cap pulled low over his craggy brow. Everything about his face looked broken – his nose, his jaw, his teeth – as if he had spent most of his life as a prizefighter, and had never once won, and had never once quit.

'Right,' he said when he saw I had finally noticed him. 'You're Eberhart. I'm Maul.' He handed me his Coyle Enterprises ID, jerked his head towards the main parking area. When he spoke, it was as if it pained him to talk. 'Car's in the lot,' he said. 'When you're ready.'

'I'm ready now,' I said.

I had never liked the kind of people Coyle employed, but I found myself liking Maul at once. Though I sensed he was not a patient man, he had waited patiently for me to notice him. He had not called me 'Colonel' or even 'Mister,' just 'Eberhart.' And as we headed for the parking lot, he made no attempt to carry my bag.

Maul, I thought. The quintessential noncom. The man you wanted in the trench with you when the shells were falling like a monsoon rain and half your platoon was shot up and the other half was dead. Sergeant Maul: master sergeant or sergeant major. I'd have bet on it, but I wouldn't ask. Sooner or later, if he decided to, Maul would tell me.

The Coyle car this time was a black Lincoln Mark IV that gleamed in the late-afternoon sun as if someone had waxed it during the time it had taken Maul to find me. It had four trunk-mounted antennae: two telephones; one TV; one four-element yagi – this latter probably for a directional scramble line. I got in front with Maul. I've

never liked being driven places, have always felt like an idiot sitting in the back seat of a limousine or staff car.

'Have we got any cigarettes on board?' I asked as we pulled away. Maul shook his head. 'I haven't been to White Oaks in a long time,' I said. 'My memory tells me it took just under an hour from Dulles, but that was when the limit was seventy. I suppose it takes longer now.'

Maul accelerated.

'No,' he said. 'It's about the same.'

I yawned, feeling grainy and edgy but too keyed-up to sleep. A well-thumbed copy of the Washington *Post* lay on the seat between us. I picked it up, scanned the front page. Most of it was devoted to the fact that William Douglas had retired from the Supreme Court. I wondered if Douglas had been a favourite of Maul's, if that was why Maul had kept the paper. Somehow it didn't seem likely. Then, as I turned to the first inside page, the reason jumped out at me from a three-column head: 'COYLE ENTERPRISES POSSIBLE TARGET OF TALBOT SUBCOMMITTEE.'

Talbot, the senior senator from Virginia, had been elected to four terms largely on the strength of his one-committee crusade against the abuses of big business. He had already clipped the wings of several multinationals, exposing their practices of influence peddling, currency manipulation, tax evasion – whatever he and his earnest staff could uncover to embarrass the fat cats. His personal feud with Coyle was legendary.

I glanced at Maul. 'I see the old man made the papers,' I said.

After a considerable pause, Maul grunted a noncommittal 'Yeah.'

'Did you read it?' I knew he had.

Again the pause. 'I read it.'

'Well?' I said.

'Well what?' he replied, adjusting his knuckly hands on the wheel.

'Well what do you think about it?' I said.

This time the pause lingered into minutes as we sped through the golden autumn of Virginia. I had forgotten how beautiful it was: the rolling hills, the white board fences, the gnarled stately oaks.

'I think the senator's got better things to do than to insult Mr Coyle,' Maul said at last. And then, after a briefer pause, he added, 'And I think Mr Coyle has got better things to do than answer back.'

It was a carefully considered, balanced reply which told me exactly nothing.

I took a chance. 'Sergeant Major Maul,' I snapped, 'I'm *not* a straight leg.'

'Where'd you go through?' he shot back.

'Bad Tolz, '57, Tenth SFG.'

He glanced at me with what could have passed for a smile at the corner of his mouth. 'And I'm no sergeant major,' he said. 'When things went to hell at Bragg, I retired as an E-8, master sergeant.'

We talked shop for a while, and when I sensed we were as simpatico as we were going to get and that I had earned something of his respect, I pressed him again about Coyle and Talbot, and he told me exactly nothing more than what he had told me before.


You visit White Oaks once and you don't forget it, not for the rest of your life. Fifteen thousand acres of rolling pastureland planted in bluegrass with artful groves of white pine and poplar, and so many miles of fieldstone fencing you would walk for a week and not measure it all. Airstrip and heliport; heavy equipment and rail spur. Fifty greenhouses, each one big enough to park an F-4, all planted in tulips (one of Coyle's numerous and profitable hobbies). Herds of black Angus, and thoroughbred hunters. Swimming pools, tennis courts, a nine-hole golf course, a trout stream with a waterfall, small lakes and ponds.

An auxiliary power station (with no aboveground lines) provides emergency power to the property. An antenna farm with satellite-tracking dishes serves the communications net. There's a sanitary landfill and waste-disposal area (where on the fences after a rain, the buzzards stand, drying their wings). There are countless outbuildings and barns, a dozen guest cottages – each cottage bigger than any of the few houses over the years I've been lucky enough to own.

And then there's the Coyle mansion itself. Set on a windswept hill, it has yellow stucco walls with black shutters and cedar shingle roofs: three stories, thirty rooms. Its gadgets and amenities range from sterling-silver ice cubes that chill a drink without watering it, to a small subway system that connects the mansion with the air and rail facilities.

The estate is protected by an electronic security system that even when I first saw it in the early '50's was advanced for its time. Attack-trained Dobermans patrol the grounds. Many of the staff of house and office help, ranch and farm hands, mechanics and pilots, are trained in small arms and self-defence, all highly paid, and as far as I knew then, all 100 percent loyal to Mr Robert J. Coyle.

'Well, Matthew,' he said after Maul had brought me to the library to wait for this old colleague of my father's who had jacked me out of a BOQ three thousand miles away, 'it was good of you to come. It's been too long.'

Except that his hair had whitened over the years, he was as I had remembered him: impeccably but conservatively dressed; a slender, almost delicate-looking man of less than average height, whose grip was deceptively powerful and whose grey eyes seemed to penetrate into the small corners of a man's soul where he is most vulnerable, where he can be bribed or bought or turned in whatever direction Coyle might want him to turn.

'If it's all the same to you, I'd like to skip the small talk,' I said. 'I'm tired. Whatever this is, I'd like to get it over with.'

'Of course,' he said. 'Take a seat. Give me a minute. Would you like something to drink?'

'Scotch-rocks,' I said. 'I could use a cigarette, too.'

'Fine,' he said. 'I'll tell Jassick. Make yourself comfortable. You do look tired.'

The library was walled with books arranged by category: lots of history, botany, and law; not much literature. There was a metal track and ladder so you could reach the books on the upper shelves. There were several small groupings of furniture, leather with brass studs, and a set of floor-to-ceiling French doors that opened on to a small patio overlooking one of the pools. It was dusk now, and the pool was illuminated with underwater spots. Steam rose from it as if from a cauldron. Coyle had a large Case desk which seemed to sit slightly higher than floor level, and I guessed he had had a small platform built under it to give him an advantage in height over his visitors.

I took a leather chair, away from the desk, watching as he worked his intercom. He told whoever Jassick was to hold his calls, then put in an order for some canapés, a bottle of Chivas, and my cigarettes. It annoyed me when he specified Raleigh filters, not only that he would know this was my brand, but that here at White Oaks he would have some in stock.

'I hope the ride down was reasonably comfortable,' he said.

'The ride down was fine,' I said. 'The rough stuff in Wiesbaden wasn't.'

He looked away.

'The next time you want me for something,' I said, 'try using the phone.'

'Please accept my apologies,' he said.

'I want to be sure I've made my point,' I said. 'Your goons used a hypodermic on a lady friend of mine.'

'Your point is well taken, Matthew,' he said. '*And* clearly made.'

'All right,' I said. 'Now I'd like to know what this is all about. You didn't shanghai me in the middle of the night and fly me halfway around the world so the two of us could drink Scotch.'

'It might have been reason enough,' he said. 'We haven't seen each other in sixteen years – not since the summer you and Diana married and we had the reception here. I really had hoped we might spend a moment or so in civil conversation before we got down to business.'

The scars on my back were heating up.

'If you've got something to tell me about Brian, tell me,' I said. 'Otherwise I'm on my way.'

Coyle's face tightened. He had a pencil in his hand and he began tapping it slowly against a grey folder that lay on the desk in front of him. I had noticed it earlier as I had walked by, had read the identifying stencil. If it was accurate, the file contained my military records. Not the short form Coyle had stored in Bonn. This looked fat enough to be the whole works.

'All right, Matthew,' he said. 'We'll put pleasantries aside and speak the harsh but simple truth. Just over a year ago, you decided to walk out on your distinguished career with the Air Force. You had your reasons – good ones, I suppose: the war had been lost, your family all but destroyed...'

I started to stand. He motioned me back.

'There was Brian, of course, but I gather you decided he was beyond hope, so you went off to sot and brawl and whore your way around the world...' He slipped a second file folder from under the first. This one was yellow, and from where I was sitting, looked to be unmarked.

'Your face mirrors your recent life all too well,' he

continued. 'If that were not enough, it's written here, chapter and verse. Some of it came to me from your father-in-law, who has been worried sick about you; the rest came from my operatives in the various capitals where you managed to make a spectacle of yourself.'

'I didn't know you cared,' I said.

'I don't. What you do with your life is your own business. During your absence, however, I've taken it upon myself to care about Brian. Do you have any idea how pathetically ill-equipped the Veterans Administration hospital is to handle a case as complicated as his?'

'They do their best.'

'Have you made any effort to find out if and where he might be more successfully treated?'

I looked at Coyle steadily, without reply.

'Well, I have,' he said. 'In Switzerland, less than an hour from Zurich, there is an advanced treatment center for quadriplegics and cases of deep coma. It's the brainchild of the most gifted neurosurgeon in the world.'

'Dr Tibor Franki,' I said.

Coyle looked disappointed, as if I had spoiled a surprise. The Franki Clinic was the place where the jet-setters got sent whenever they wiped out on their skis or cracked up in their sports cars or fell off their hotel balconies the way a well-known American actor had recently after a fight with his boyfriend in Rome.

'Perhaps you haven't been as lax as I feared,' Coyle said.

'I can still read a newspaper,' I said.

'Then you may also know the treatment involves pressure relief through the use of laser. Dr Franki and his staff have done a complete workup on Brian. They are ready and eager to receive him at the clinic. They say although it may take several years, there is no doubt in their minds that he can be helped.'

'I looked into the Swiss clinics as soon as I came back

32

from Phnom Penh,' I said. 'They come high. There's no VA assistance, no CHAMPUS, and you know as well as I do my retirement couldn't handle a down payment on something like this.'

I took a deep breath, let it go. It sounded like a sigh. My father-in-law and I had talked the situation over endlessly. The bottom line was that even between his salary from the CIA and my retirement from the Air Force we couldn't begin to swing it. I was going to remind Coyle of this, when his man Jassick came in.

Jassick was about my height, but cadaverously thin. He wore plaid slacks and a blue blazer, had large eyes and a small mouth and patches of mouse-grey hair that looked as if they had been swept up from under a barber's chair and glued to his skull.

Without saying a word, he fixed me my Scotch on the rocks. The rocks were silver and glinted through the glass when the light struck them. The last time I had seen anything like them had been at the wedding reception here at White Oaks when Diana and I had toasted each other. Long life and happiness. 'I love you, Matt,' she had whispered. Her eyes had shone.

My cigarettes were on the tray. I got one out and lit up, hands trembling. Coyle, in his inimitable way, was watching me.

'Well,' he said after Jassick had left, 'where were we? Oh, yes, the expense. I've looked into that too.' He rested his elbows on his desk, touched the tips of his fingers together. It was obvious he was enjoying himself.

'How much?' I said.

'Nine thousand a month. That includes everything.'

Coyle said this matter-of-factly, as if it were a negligible sum – 108K a year. If Brian had been his son, Brian would have been sent to the Franki Clinic in the first place, and maybe by now he'd be able to talk or breathe on his own or even get around in a wheelchair.

But he wasn't Coyle's son, he was mine; and that was bad luck for Brian, whose luck had been as bad as any kid's could be.

'I'm not a charitable man,' Coyle said. 'And even if I were, I suspect you will have too much of your father's stubborn pride to accept a gift.'

Try me, I thought.

'And as for a loan,' he continued, 'with the figures we're talking about and the size of your pension...'

I stubbed out my cigarette. I think there was something in the way I did it that made Coyle get to the point.

'I have a job that needs doing,' he said. 'I think you're the man for it. If you agree to help me, I'll agree to help Brian. It's as simple as that.'

Nothing Coyle ever did was as simple as that. I emptied my Scotch, lit another cigarette.

'What's the job?' I said.

'I've been reviewing your records,' he said, tapping the grey folder again. 'There's a notation that interests me towards the end of your tenure as air attaché in our embassy in Phnom Penh. It says you spent a week's convalescent leave at the International Hotel at Kampong Som. That's the one Prince Sihanouk had built during his salad days, isn't it?'

'That's right,' I said.

'There doesn't seem to be any indication here as to what you were convalescing from,' Coyle said.

'There wouldn't be,' I said. He paused as if he hoped but didn't expect I might fill him in, that I might tell him how it had been after I came back from burying Diana and accompanying what was left of my son to the VA hospital in DC: how I did things in Cambodia then that were never a part of my charter as air attaché; how I went on ground patrols with Kam, one of our Cambodian forward air controllers (Kam the Fac, as I called him); how we were caught in a Khmer Rouge mortar barrage

one day south of Route 3 and Kam dragged me out with two 60mm mortar fragments in my back; how Kam and Jillion Leggett and I spent a week very drunk at Sihanouk's International Hotel while I was on the mend.

'Why the interest in the hotel?' I asked. 'It's been abandoned since the Khmer Rouge overran the country.'

'Yes, unfortunately it has,' Coyle said. 'Shortly before that happened, one of my companies was negotiating with members of the Lon Nol government to receive rubber shipments from the Chupp plantation and arrange sales. Since the Cambodian *riel* was so unstable at the time, we agreed to make our payments in diamonds.

'We conducted our business at the hotel. Our courier would go there, check into his usual suite, arrange a shipment of rubber from the Kampong Som deep-sea port, and deliver the diamonds.

'As you well know, Kampong Som was cut off and overrun just before Phnom Penh on April 17. Our man never got out.'

'And you think the diamonds he had are still there?'

'I'm sure of it. According to our sources, the last payment was never made. Our man's name was Dennis Capps. Did you ever run into him over there?'

'No.'

'Too bad. I think you would have liked him. He was trustworthy and tough, one of our best. He carried the diamonds in a pouch, along with a detailed record of the transaction: shipping manifests, delivery schedules, the bonded appraisals of the gems. During his negotiations, he would keep the pouch locked in a wall safe hidden in his suite.'

'How much are the diamonds worth?' I asked.

'That's difficult to say,' Coyle replied. 'They've been

increasing in value, of course. The last best estimate we had put them at just under two million.'

I whistled at that, poured myself another drink. I had no idea how much two million might mean to a man as wealthy as Coyle, but I knew very well what it would mean to me.

'I want the diamonds back,' Coyle said. 'The pouch, the papers. Everything.'

'And you think I can get them for you?'

'Yes.'

I shook my head.

'I think you're perfect for the job,' Coyle said. 'You know the area. You speak some of the pertinent languages. You have the contacts—'

'No way,' I said.

Coyle looked genuinely disappointed.

'You must be nuts,' I said. 'There's a bloodbath going on in that country. The Khmer Rouge are slaughtering their own people, driving them out of the cities—'

'I said I had a job for you. I didn't say it was going to be easy.'

'How come you waited this long to dig me out?' I said. 'Cambodia fell seven months ago.'

Here Coyle hesitated, as if he had not been prepared for what seemed to me an obvious question.

'The first attempt ... our first attempt failed,' he said finally.

I laughed.

'I'll bet it did,' I said. 'What happened?'

'We're not sure. Apparently our man was discovered by a Khmer Rouge patrol. They hacked him to death ...'

'With hoes,' I said.

'Yes. His body was found by the Thai border police. He'd been decapitated, so for a while identification was difficult, but finally there was no doubt. He was Chinese, I believe.'

36

I was silent. The story Coyle had told was plausible enough.

He watched me. 'Do I have your attention?' he asked.

'You know damn well you do,' I said.

'Good,' he said, hurrying now. 'This is my proposition. You'll either take it or leave it – I'm not prepared to haggle with you. If you agree to accept the job, I'll have Brian flown at once to Zurich, where he will be admitted to the Franki Clinic with six months' treatment prepaid. Once you've returned the pouch to me, I will pay for an additional six months. We will, of course, cover all your expenses; our people will be at your disposal anywhere in the world. Finally, to sweeten the pot, if you bring the pouch back safely, ten percent of the current value of the diamonds will be yours.'

'That comes close to sounding charitable,' I said.

'Assuming you take the job, you'll earn it,' he said.

'How much time do I have to think it over?'

'None. You'll have to decide now. If you accept, you'll leave for Zurich tonight.'

'Why the rush?'

Again Coyle hesitated.

'We have information there are others who are interested in the pouch as well,' he said finally.

'Who?'

'An international syndicate that deals in gems and treasure. We'd be very unhappy were they to reach the hotel before us.'

'If I go into Kampong Som,' I said, 'I go my own way. No interference.'

'Of course.'

'Have you got a staging area?'

'Yes. The Adune plantation southeast of Bangkok.'

'I'll need some Cambodians. One in particular—'

'We located your friend Kam in San Antonio. He's en route to Dulles.'

I shook my head. Coyle punched a button on his intercom.

'Jassick?' he said. 'Call the hospital. Tell them the project is on.'

'You never had much doubt, did you?' I said.

'I was relying on your fighter-pilot spirit,' Coyle said. 'Your attitude of can-do. I admire that.'

'How did you manage to get my complete dossier?' I asked.

'From Campbell Cooke, naturally.'

I glanced up at that. My father-in-law was usually discreet.

'I told you he was concerned about you,' Coyle said.

'He's that kind of man,' I said. 'He worries about people. He may even be worried about you these days.'

'Why should he be?'

'Talbot's subcommittee, for one.'

Coyle snorted. 'That's nothing more than a cheap grab for publicity.'

'The Washington *Post* seems to be taking it seriously.'

'Those unspeakable sons of bitches would bribe a pope to fill a column.'

'Is there good security on this Cambodian operation?'

'Of course.'

I stood up, lit a cigarette. Through the French doors I could see the steam rising from the pool.

'Somebody knew I was coming here,' I said.

Coyle whitened. 'That's impossible,' he said. 'Dieter and Karl are two of my best men. They were the only ones outside this house—'

'Somebody booby-trapped my seat on the plane. I wasn't in it at the time. The guy who was came close to losing his hand. When that didn't work, I got a warning

38

through the intercom telling me to abort this trip. The warning came in French with a German accent.'

Coyle was silent. For the first time since I had come in, he looked like a man who might lose.

'Then someone very close to me is a traitor,' he said finally.

'Any idea who?'

'No. But you may be sure I will bend every effort to find out.'

'I'd like to be the first to know,' I said. 'It's a long way from here to Bangkok. I don't want to have to keep looking over my shoulder.'

Coyle nodded. 'Maul will drive you to the airport,' he said.

I stubbed out my cigarette.

'At least your international scum, whoever they are, aren't perfect,' I said.

'What makes you so sure?' Coyle said.

'They didn't know what I looked like.'

# 5

The Coyle Enterprises jet that would take me to Zurich was the pride of Coyle's fleet. It was a Boeing 727-200, one of the big stretch versions designed to carry up to two hundred passengers. Coyle's particular plane had been customized to suit his specifications. The exterior paint was black and red, the interior appointments – Maul assured me – as lavish as those of an oceangoing yacht. It was maintained by Page Aviation at Dulles, parked now on the civilian flight line.

Huge flakes of snow were drifting down into the lighted ramp area by the time we pulled up just short of the jet's wing. As we got out of the Lincoln, a guard in an orange parka approached.

'Too friggin' early for snow,' he said.

'Yeah, right,' Maul said.

'You have any trouble on the road?'

'No trouble,' Maul said. 'Call base. Tell them I'm on my way back. I don't want to get stuck out here.'

The guard carried a Hewlett Packard 250 hand radio in a leather holster on his belt. He keyed it and I listened as he made his call: 'Base, Hubcap one-zero. Tie Rod has arrived, acknowledge.'

'Hubcap one-zero, Base,' the radio crackled. 'You're acknowledged.'

'We've got some weather here. Can you give me an update on the ETA of Westwind two-four, over.'

'That's a roger, Hubcap one-zero. Westwind two-four estimates touchdown in eighteen minutes, acknowledge.'

I looked at Maul. He was standing with his hands stuck into the pockets of his leather coat. Snow had begun to build on his cap.

'Is Westwind the exec jet out of San Antonio?' I asked.

'Yeah, right,' he said.

I smiled.

'And you're Tie Rod?' I said.

'Yeah, right,' he said. He reached up and tugged on the lobe of his ear, as if the code business embarrassed him. He said Coyle and each staff member had individual call signs that were, this month, parts of a car. Coyle was Bumper, the guards were Hubcaps, Jassick was King Pin, I was Piston. Coyle changed the signs each month and always gave the name that sounded most like the leader to someone else.

'Kind of funny,' I said.

'Since they tried to kidnap him,' Maul said, 'he takes it serious.'

'I read about that. They were Sicilians, weren't they?'

'No,' Maul said. 'They were Krauts.'

He turned to look at the guard. 'What have you got on the ambulance?' he said.

'They were in and out of here twenty minutes ago,' the guard said. 'The colonel's son is on board with his nurse.'

I wanted to go see Brian at once, but I had learned from painful experience it was better to psych myself first.

I shivered, raised the collar of my trench coat against the snow.

'Who's the nurse?' I asked. Coyle hadn't mentioned one.

'Some old dike from Walter Reed,' the guard said.

'Stocky, mid-fifties, with steel-grey hair? Barks when she talks?'

'That's her.'

'That's Major Wilma O'Neill,' I said. 'She's a personal friend of mine. You won't want to call her a dike again. At least not where I can hear you.' I felt a surge of anger. The guard looked at me, then turned and spat once on to the tarmac under the wing.

'You got some beef with this nurse?' Maul asked him.

'I lost my grip on the friggin' gurney going up the ramp,' the guard said. 'I didn't drop it or anything like that, but the stairs were slick and I started to slip—'

'She chew you out?' Maul asked.

'Chew me out, hell,' the guard said. 'She tore me a new asshole.'

Maul chuckled at that, shook hands with me, and left. I carried my bag up the Weber air stairs of the plane. I could hear the muted turbine sound from the auxiliary unit that provided electrical power when the engines weren't turning. And I thought of Brian and how without electricity he would die.

Wilma O'Neill was known affectionately as 'Whisky Oscar,' her initials in the phonetic alphabet used by the military. She was boot-tough, had served in the field in Korea and then with distinction in the 93rd Evac Hospital at Long Binh in Vietnam.

Using her seniority, she had returned to ward duty at Walter Reed, intending, as she had told me, to relax out her days before retiring from the Army. Top surgical nurse that she was, she had never been willing to play the game, had always refused to recognize rank over competence. That was why she was and always would remain a major. No promotions for the independent. She ran the intensive-care unit on the late shift, had been with Brian from the start.

She was drinking a cup of coffee in the forward lounge of Coyle's plane when I came in. She had a civilian

42

nurse's uniform on, striped cap pinned firmly to her grey hair. She stood up as I approached, stuck out her hand.

'Hey, Turkey,' she growled. 'You're late. You said you'd be back in three months. How come it took twelve?'

I took her hand and pulled her towards me. There weren't too many people close enough to Nurse Whisky to risk giving her a hug. I was glad I was one of the ones who was.

'You look terrible,' she said.

'I skidded for a while,' I said. 'Got behind the power curve. I'm coming back.'

'When was your last physical?'

'Hate to tell you this,' I said, 'but I can't remember.'

'If you don't schedule one, I'll schedule one for you,' she said. Her voice was raspy from years of too much coffee and cigarettes and booze and shouting over voice-operated telephones in the field. It could cut like a saw and be gentle too, depending on the effect she wanted to have. Right now it was somewhere in between as she ticked off the things she would want me to have done: 'Blood workup, chest X-rays, lower GI, sigmoid—'

'The hell with the sigmoid,' I said. 'I had one of those last time. The viewing instrument is a yard long and cold as an icicle. I damn near went through the ceiling.'

'And I thought you jet jockeys were iron-ass,' she said.

We laughed at that.

'All right, Whisky,' I said. 'What are you doing here?'

'Where the kid goes, I go,' she said. 'I guess it's as simple as that. When I heard this Franki Clinic thing was in the works, I put in my papers for retirement. I'm on terminal leave.'

'That quick?'

'I had a couple of weeks.'

'I hear Switzerland is pretty expensive. Can you handle it okay?'

'The chief of surgery at Walter Reed has a couple of lines to Franki. The chief owed me a favor, and when I asked, he made a call to the clinic and got me on the staff. Like I say, where the kid goes, I go.'

I hugged her again.

'How's he been doing?' I asked.

Wilma always told it straight. She didn't know any other way. She said that Brian's alpha and beta waves continued to indicate that his brain was alive, but he remained in a deep coma. Though his heartbeat was strong, he could not breathe without the help of a respirator. His bones had begun to turn brittle and his muscles were atrophying. He was increasingly susceptible to respiratory infections, skin care was difficult; according to the doctors at Walter Reed there was little hope for even partial recovery.

There were only two remotely encouraging signs: the fact that his pupils were still light-sensitive and the fact that his brain waves still showed actively on an electroencephalogram. Until the EEG charted a flat line, there was at least a chance in a million that Brian might regain consciousness one day.

'Come on,' Wilma said. 'Let's go see him.'

He had been placed in the master stateroom just aft of the lounge, port side. The room had been painted off-white. The furniture was upholstered in red. Except for the decor, nothing had changed for my son. He lay on his back in soft light. His blond hair looked clean but lifeless. His eyes were closed and his skin was very pale. There were IV tubes running into both arms. A larger tube ran from his mouth to the portable respirating machine that hissed quietly beside the bed. I knew there were other tubes that I could not see under the scarlet

blankets that covered him. I touched his hand. The hand was limp and the skin felt cool.

'Brian,' I said. 'It's Dad. How have you been doing, son? You sure have a nice room here. Have you been behaving yourself?' I felt a welling in my throat, a sense of rage. I wanted to say: *What's the use*? I wanted to tell Wilma to shut off the respirator and let Brian go in peace and with as much dignity as he had left; but I knew what Wilma would say. In many ways old Nurse Whisky was a whole lot tougher than me.

'He looks good,' I said.

Wilma beamed. 'Of course he does,' she said. 'I see to that.'

'Have you got everything you need on board?'

'You bet,' she said. 'This guy Coyle is no piker. When I found out somebody had had Brian's charts pulled, I peeled ass all over the hospital until I found out who it was. Hey, Tiger,' she said, 'if you don't mind me asking, what's your connection with him?'

'He was in the war with my father.'

'So he's footing the bill for all this?'

'He's going to let me work it off.'

'Doing what?' she said. 'Robbing Fort Knox?'

'I could tell you,' I said. 'But then you'd be part of it. I'd rather you weren't.'

She looked at me with worry and disapproval.

'So it's that kind of work.'

'Yeah,' I said. 'It's that kind.'

The passageway and lounge section were chilly as I walked forward to the open-air-stairs door, where, through the falling snow, I saw the twin landing lights of the Westwind executive jet taxiing up. Page ground crews, using lighted wands, brought it to a halt as the guard used his radio and the side door of the small plane opened. The engines were still running. A slender figure stepped out, and the door closed behind him. At once,

the jet increased revolutions and taxied away. Home to White Oaks, I thought. Before this snow gets any worse.

I went down the stairs to greet my old friend Kam. He wore a brown silk suit and black ankle-high dress boots.

'*Chum rip seur*,' I said.

'*Chum rip seur, Lōk*,' he replied. We embraced. He was shivering from the cold.

Kam is not your basic Cambodian. He has some White Russian and Harbin Chinese blood in his veins. He is taller by half a foot than most Cambodians, several inches wider at the shoulder. He has high cheekbones and skin the colour of caramel. His hair is black, eyes even blacker. He does not talk a lot. When he does, it can be in English, Chinese, Vietnamese, Thai, Khmer, Russian, or French.

Off the battlefield, he resembles a collection of spare parts – all sharp circles and pieces of a body that, when he walks, generally move in the same direction. A leg goes forward, followed by a hip, then an arm, another leg, another arm, and so on. The movements are as jerky as those of a puppet. Off the battlefield, Kam moves as if suspended from strings.

But on the battlefield, he has the grace of a panther. Once, when we were pinned down by AK-47 fire in a cemetery near Slap Deng by two Khmer Rouge perched in palm trees, I watched Kam as I crouched behind a tombstone, bullets whanging. I was fascinated as he slipped from stone to stone, then to the wall, then back, looking for a way out. He didn't move fast, he simply flowed, as natural a part of the landscape as a lazy brook.

And he was a silent killer. He disdained guns, grenades, noisemakers of any kind. He carried a Morseth number-8 boot knife, a twenty-inch steel-wire saw, and a throwing star. I had seen him use all three,

each with the deadly effect of a cobra. I don't think Kam is by nature a violent man. I think he became violent in a violent world. He had lost everything in the war. His wife. His children. His country. I knew he'd want to go back.

'Come on,' I said. 'I want you to meet somebody.' We ascended the stairs to the lounge and went to Brian's stateroom.

When Kam and Wilma shook hands and eyed each other, I think they liked what they saw. Kam went to Brian's bed then, and put his hand gently on my son's brow. He stood that way for several seconds, head cocked as if he were listening.

Finally he took his hand away and turned to me. 'Brian sleeps in earth, deep, warm,' he said. 'But he is strong and will awake when he is told.'

'You bet your boots,' Wilma said.

'I will go now to inspect the plane,' Kam said.

Anyone who has known sustained combat seeks and finds his personal survival mode. It is a mental state based on the unflinching will to live regardless of hazards. On this base you build your sensing devices, which automatically sound the inner alarm that puts the body and the brain on alert. Experience, often painfully gained, tells you how to interpret the data input. A flash from the ground can be sun reflecting from water in a shell hole, or from the muzzle blast of an unfriendly gun. An arm movement in downtown Phnom Penh can be a greeting wave from a friend or the toss of a terrorist grenade. A car following too closely can be that of an inept driver or that of a suicide squad. An empty pack of cigarettes lying innocently on the sidewalk can blow off a foot.

I was still working back into my survival mode. Kam I was sure, had never abandoned his. Before we took off, he would know every exit on the plane, every nook,

47

every cranny. He would nose around like a flop-eared hound, would smile happily if anyone should notice him, as if to say: *Please, there is no problem here. I am only curious.*

He had no sooner gone out of the stateroom than our hostess and Coyle's chief pilot came in. The hostess was an attractive brunette with blue eyes. She wore a black, skirted uniform. The pilot, maybe twenty years her senior, was tall, lean, had similarly blue eyes and white hair. His uniform was black, with four gold stripes on the sleeves. He said his name was Pat Flahaven. Hers was Monica Eklund.

'How many crew members are there?' I asked.

'Four,' the captain replied. 'My copilot and engineer are on the flight deck.'

'I've never done a walk-around on anything this big,' I said. 'Would you mind taking me through your external pre-flight?'

'I'd be happy to,' he said. 'We'll want to get off the ground as soon as possible. This weather seems to be going to hell.'

He started to leave.

'Will Colonel Eberhart wish to have a hot meal once we are under way?' the hostess asked. Her accent was Scandinavian. She was the sort of woman who combined efficiency with sensuality in a way that had never failed to interest me.

'My name's Matt,' I said. 'I'll skip the hot meal. If you can scare up a Scotch-rocks and a sandwich once we're airborne, that will suit me fine.'

'Same here,' Wilma said. 'And with me, you can double the Scotch.'

I went outside with Flahaven. He walked me through the external check: wheel wells, struts, air stairs, accumulator pressures, engine inlet and exhaust, flaps, brakes, antiskid devices and tail skid.

I saw nothing out of the ordinary, but as I followed

Flahaven through the pelting snow, with my hands deep in my pockets and my collar up, I remembered all too clearly what had happened to Myron Bennett on the flight from Frankfurt, and how Coyle had whitened when I told him about the warning I had received.

'Looks like we're ready to fire up,' I said, once we were back inside.

'There are intercom hookups throughout the plane,' Flahaven said. 'Anytime you want to talk, give me a buzz.'

'I'll do it,' I said. 'What's our time in the air to Zurich?'

'Eight and a half hours. Once we're out of the storm system, we should have smooth sailing over the Atlantic. Zurich is wide open and forecast to remain so.'

I looked in on Wilma. She was strapped into a comfortable-looking seat next to Brian's bed.

'How come my hands sweat?' she said. 'After all I've seen. Kids with their guts hanging down to their knees, their ears shot off, their EMT cards stained red.'

'It's just another plane, Whisky,' I said.

'Yeah,' she said. 'Well, I'll be glad when we're up. Once we're up, I don't worry about it.'

Kam was in the lounge. I joined him there, strapped myself into one of the sofas. I could hear the engines spool up as Flahaven's voice crackled over the intercom, telling us we were ready to go.

I gave Kam the thumbs-up sign. 'How much of a briefing did they give you about all this?' I asked.

'Only that I was needed by you. There will be for me from Mr Coyle two hundred dollar each day.'

'Good. I'll fill you in on the rest, once we're airborne.'

He leaned closer to me and said quietly, '*Lŏk*, there is a parachute in the crew cabin.'

'Concealed?'

'Yes.'

'What kind?'

'A large one. A Para-Commander, I do think.'

'Did you leave it the way you found it?'

'Yes. But I do think one does not have such a thing on so large a plane as this.'

I nodded. 'Kam, my old friend,' I said, 'you are absolutely right.'

# 6

By the time the big jet had reached a cruising altitude of
34,000 feet, I had quietly told Kam about Coyle, the
mission, how it could affect Brian's chances for recovery, and of the warning I had received on my flight from
Germany. Kam listened intently. He made no comment
until I mentioned Cambodia. Then his eyes became
obsidian and he nodded. '*Baht, Baht.*' Yes. Good.

He said he had found the parachute hidden in the linen
locker in the crew quarters. Also a jumpsuit, boots,
helmet, goggles, and oxygen mask. Clean linen had been
balled up and dropped into the locker to cover this
equipment. There were two storage bins adjacent to the
linen locker. Both were empty and would have provided
room for anyone's legitimate chute and gear.

I asked Kam to give me the layout of the plane's
interior. He said the crew cabin was attached to the flight
deck. Next came the spacious lounge where we were
sitting, with its blue sectional sofas and rows of gold
chairs. Next came Brian's stateroom, located amidships
over the wings. Beyond that there were two smaller
staterooms. These three rooms opened to a long passageway on the starboard side of the aircraft. The passageway ran from the forward lounge section to the open
office and communications area at the rear of the plane.
Beyond that, still going aft, were a master galley and two
heads.

'Were you able to look at everything?' I asked.

'Everything except cockpit.'

'Any chance we might have a stowaway?'

'I think no way chance of that.'

'Okay,' I said. 'We've got four crew members and one chute. We can assume whoever the bad guy is, he's a pro. We're not going to get anywhere trying to flush him out by letting him know we've found his gear. Let's keep that between the two of us. I don't see any reason to get Whisky all upset. Whoever we're dealing with damn sure isn't going to jump into the Atlantic. We've got some time.'

'Yes,' Kam said. 'You are right, I do think.'

The door to the crew cabin opened just then, and a man I had not seen before ambled towards us. He looked to be in his early thirties, had two gold stripes on his sleeves, a beer drinker's belly, and a face as round and shiny as a pan. He introduced himself as Sandy Johnson, our flight engineer.

'Y'all comfortable, Colonel?' he asked.

'Hard not to be on this bird,' I said.

'Ain't she a honey!'

'This has to beat hell out of commercial flying,' I said. 'How does a fella manage to land a job like this?'

Sandy smiled. When he did that, the flesh of his cheeks squinched up under his eyes.

'Hell, Colonel,' he said, 'I don't rightly know. The captain tells me in my case it's because I graduated from Virginia Tech. Old Coyle, I guess he thinks that school's the cat's meow. Anyway, I've been with him going on ten years.'

'Do you fly?'

'Hell no! I've got me a case of acrophobia you wouldn't believe! I don't even like to look out the damn window! I've got to check my dipstick in the ass end. Y'all take care!'

He disappeared down the passageway off the lounge just as Monica appeared with our whisky and sandwiches.

'I made three kinds,' she said. 'Ham, chicken, and corned beef. I hope that's all right.'

'That's fine,' I said. 'Can you join us?'

'Thanks,' she said. 'Maybe in a little while. I've got another batch to do for the crew.'

'I've met everyone except the copilot,' I said. 'What's he like?'

'Well, let me see,' she said. 'He's the strong, silent type, I think. When we first met, he asked me if I would to go bed with him. I told him no. He hasn't spoken three words to me since.'

I laughed. Direct people, the Scandinavians.

'When was that?' I said.

'Over a year ago. Oh, by the way,' she said, 'I gave Major O'Neill her tray. She asked me to tell you she was going to try to get some sleep. I think she may be feeling a little airsick.'

'I'll look in on her,' I said. 'Is everything all right with my son?'

'Yes.'

Monica caught her lip in her teeth and looked away.

'What's wrong?' I asked.

'Nothing.'

'If it's about Brian,' I said, 'go ahead. I don't mind talking about it.'

'I was told once,' she said, 'that people like him are actually awake inside their bodies – that they can hear and understand, but they can't respond.'

'I've heard that too,' I said. 'The doctors at Walter Reed tell me there's very little to support that theory. They say the odds overwhelmingly favor the notion that Brian is in a sound and dreamless sleep.'

'That would be better,' Monica said.

I agreed that it would. She told me to use the intercom if I should want anything, that she would be in the galley, aft.

'How about calling me Matt next time,' I said.

'All right,' she said.

She went away. I looked at Kam. 'Any vibes?' I said.

'She is what you say a very pretty girl.'

'How about Johnson?'

Kam shrugged.

'Copilot?'

'He has spoken with rudeness to Miss Eklund, I do think.'

'It's all part of the hustle,' I said. 'What kind of sandwich do you want?'

'Beef,' Kam said. 'With corn.'

We continued to cruise without incident through a gentle night and towards the dawn. On his way back to the flight deck, Sandy Johnson told me the Coyle jet was powered by three big Pratt and Whitney turbo-fan engines, each delivering over 15,000 pounds of thrust. He said the captain was maintaining an altitude of 34,000 feet. The plane's interior, pressurized and warm, offered most of the comforts of home. All very snug.

'I didn't catch the copilot's name,' I said.

'Phil Lopez,' Sandy said. 'You meet him yet?'

'No. Monica was telling me about him.'

'You know, I believe old Phil's got a thing for her,' Sandy said. 'Now, I told the captain the only female crew I want around me are the old ones. Fat and forty and haired-up and healed-over. That's one of Johnson's rules. Now, you take a fox like Monica and put her on board, and first thing you know, you got yourself a copilot up there with only half his mind on his work!'

We all chuckled at that.

'What is fox?' Kam asked. Sandy told him, and we chuckled some more. Then I asked Sandy how long he had known Lopez.

'You know, I can't remember just when it was we first met. Mr Coyle, he uses Phil here and there, wherever he

needs somebody to get an aeroplane off the ground. I guess it was maybe five, six years back. You want to meet him, you'll have to go up front. He sticks to the cockpit and crew cabin. He doesn't like to talk much. Now, this old pea-picker never had that problem. My wife tells me I've got a mouth that'll run four days into next week. Give us a honk if you want to tour the cockpit, hear?'

'Okay,' I said. I yawned.

Sandy looked at me. 'Hey, old buddy,' he said. 'You just about swallowed yourself with that one.'

'Sleepy,' I said. 'I may have to bag it for a while.'

'Help yourself!'

Monica came by shortly after that and freshened my drink. Kam hadn't touched his first.

'Is everything all right?' she asked.

'In the same way I am feeling as Nurse Major O'Neill,' Kam said. He patted his stomach.

'I'm sorry,' she said. 'Would you like a motion-sickness pill?'

'Perhaps later,' he said.

'The captain expects to encounter some turbulence over France,' Monica said. She produced a small vial from one of the pockets of her uniform, gave it to Kam. 'We'd probably all do well to take one before we're over land,' she said.

I sipped my Scotch, had my first cigarette since coming on board. I did feel sleepy, and Kam had reminded me by not touching his drink of the possibility of being doped.

So. We had four crew members and one chute. Flahaven had struck me as the totally professional pilot: thousands of hours logged in the air; crisp, assured, dependable. Johnson seemed like a good old boy from a small town in the South, the kind who is smarter than he seems, who does his job well for five days, then lies back on the weekend with a case and a half of beer.

Monica was Monica. The kind of woman who had liberated herself a long time before it had become fashionable to do so. Sexy and tough. I didn't rule her out.

Then there was the one I hadn't seen. Lopez. The copilot.

Kam got up to prowl around the plane. By the time he came back, he had covered everything again. Nothing had changed. The chute was still in the locker. Brian's life-support systems were purring away. Wilma had stretched out on the bed next to him, Kam said, and had fallen asleep. The guest staterooms were empty. So were the office and communications area, the master galley and heads. All four crew members were up front.

'I have to get some sleep,' I said. 'How are you doing?'

'I will sleep only when plane is on ground,' Kam replied.

'Give me a couple of hours,' I said. 'Then wake me up.'

The lights in the room where Brian and Wilma slept were dim. There was a two-seater couch across from the bed, and I curled up on it as best I could, too tired to care about comfort. Kam would keep as sharp a watch as any man I knew. I trusted him completely.

I wanted to sleep so much I couldn't at first. I tossed and squirmed. Images came to me of the first time Kam and I had met. It was in the Cambodian village of Kampong Thom, north of Phnom Penh. The village had been surrounded at the time. I had flown there by helicopter as part of my war-zone orientation. Kam had met my chopper with his jeep, proud of his English and of his ability to control American air strikes.

I liked him at once. He told me he had been a teacher before the war, but that now it had become necessary for him to fight for his country. And fight he did, springing

from shell hole to shell hole, boring in on the enemy until even the pilots overhead whose cause he was serving warned he was getting too close.

A year later, I asked him to join me as a special aide in the overseeing of all the fronts that were using American air. We became like brothers. When I finally had to leave his country, he held my arms, looked into my eyes, and said in his curious English, 'Too soon to know, too soon you go.'

At least he was one person I hadn't lost.

I squirmed some more, my thoughts jumbling. Once, I half sat up and squinted at my watch. A little over three hours to go.

Okay, Eberhart, I thought. Rack it up.

And I slept.

At first, I slept as dreamless a sleep as Brian's. Then – how much later, I could not have said – I was at the controls of my Phantom and we were going up. We were going up past the cumulus, up past the anvil-headed thunderstorms, up into the sunlight so intense it tightens the skin. I had the burners lit, and we were climbing, climbing, climbing, until, past the clouds, over the tops, I levelled off with an easy wing roll.

Now I could see the curve of the earth, could see where the blue sky becomes deep azure at the edge of space.

I grinned happily, rolling left and right and left again. I pulled back on the stick and zoomed even higher, went over the top, pushed forward and went weightless, dizzy weightless, fuzzy weightless, blacking-out weightless, cold weightless . . .

Floating, sleepy and cold. My lovely Phantom gone. All the sensations of flying, without a plane, because . . . A word swam in the black night of my brain. It had an important answer for me if only I could remember it. I smiled, hearing myself laugh as if from a great distance.

Go ahead, Eberhart. You know that word. You've heard it a million times.

It'll come to me. In the morning. I'm too sleepy now.

And then it came, like the clanging of a bell.

*Hypoxic.*

Even as I came up from the deep, even before I opened my eyes, I was doing the M-1 manoeuvre – filling my lungs with air, then grunting; fill and grunt, fill and grunt; force the oxygen into the alveoli of the lungs; clear the brain, the cold sleep . . .

I rolled off the couch. We had lost our cabin pressure. My time of useful consciousness was all but gone.

TUC- Get O

*Get oxygen.*

I found the emergency-oxygen panel, grabbed one of the portable bottles, jammed the mask to my face, spun the yellow valve. One hundred percent pure oxygen flooded the mask and forced open my lungs. I breathed the cobwebs away in a split second, already crawling towards Wilma and Brian.

Brian's chest respirator and portable system were sustaining him. I held a deep breath and slammed the hissing mask over Wilma's face, pushing my free hand into her solar plexus, releasing, pushing again, releasing again, forcing her to exhale.

I was cold. I guessed the pressure altitude was over thirty thousand. That meant the time of useful consciousness would be less than two minutes. Then the good sleep. Then death.

Wilma's hand came up and caught my wrist.

'Exhale!' I shouted. 'Work at it!'

At this altitude you have to pressure-breathe, since the air pressure is so much less than at sea level. The oxygen enters the lungs under pressure. You have to breathe out against the mask. The resulting pressure forces oxygen molecules into the alveoli sacs in the lungs and hence into

the bloodstream. Brian's lung machine was doing it for him. We had to do it for ourselves.

'Keep this bottle!' I said. 'There's another behind the panel! I'll use it! I've got to go for Kam!'

I found him on the floor of the passageway not far from the door. He was making swimming motions. I slapped the mask over his face. He cleared in an instant. We traded off, going back into the room. I shut and locked the door. Wilma was on her feet, checking Brian's regulator, piling blankets on him against the high-altitude cold.

Kam and I stood by, alternately breathing and exhaling. He pointed at the emergency-oxygen-mask panels in the ceiling. They should have opened automatically as soon as the cabin pressure reached fourteen thousand.

'Why not work?' he asked.

'They can be cancelled from the cockpit,' I said. 'Were you in the lounge when it happened?'

'Yes.'

'Were all four crew members on the flight deck at the time?'

'Yes.'

Sunlight was streaming through the window. I checked my watch. It was twenty past nine in the morning, Washington time. I had been asleep for over five hours. It was two-twenty p.m. in Zurich. Although we were due to land in ten minutes, we were still at altitude. I glanced through the window again, through the port plug and along the wing. As I did, I felt the engine vibration begin to diminish. Then the nose tilted down, and I knew the aeroplane was starting a descent.

'What's going on?' Whiskey growled, pulling her mask away, then shoving it back.

'I don't know,' I said.

I went to the intercom panel near the bed and picked

up the handset. Although we had no pressurization, the plane was under control. Someone had pulled the throttles back and had started us down. I knew if my time estimates were right we were somewhere near Zurich, descending towards mountains that rose to fifteen thousand feet.

And we had a bad guy on board with a chute.

I switched from intercom to the external radio receiver. It was silent for a moment; then a voice crackled on. 'Boeing Two-Niner Charlie Echo,' it said. 'Boeing Two-Niner Charlie Echo, this is Zurich Control. Come in, please.'

I waited for Flahaven to reply. He did not. After several seconds of dead air, Zurich crackled on again.

'Two-Niner Charlie Echo, if you read squawk ident. Two-Niner Charlie Echo, squawk ident for Zurich Control.'

Again there was no reply from Flahaven or from the copilot.

Kam borrowed the mask, took a slug, handed it back. We were both shivering from the cold.

'There is difficulty?' he asked.

'They figure our transmitter may be out. They're asking the captain to activate his radar identifier.'

'Has this been done?'

The answer to Kam's question crackled back from Zurich Control. 'Boeing Two-Niner Charlie Echo, we do not have your transponder. Repeat, we do not have your transponder. If you have problems, flash emergency for ten seconds.'

I looked at Kam. He shrugged.

'Have you ever flown one of these?' Whiskey asked, peering out from behind her mask.

'No,' I said. 'I haven't.'

# 7

I filled my lungs with sweet oxygen, returned the mask we were sharing to Kam. Then I went to the window of Brian's stateroom and looked out. I was pretty sure I recognized the lay of the land. Beyond the leading edge of the wing, I could see Kreuzbach in miniature. We were between the Zurichsee and the Bodensee, heading towards the mountains west of the Zugspitze. Zurich itself was behind us.

Our angle of descent was shallow – no more than five degrees. I guessed we were losing about a thousand feet per minute. If I was right about that, and nothing else changed, we would have about ten minutes before slamming into one of the Alps.

Kam came to the window to offer me the mask. I took it, shivering, and breathed deeply.

'The mountains approach,' he said.

'Sweet Jesus,' Wilma growled.

'Take it easy,' I said.

'I want to know what's going on!'

'We've got a bad guy up front, Whiskey. The depressurization was no accident. Neither is the radio silence.'

'Who is it? Flahaven?'

'I don't know. I doubt it, but I couldn't say for sure. Whoever it is, he's got a parachute. Kam found it after we boarded at Dulles. It was tucked away in a laundry bin in the crew cabin.'

'How come you didn't tell me?'

'Would it have helped?'

'I could have worried a lot.'

'I didn't want you to worry.'

'I'm worrying now,' she said. 'I'd like to know just where in hell he thinks he's taking us.'

'Towards a prearranged jump zone, would be my guess. A circle of orange dye on the snow of a pasture. Something like that. When we reach it, our friend will level off and out he'll go.'

'What about us?'

'He figures we died above thirty thousand feet,' I said.

'The rest of the crew too?'

'Probably.'

'And there aren't any other chutes, are there?' Whiskey said.

'No,' I said.

She had been pulling her mask away in order to talk, then shoving it back to breathe. Now she let it fall to her lap, clenched both fists, and glared at me.

'I'm sorry, Whisky,' I said. 'You and Brian got caught in the wringer. If I could have stopped it, I would have.'

'I've always hated these goddamn planes,' she said. 'I'd rather put my ass in a Jeep. Every time I get a yard off the ground, I feel like I'm going to barf.'

I looked at her. She sat on the bed next to my son, her nurse's cap askew.

'How do you feel now?' I asked.

'You tell me we've got no chutes and no pilot and we're heading chop-chop for the Alps, and you're asking me how I feel?'

I shook my head. 'I didn't mean about that,' I said. 'I meant about breathing without your mask.'

She looked surprised. The mask was still in her lap. She looked down at it and then sniffed the natural air of the cabin as if to determine whether or not it was fresh.

'Not too bad,' she said.

'Also now less cold,' Kam said.

'We're losing altitude,' I said. 'Our air and temperature are going to get better all the way down.'

'I'd rather not think about that,' Wilma said.

'You stay here with Brian. Kam and I need to get to the flight deck. It may take us a while. We'll buzz you on the intercom once we're there.'

'How long is a while?'

'A few minutes. It may seem like a lot more.'

'What do I do if I don't hear from you?'

I didn't answer at first. Then, without looking at Wilma, I said, 'Stay away from the window. Lie down with Brian.'

Kam and I took our final deep slugs from the oxygen. There was a small carbon dioxide fire extinguisher on a rack next to the bed. I took it down. Kam nodded to me as if he approved. He had his weapons and now I had mine.

From a crouched position, I eased open the stateroom door. Kam positioned himself behind it. We would move forward like infantrymen in a zigzag advance, each covering the other. What we lacked in firepower we would try to make up for by surprise. We did not have to discuss these things. We had done them together many times before.

The passageway was clear. As I started forward, the aeroplane began to level off. I cocked my ears, waiting to hear an increase in the engine rpm. It didn't come. We were slowing down, and unless somebody corrected that in a hurry, we were going to stall. Then flip over on a wing. Then go into the final spin.

I ran up the passageway and ducked behind the first row of gold chairs in the lounge. Kam darted past me. He was a born sprinter and I sensed he was going to take all thirty feet to the door of the crew cabin, when I saw that door begin to open.

I wanted to shout a warning, but for a half-second I froze. In that half-second the door opened the rest of the way and I saw a man in full sky-dive rig: helmet, goggles, HALO oxygen mask and tank, reserve chute in front, the big Para-Commander chute strapped to his back. All his equipment was white except for the gun he held in his right hand. The gun was black, with an elongated barrel. He looked at Kam through the goggles of his mask, obviously startled to see someone alive in the lounge. He pointed the gun and fired once.

He fired just as Kam had been about to spring away. The gun carried a silencer. I heard the *phut* sound clearly above the wind rush of the plane, saw Kam fall towards one of the sectional sofas and lie still. I crouched behind my seat row, the small carbon dioxide extinguisher clutched in my hands.

I knew whoever this gunman was, he would be in a hurry. The plane continued to slow. That meant the other three crew members were too disabled to get to the controls. The jumper would have to remove one of the exit plugs and bail out just prior to stall. After that it would be too late.

He advanced towards my position quickly but cautiously. He checked behind each of the seat rows, swinging the elongated barrel of the gun like a flashlight. I held the cold carbon dioxide canister in both hands. It seemed to take him forever to get to my row. I watched him through the narrow gap between the chairs. He kept coming closer and closer. I tried to move my legs in order to be able to spring more effectively. They were cramped. Then he was two rows away, and I knew he had seen me.

He began to shoot. The first slug ripped the deck upholstery next to my knee.

Christ, this is it, I thought as I scrambled out and came up spraying a cold fog of carbon dioxide.

In that instant I saw the man lower his gun and look

at me and nod. He kept on nodding as he knelt in front of me, his goggles masked with white frost. I snatched the gun away from him. He held his arms at each side in a supplicating gesture, still nodding. Then he sat back on his heels and leaned slowly against the side of the seat row.

'Kam!' I shouted.

My Cambodian friend was already coming down the aisle, padding along as if there was no reason to hurry. I saw him stoop and retrieve his throwing star from the back of the gunman's neck, just below the helmet and above the parachute harness. The target area had been less than two inches square. The gunman shuddered once and stopped nodding.

'Reflex from neck and back cord,' Kam said. He pulled the helmet off and I saw it was Monica. Her black hair spilled over the bloody wound at her neck. Her eyes were open and thoughtful.

'Christ,' I said.

'She felt nothing,' Kam said. 'The quick sting like a bee. The rest was reflex only.'

'Are you hit?'

'Only through my sleeve.'

The aeroplane started to shudder, gently rocking Monica's body.

'Get back to Wilma,' I said. 'I've got to get forward.'

I didn't want Kam to sense the panic I felt as I ran up the aisle towards the flight deck. The shuddering motions had increased, the first nibbling of a fatal stall. I vaulted through the crew cabin, yanked open the flight-deck door.

All three crew members were sitting in their flight positions: Sandy Johnson at the engineer's panel, Phil Lopez in the right seat, Pat Flahaven in the left.

Each had been shot once at the base of the skull.

# 8

I didn't have time to unstrap Sandy Johnson's body from the engineer's position so I could reach the controls. The plane was quivering badly and had started to buck. I climbed over the body to the centre console between the two dead pilots.

I had never flown a plane anything like this big, but it was obvious which three levers were the throttles. I slammed them forward. As I did, I saw the engine exhaust and rpm needles on the centre panel begin to advance and felt the big engines spool up. The quivering stopped and the airspeed began to increase, knot by beautiful knot.

'*That* was close,' I said.

Kam had come to stand at my shoulder. He had unstrapped Johnson, had dragged him into the crew cabin.

'You fly now?' he asked. It was as close as I had ever heard him come to sounding urgent.

'Help me get the captain out of his seat,' I said. Flahaven sat, head back, eyes closed. Kam moved behind him. I leaned over the body, rotated the lap belt buckle, and laid the strap ends aside.

'We'll ease him up and over the back of the seat,' I said. 'Are you ready?'

'Am ready,' Kam said.

As we started to lift the body, I heard two loud snaps like the breaking of sticks. At once the plane's nose bucked up, sending me sharply to my knees.

'Pull him back!' I screamed at Kam. 'Pull him back!'

I had to get to the control yoke and couldn't with Flahaven in the seat. Kam jerked him up and over. Still kneeling, I pushed forward on the yoke until the plane levelled again. Then, keeping pressure on the yoke, I eased into the seat and placed my feet on the rudder pedals. I found the trim buttons on the left side of the pilot's wheel. Fortunately, Lopez had fallen back in his seat. His body would not interfere with my movements.

'Plane in control now,' Kam said. He sounded hopeful.

'Better check in with Wilma,' I said. 'Be sure that last buck didn't foul up Brian. Get back to me as soon as you can.'

'I will tell Nurse Whisky that all is well. We are again with pilot.'

Good old Kam, I thought. We were again with pilot, all right, but pilot didn't know shit from Shinola about flying a 727. We could probably strap Whiskey into the Para-Commander and boot her through one of the exits, but as for the rest of us, we were a long way from home.

I looked at the instrument panel. The airspeed, which had been too slow, was now building up too high. I didn't know how much fuel I had, so I pulled all three throttle levers back to 82-percent power on the rpm gauges. Then I eased the aeroplane into a left bank to orbit while I figured out what to do next.

There was a microphone hanging on the left side of my seat. I couldn't find a headset or cockpit loudspeaker. I began to transmit.

'Zurich Control, this is Boeing Two-Niner Charlie Echo, somewhere east of your location in a left-hand orbit at sixteen thousand feet. The crew is incapacitated and I have taken control of the aircraft. I'm going to need help from a 727 pilot. I can't find a headset. Repeat. I can't find a headset. I am transmitting in the blind.'

I repeated my message twice, voice shaky. As the big plane turned in the left bank, I could see mountain peaks all around me. They rose like teeth, two thousand feet below the plane. The snow cover gleamed in the sun.

I found the radio control panels on the centre console near the autopilot control. There was no position for cockpit loudspeaker. Before I could receive a reply from Zurich Control, I had to find a headset.

As I looked at the autopilot panel, I saw what had caused the two loud snaps when I had leaned across the console to help lift Flahaven out of his seat. I had brushed against the big paddle switches that disengaged the automatic flight control, causing the plane to pitch up.

I placed the mode selector on 'Altitude Hold,' engaged the two paddles, and dialled in a twenty-degree bank for a continuous left turn on the turning control knob. Having done that, I was free to let go of the yoke.

I knew Flahaven had to have some way to receive radio communications. As a fighter pilot, I was used to having earphones built into my helmet; 727 pilots did not wear helmets, they usually wore caps. The smaller planes I had flown that were not fighters had a cockpit speaker or a headset. Flahaven had neither. What he had, and what I finally found, was a small clear plastic earpiece attached to a wire and alligator clip. This had been pulled free when Kam had dragged the dead pilot up and out of his seat. I put it on and picked up in the middle of a transmission from Zurich Control.

'. . . Echo. If you read, squawk ident.'

I keyed the mike switch and replied. 'Zurich Control, this is Boeing Two-Niner Charlie Echo. I now read you loud and clear, over.'

'Two-Niner Charlie Echo, this is Zurich Control. Repeat the nature of your problem, please, over.'

'Roger, Zurich. The flight crew of Charlie Echo is incapacitated. I am a pilot, but I am not checked out in

the 727 or any similar large aircraft. I will need assistance from a 727 pilot in order to land. Would you bring one up on frequency, please, over.'

Kam returned, gave me the thumbs-up sign, stood quietly behind my seat. He had dragged Flahaven's body into the crew cabin.

I pointed to Lopez. 'Get him out of here too,' I said.

'Nurse Whiskey wants no more jolting,' he said as he moved to do that.

'Is Brian okay?'

'He is fine.'

'Good-looking range of mountains down there,' I said.

Kam peered through the windshields. Drops of moisture were beading off the glass.

'Yes,' he said. 'They look finer now than before.'

He was dragging Lopez aft when Zurich Control came back on. 'We understand your problem and are vectoring Condor Delta Bravo to your approximate position. Can you locate the IFF and squawk code two-two-four-four.'

I searched the centre console and finally found the IFF panel to the right of the weather radar. It had been turned off. Monica had been very well briefed on the 727 cockpit. I turned it on and dialed 2244 as Zurich had requested. Then I called them back.

'I've got two-two-four-four set in the transponder,' I said. 'I'll be off the air for a minute or so. Do you copy?'

'Roger, we copy. We have you on radar. We show you east of Zurich at seven-two miles.'

I checked the autopilot, got up, eased myself to the engineer's panel. I wanted to have a look at the cabin pressurization controls. Kam watched me.

'Here it is,' I said. The cabin altitude had been set to match flight altitude. I turned the knob below the 'Cabin Altitude' indicator to five thousand feet and felt my ears

fill as the pressure built up. Kam opened and closed his mouth. The passenger switch on the 'Oxygen System' panel was in the off position. I flipped it to normal. Now, if they were needed, the oxygen-mask doors would open.

'Our friend Monica didn't miss a trick,' I said.

'It is good to be professional,' Kam said. He was eyeing the empty pilot's seat.

'I'll bet you'd feel better if I was sitting over there,' I said.

'Yes,' he said. 'I do believe I would.'

'I'm pretty sure I can fly it,' I said. 'I'm not at all sure I can land it.'

Kam was silent.

I got back into the left seat, and called Zurich.

'This is Two-Niner Charlie Echo back on the air,' I said. 'Give me a steer to the Zurich airport, please, over.'

'Two-Niner Charlie Echo, this is Zurich. Remain in your left turn. We are vectoring Condor Delta Bravo to your position. Break, break. Condor Delta Bravo, are you up on this frequency?'

A British voice responded. Very crisp. 'Zurich, Condor Delta Bravo here and coming up on Charlie Echo's five-o'clock position. Do you read me, Charlie Echo?'

'Roger, Delta Bravo. I'm holding two-twenty knots.'

'Good show, Charlie Echo. We've been listening up on this frequency and think we grasp the nature of your problem. Can you give us some background on your experience, please, over.'

'Condor, I'm a retired USAF fighter jock. The only thing I've flown that's even close to this is the T-39 Sabreliner jet. The rest was all fighters and some Gooney, ah, Dakota time.'

'Very good, Charlie Echo, we understand your background. Zurich Control, we would like to buy a discreet

frequency to work our show. No point cluttering up this channel, over.'

'Condor Delta Bravo, this is Zurich. We copy your request. Go to one-twenty-four-decimal-five-five. We will monitor and will clear all traffic for you. Do you wish to declare an emergency at this time, over.'

'Zurich, Condor, that is affirmative. Please have the full complement of crash equipment by the runway. I'll bring Charlie Echo down on a long, straight-in approach. Charlie Echo, can you find the radios and meet me on one-twenty-four-decimal-five-five, over.'

'Stand by, Condor,' I said, looking for the radio console. 'Roger,' I said. 'I've got four of them just below the throttles here. It looks like two of them are navigation and two communication. Okay, I've got it now. I'm going over to one-twenty-four-decimal-five-five.'

'Very good, Charlie Echo. Dial in both comm radios, and if we lose you, come back to this frequency.'

I dialed in the numbers and heard the tuner tone as the radio locked in on the new frequency.

'Condor, do you read Charlie Echo?' I transmitted.

'Roger, Charlie Echo. I read you very well. We can relax and enjoy ourselves now. I suggest you take up a heading of two-nine-five degrees for your return to Zurich.'

I scanned the pilot's instrument panel and cross-checked the basic flight gauges: airspeed indicator, altimeter, vertical speed needle, altitude and directional gyros. The FSI indicated we were passing north, 360 degrees.

'Roger, Condor,' I said. 'I'll roll out on two-niner-five.'

I reached over and pulled the autopilot switches back and off. They made their now familiar snapping noises. I corrected the slight nose rise and prepared to roll out, when Condor came back on.

'Charlie Echo, what is your fuel status, over.'

'I don't know, Condor,' I said. 'I was wondering about that myself. Where are the gauges, over.'

'In rather a poor place, actually. Lean back and look over on the lower left of the flight engineer's panel and you will see three gauges about poker-chip size.'

I twisted back in my seat. 'Okay,' I said. 'I've got them.'

'Give me a reading on each, if you will.'

'Facing the panel and from the left, the needles are below one, below two, and below one.'

Condor was silent at that.

'Repeat,' I said. 'I read below one-two-one with the needles.'

'All right, old chap. You are fuel-critical. We'll want to get you on the ground as quickly as we can.'

'Roger that,' I said.

'We'll be with you all the way to touchdown. I'll be giving you your vectors, your altitude, your control requirements; and I'll be handling the radio calls. You're flying a very good aeroplane. Your Sabreliner experience should see you through nicely.'

'Let's hope you're right about that.'

'Just stay as relaxed as you can. Shouldn't be any more difficult than fucking a tame duck, actually.'

I laughed. It wasn't too hearty a laugh, but it helped break the tension. Condor's voice was calm and assured, and like most of the Brit pilots I had known, he had a ribald sense of humor.

While I had been busy with the radio, Kam had disappeared somewhere aft. He returned now with Whisky in tow.

'I have seen this other aeroplane,' he said. 'It is visible from the galley.'

'Are they carrying passengers?'

'Yes. Each window has a face.'

'Pretty big show,' I said.

'How big's it going to get?' Whiskey growled.

'The Brit captain says it shouldn't be any worse than fucking a tame duck.'

'What the hell would he know about that?'

'These Brits are into everything,' I said. I glanced back and smiled. Whiskey's face was as white as her uniform.

'I don't like this,' she said. 'I'd rather be shot.'

'I guess we're lucky we weren't,' I said.

'Does Zurich know we're coming in with four DOA's?'

'I thought I'd save that until we were down.'

'This is the first time I've ever been glad that Brian's the way he is.'

'How's he doing?' I asked. 'Breathing okay?'

'Fine. I came up here to ask if there was any chance we might lose the electrical power.'

'I hope not. There's always a chance. Have you got a backup system?'

'We can go manual anytime. If that happens, I'll need help. My arm isn't what it used to be.'

'I will help,' Kam said.

Whiskey sighed. 'You could park one of those fighters you flew in the lounge of this thing,' she said. 'Do you really think you can handle it?'

'No problem, Whiskey,' I said.

'Yeah, I know,' she said. 'Like fucking a duck.'

Condor had been busy on the radio with Zurich Control. Now he came back and asked me how I was making out.

I keyed the mike. 'Okay, Condor,' I said. 'I'm with you all the way. Get us down and I'll buy the bar.'

'Roger on the bar, Yank. Now, then, I want you to pull your middle power lever, repeat, the middle lever marked two, all the way back to idle. This will conserve fuel.'

'Got it.'

'Now, place the two outboard levers to about sixty percent; then lower your nose and pick up two hundred and fifty knots. We're going to start our descent to eight thousand feet.'

I arranged the throttle levers as he had told me to do, and with Whisky and Kam peering intently over my shoulder, I started us down. Condor had obtained clearance from Zurich all the way at the altitude of our choice. The crash equipment was standing by. I held the descent, trying to get a feel for the big bird without too much control movement. I repositioned the seat.

'All right, Yank, we are at thirty-five miles now. We'll want you level when we reach eight thousand feet. The QNH is ten-twenty.'

'Say again QNH?' I asked.

'Oh, sorry about that. You call it the altimeter and you want it in inches. That will be three-zero-decimal-one-two. Field elevation, fourteen hundred feet; runway length, ten thousand; wind from your left at ten knots, runway heading three four zero.'

I was about to acknowledge when all of a sudden I felt a loss of thrust and had two red lights in the cockpit. Jesus! I scanned the centre console and saw the left rpm gauge unwinding and the exhaust temperature decreasing.

I keyed the mike. 'Condor! I've just lost my port engine!' I shouted.

'No great problem there, old chap. She's probably flamed out from lack of fuel. Keep your number-two lever back so we know what we have. Advance your number three a bit. We are passing through ten thousand now, so you'll be breaking your descent soon. When you level off, let your airspeed bleed off to two hundred knots.'

Condor's voice remained steady and calm. Mine had gone up an octave. When I glanced to my right, I saw that

74

Kam had taken the copilot's seat. He sat in his brown silk suit, staring through the windshield at the mountains below. They looked like jaws waiting to snarf us up. The sun was dazzling bright on the snow. There were lakes, and dark wedges of trees, and small villages, any one of which would look fine on a calendar. I turned to glance at Whiskey.

'Party's over,' I said. 'Go back and pile cushions around yourself and Brian. Secure all loose objects in the cabin. Make sure you're strapped in tight.'

She bent down and stuck her jaw at me and said, 'Turkey, don't bash this thing.' Then she punched me once on the shoulder and left.

I had no idea how long our fuel was going to last. Obviously the gauge readings were off or there was certain valving or bypassing that had to be done in order to get fuel from one engine or tank to the other. The flight engineer's panel was a maze of dials, levers, and gauges. No one alive on board knew how to operate any of the switches or fuel-bypass controls. And there was no time for instructions from Condor.

'You're doing fine, Yank,' he radioed. 'This bird will fly successfully on one engine, and you still have two. Quite like your fighters, actually. You have all kinds of systems to back you up. We're at eight thousand now, so raise the nose, and bleed off your airspeed to two hundred. We'll coast a bit, then start final approach.'

I did as he said, easing back on the control column and pushing the right throttle forward a tad. Flying a 727 felt like flying the monorail at Disneyland. It was so long, I was sure it was bending in the aft section someplace. Over one hundred and fifty feet in length, it was about two and a half times longer than the F-4 Phantoms I was used to, and three and a half times as long as the Sabreliner.

Condor came back.

'Very good, Yank. We're twenty-two miles now and

we'll be starting down soon. First I want you to lower your flaps. The handle is on the far side of the centre console.'

I found it and placed my right hand on it. Though the air in the cockpit was cool, my hand was sweaty.

'Now raise up on it and work it back to the place where it reads twenty-five, and leave it there in the little gate. All right, I see your flaps coming down, you're looking good, that's it. You're decelerating, trim the nose up. We're coming through one-sixty knots now, so give your number-three engine more power; keep your number two in reserve. Now look to the right of the engine gauges for the handle and put the landing gear down.'

The handle had a miniature aircraft wheel on it. I reached over and pulled it out slightly, then slammed it to the down position. While I was doing this, I must have relaxed pressure on the control column.

Condor crackled in my ear. 'Watch the nose, Yank. Bring her up. Hold her up until your gear locks into place and you have all green lights above the handle. They may be a bit slow, since you lost one of the hydraulic pumps with your number-one engine.'

An hour seemed to pass before the big wheels finally thudded into place and the lights were green.

'Three down and green,' I said.

'Very good. We are now at eighteen miles from runway and at one-fifty knots. Take up a heading of three-four-zero.'

'Roger. Three-four-zero.'

'Now we will want you to hold the nose up until you have one hundred forty knots, then start down. You'll want to attain about nine-hundred-feet-per-minute rate of descent. Use whatever power you need to maintain one-forty knots. Give it some nose-up trim.'

The trim buttons were on the left side of the yoke. I thumbed the two simultaneously and felt the back pressure come off the yoke. I had had a death grip on the

big column and now forced myself to try to relax. I even trimmed to hands-off flying.

I cross-checked the instruments as best I could. I had about one-forty-two knots and nine-hundred-fifty-feet-per-minute descent. Now it was time to look ahead and see if I could pick up the runway visually.

At first I didn't see it, and then I did. It lay on a flat plain northeast of the city of Zurich. I pointed it out to Kam.

'The plane seems too big, the runway too small,' he said.

'It always does,' I said.

'Once we are down,' Kam said, 'I believe I will wish to speak to Mr Coyle.'

'That's two of us,' I said.

I radioed Condor that I had the runway in sight.

'All right, Yank. But watch your airspeed.'

I looked back into the cockpit to see more red lights, striped instrument warning flags popping up and down, gyros tumbling, and my airspeed indicator at one-thirty-five and dropping.

Christ! I was losing another one!

I lowered the nose with my left hand, slammed all three throttles to the fire wall with my right. I hadn't felt any loss of thrust, but the aeroplane felt heavier. I keyed the mike in a hand so slippery now with sweat I could barely grasp the plastic.

'Condor! I think I've lost another engine! I've got red lights all over the place, and my instruments are going out!'

As I unkeyed, I could feel thrust build and the airspeed increase. My rate of descent was now approaching fifteen hundred feet per minute.

Condor came back. 'I say, Yank, you did perform a bit of a manoeuvre there. Almost threw me off your wing. I see by the exhaust and your airspeed buildup that you do have a live engine. Check your engine instrument

panel and see what looks cold. You probably lost number three, but take a look to be sure. And do pull up, you're descending too fast. My passengers are complaining.'

I looked at the center console. Condor was right. The needles on the gauges of the five instruments stacked vertically in the centre were up. Those on both sides were down. I still had my number-two engine. One and three were out.

I eased back on the centre throttle while pulling up until I could find and maintain nine hundred feet per minute. As the nose came up, the big plane felt like it would break in half. The airspeed needle hovered at one-forty.

'I've got power on number two,' I said.

'Fine, Yank. It's like one of your fighters now. Pull the two outboard throttles back to get them out of the way. You are much too low on the glide path. Level off until I give you the word. Use whatever power you need.'

I levelled the big aeroplane until Condor came back and told me to start down again. I did. With him in my ear.

'You're looking good, Yank. Keep the runway in the centre of your windscreen. Hold what you've got.' He paused for a moment. 'I'm starting to get my glide-slope alignment needle in the top of the case now. We'll be on course and glide path shortly. You still have main hydraulics and essential electrical power, but not enough fuel to circle. Only one chance to shine today.'

So there it was. I was committed to land. When you fly a single-seat fighter with an ejection mechanism that will rocket you out of trouble even on the deck, you can afford to be fearless. But the only way out of this giant cigar was through one of the exit doors. I wasn't looking too steelyeyed right now. There hadn't been time for Condor to brief me on how to activate the speed brakes, if there were any, or how to put my one remaining engine into reverse thrust once we were on the ground.

And the ground was coming up. Fast. And I didn't even know how to steer on the roll-out.

I glanced over at Kam. He raised his chin and smiled. I wasn't sure just how much of the situation he had been able to grasp. Judging by the look on his face, he thought things were fine.

I picked up the mike. 'Condor,' I said. 'Couple of last questions here. How do I steer and brake this thing once we're down?'

'We'll cover that as we go. I'm going to follow you all the way. We're on short time now. When you cross the runway-approach lights, decrease descent to five hundred feet per minute. Keep your power where it is, keep aligned, and let it slam down. Lower the nose instantly and get on the binders, hard. You have antiskid, so you can't blow your mains. You'll have rudder steering to about fifty knots, then some nose-wheel steering and your brakes. Oh, yes, Yank, do remember to bring your throttle back when you touch down.'

'This bird is bloody long. I won't hit tailfirst, will I?'

'No problem, old chap. Too much airspeed. I'll meet you at the bar.'

We were so close to the ground now that Condor had to add power to go around. I saw his big plane peel off my starboard side, all three engines roaring at max power, gear starting to retract. As Kam had said, each window had a face.

I dropped the left wing to counter the slight crosswind. The runway was coming up fast. I could see fire trucks and foam-spreaders at the intersections. A dozen planes had been held on the taxiways. I had to work the controls to overcome some turbulence and ground effect as the approach lights flashed under us.

I raised the nose slightly to get my five-hundred-foot descent. The end of the runway disappeared in a flash beneath me. It took all the willpower I had to follow Condor's instructions, to maintain that attitude to

touchdown. I wanted to add power and climb back to altitude and think things over.

'Now we are going very fast,' Kam said.

My teeth were clenched. My right leg was bouncing on the rudder pedal. The concrete rushed up to meet us and we hit with the force of a building falling out of the sky. I pulled the number-two throttle back, sure I had driven the gear up into the wheel wells. I let go forward pressure on the control column and tried to ease the nose down.

Then Condor was in my ear. 'Let her drop, Yank! Get your nose wheel down! Now!'

I slammed the nose down and stood on the brakes. The big bird veered towards the left side of the runway. I eased up on the left brake and jammed the right rudder. It straightened and I continued braking.

'More brake, Yank! More brake!'

Runway was flashing by. I could see the crash equipment, red lights blinking at each intersection. They were falling in behind, following at max speed down the runway. Kam was sitting in the copilot's seat with his arms folded, gazing through the windshield as if at a television show he didn't much like. I could hear the shriek of sirens. I felt like my teeth had split.

'You're drifting left again. Use the nose wheel. Keep the binders on, Yank.'

We ground to a halt slightly to the left of the centre line and not far from the end of the runway. The nose popped up some as I released the brakes. The fire equipment surrounded the plane. I heard Kam sigh.

Then Zurich Tower came on. The caller was a Swiss who spoke English in precise accents. 'Two-Niner Charlie Echo,' he said. 'If your emergency is over, please clear the runway.'

# 9

I was so relieved to be on the ground, I hardly noticed the fact that we had a clown in the tower. Kam unbuckled at once and went aft to check on Wilma and Brian. I had to peel my hands off the yoke, finger by finger. Through the windshield I could see various members of the crash crew. When one of them caught my eye, he gave me the thumbs-up sign.

No brake fire.

No gear damage.

I yawned so big, as Sandy Johnson might have said, I almost swallowed myself. Then things got busy in my ear.

'Charlie Echo, this is Condor Delta Bravo. Good show . . .'

'This is Zurich Ground, Condor. Can you help Boeing Two-Niner with his shutdown, please.'

'We've got a patient with an electrical respirator on board,' I said. 'We'll need our auxiliary power before we shut down the engine.'

'This is Condor Delta Bravo to Zurich Ground. Boeing two-Niner is fuel-critical. We suggest you bring up a ground power unit as soon as possible.'

'That is affirmative, Condor. We will want to board Boeing Two-Niner with a mechanic for the towing procedure. We suggest an immediate shutdown and transfer to auxiliary electrical power.'

'We're equipped with Weber air stairs,' I said. 'I'll need instruction on working the hydraulics.'

'We understand. We will patch in our runway supervisor.'

'Two-Niner Charlie Echo, this is the Swiss border police. Do you copy, over.'

'Reading you loud and clear, Swiss police.'

'Are you able to transmit freely?'

'That's affirmative.'

'We would like for you to identify the difficulty with the regular crew.'

'I'd prefer to maintain a discretionary silence until you board.'

'Are you dealing with a hijacker?'

'That's negative.'

'Stand by, Charlie Echo. . . .'

'Charlie Echo, this is Condor Delta Bravo. Let's get your number two shut down.'

'Okay, but brief me on the auxiliary power first.'

'Two-Niner Charlie Echo, this is Zurich Ground. We are bringing up a tractor—'

'I've got too much traffic in my ear,' I said. 'Let me deal with Condor first.'

'You should prepare to be boarded by customs and police. Your aircraft is in quarantine until further notification.'

'Okay, okay, hold it down.'

'Charlie Echo, can you read me through the bleeding traffic?'

'Loud and clear, Condor, I'm ready to copy on the shutdown.'

'Jolly good. We've got an aggressive situation with the passengers up here. They've been toasting your show. I understand there's a bird in first class with her knockers out.'

'Hope she's a pretty bird,' I said.

'We're sending our copilot to confirm. Now, here's your procedure, Charlie . . .'

I spent the next few minutes hopping from the pilot's

seat to the APU starter on the engineer's panel and back, getting my instructions from Condor, carrying them out. While I did this, the ground crew brought the tractor up and hooked the tow bar to the twin nose wheels of Coyle's big plane.

Nobody seemed quite sure how to operate the Weber air stairs, but with a lot of help from Kam I finally found the combination and the door swung open and the stairs went down. The first thing I remember thinking was how fresh the outside air seemed: crisp and cool.

There were riflemen stationed around the aircraft. Two Swiss border police came up the stairs with their pistols drawn. They were followed by the airport manager, the ground mechanic who would help with the tow on to the civilian flight line, two customs officials, and a doctor.

The airport manager was a slender man in a blue wool suit, topcoat, and hat. The air stairs opened into the lounge, and he faced me there, puffing as if he had run to catch up with the emergency. The police stood on either side of him. They looked uneasy and did not holster their pistols. The rest of the party had paused on the top platform of the stairs. They were bunched up there, peering in.

'There's no danger,' I said. 'You won't need the guns.'

'Please identify yourself,' the airport manager said.

'My name's Eberhart. United States Air Force, retired.' I handed him my ID card.

'You are employed by Coyle Enterprises?'

'Correct.'

'What happened here?'

'We had an assassin on board. She shot both pilots and the engineer. Then she tried to kill the rest of us by depressurizing the cabin while we were at thirty-four thousand feet. She was equipped with a parachute and

was on her way to bail out when we managed to overpower her.'

The airport manager pursed his lips. 'She?' he said.

I pointed down the aisle where Monica's body now lay. I guessed Kam or Wilma had positioned her that way.

'There will be an interrogation,' the airport manager said.

'Fine,' I said. 'Before we get started on that, I'd like to look in on my son. He's in the master stateroom.'

The airport manager nodded, then looked at Kam. 'Is this gentleman also an employee of Coyle Enterprises?' he asked.

'Correct,' I said.

Kam smiled sweetly. In his brown silk suit, he looked like a dealer in Oriental rugs.

'My name is Kam Trak,' he said. 'I am Cambodian.'

'Can you vouch for him personally, Colonel Eberhart?' the airport manager asked. He had returned my ID.

'Yes,' I said.

'Who else is alive on board?'

'My son's nurse, Major O'Neill. I can vouch for her, too.'

'Very well, Colonel. We will take charge of the aircraft now. You are free to visit your son.'

'This flight was to be met by an ambulance from the Franki Clinic,' I said. 'Have they been cleared?'

'Yes,' the airport manager said. 'All those arrangements have been made.'

Kam and I walked through the lounge, past Monica's body. The doctor was kneeling over it, exploring the wound at the base of the neck, making small clucking sounds as he did. I guessed it was probably the first time he had seen the effect of a throwing star.

'Mr Coyle will authorize my weapons?' Kam asked me as we entered the passageway.

'Pretty sure he will,' I said. 'If you hadn't brought them on board, he'd have lost his plane.'

'We will speak with him soon?'

'He's got people on the ground here. I imagine they're keeping him posted. I don't know how sophisticated their equipment is, but I'll bet they've got good ears on the Swiss police. It shouldn't take them long to figure out what happened.'

'Mr Coyle will know who has been responsible?'

'My guess is Mr Coyle has known from the start. Not about Monica, but about whoever it is she was working for: someone who will go to this much trouble to keep us away from Cambodia and Sihanouk's hotel.'

'This occurred to me,' Kam said. 'For if I wished to acquire the diamonds, I do think I would happily let someone else go to the hotel and bring back.'

'And you'd be waiting for them at the border, with that number-eight knife of yours, and you'd say thank you kindly.'

Kam smiled. 'This is true,' he said. 'I would thank them very much.'


We went into the master stateroom. The room was cool, the lights dim. Wilma stood with her back to us, monitoring the portable support system that was keeping my son alive.

'Everything okay?' I asked.

'Everything *not* okay,' she barked. 'We need heat. I've got every blanket on him I could find, but if he gets a chill . . .'

'They're going to hook us in to ground power,' I said. 'We should have it in a couple of minutes.' I went to Brian's bedside. He slept his sleep, oblivious. 'We made it,' I said.

'That landing of yours was pretty goddamn shabby, if you ask me,' Whiskey said.

'Sorry about that,' I said.

'I banged my shin on the kid's respirator...

'You were supposed to be strapped in.'

'How am I supposed to take care of him when I'm tied to my seat?' She turned to glare at me. Her face was ruddy again.

I smiled. She clunked her arms around me. She smelled of sweat and faded perfume. I held on to her.

'You really got me scared that time,' she said.

'Got myself scared, too.'

'Are the Swiss cops going to hassle us?'

'They'll be asking some questions.'

'What do you want me to say?'

'Nothing but the truth.'

'Good. I'm not worth a flat damn as a liar. It's not that I mind lying, you understand. It's just that I'm no good at it.'

'I know what you are, Whiskey,' I said. 'You don't have to tell me.'

She pushed herself away and looked me in the eye. 'And what are you, Turkey?' she said. 'Getting mixed up in a thing like this.'

'Tough question,' I said.

'Can you give me an answer?'

'Sure,' I said. 'I can give you a bunch. The trouble is, I don't know which ones are real anymore.'

'You used to do it for flag and country. Maybe I'm just an old-fashioned broad, but I can still dig that. But this...'

She looked distastefully at the door, made a vague gesture with her hand. I knew it was meant to include the four people on board who were dead. 'This isn't for flag and country,' she said. 'This is free-lance. Guns for hire. I don't like it, Matt. We've been through enough together so I can tell you.'

I went and sat on the edge of the bed, away from the tubes and wires that connected the life-support system to my son. I could see his blond hair, straggly-looking

86

now, and his pale inert face just visible above the scarlet blankets that covered him.

'I gave it twenty years, Whiskey,' I said. 'There were better pilots than me, but nobody I knew who worked at it harder. I hung it out there and kept hanging it out until there wasn't anything left. Twenty years ago you could talk about these things and not feel like an asshole. I mean patriotism and dignity and courage. Twenty years ago it was still an honour for a man to serve his country, and if he had to die for his country, that was an honour too. Then things went sour. You get me started on this, and I can go the whole nine yards: what I think happened, who was responsible and why. I don't know how right I am, or even if I'm right at all. After the losses, after the failures, after Diana was killed, I began to burn out. And when I saw I was burning out, I began pushing myself harder and harder, trying to keep it from happening, and all I accomplished was to make it happen sooner.

'I'm stuck in the old mode, Whiskey. I still believe in good guys and bad guys. And even though I've been both in some ways, I can't shake it.

'So, you wanted an answer and I'm getting to it the long way around. I think Brian's a good guy. I think he deserves to live. Not like this, but in the same way most fifteen-year-olds live: with perceptions, and pleasures, and pain. If I can help him do that by selling my gun to Coyle, then I will, without hesitation.'

She stood, impassive. I could not tell whether I had reached her or not. The respirator hissed quietly. The plane was moving now, under tow.

'Those are more words than I've put together at one time in a year,' I said.

'We disagree about some things,' she said. 'But we don't disagree about him.' She came and sat next to me on the bed, put her hand on mine. Kam stood by the window.

'What's happening?' I asked.

'We are coming into place before a hangar,' he said. 'There are many police.'

The interrogations by the Swiss authorities were conducted on board Coyle's 727 in three different rooms. Whisky stayed where she was, with Brian. Kam was taken to one of the guest staterooms. I was taken to the office and communications area at the rear of the plane. It was very plush, with deep shag carpets and red leather chairs. The lights had brightened and the plane's interior was warm again now that we had tapped in to the ground power unit.

I would be questioned by a Swiss inspector in civilian clothes, a smallish man who spoke English so well I thought at first it might be his native tongue. A uniformed member of the Swiss border police stood, parade rest, just inside the room. A male stenographer took down my statement as I gave it.

'An elaborate case of sabotage,' the inspector said when I had finished. 'Don't you agree?'

'Yes. I do.'

'We are checking the stewardess's credentials. I suspect they will turn out to be forgeries. We understand she has worked for Coyle Enterprises for over a year. Is that correct?'

'I believe so.'

'Then certainly she had many other opportunities to scuttle the plane. Why do you suppose she picked this particular flight?'

'You're asking me to get inside the head of a professional assassin,' I said. 'I really don't have a clue. Whoever she took her orders from must have decided this was the time.'

The inspector nodded. 'What sort of work do you do for Mr Coyle?' he said.

'I'm sorry,' I said. 'I've been asked by Mr Coyle to keep that confidential.'

'It would be easier all around if you would not.'

I glanced at the communications panel behind me. 'He should be easy to reach,' I said.

The inspector smiled. He had a pipe which he now tamped down with his thumb and lit up. The tobacco was aromatic. I got out my cigarettes.

'We have, of course, already spoken with Mr Coyle,' he said.

'Is that right? What did he tell you?'

'He said you were an old family friend who had been down on his luck in recent months. He said he had felt a great deal of compassion for you and had offered to finance your son's stay in Switzerland in exchange for your services as a special courier.'

'Did he say what I'd be carrying?'

'Industrial diamonds.'

I inhaled deeply, and released the smoke.

'Which you will pick up in Thailand,' the inspector said. He had a twinkle in his eye, as if he believed very little of this.

'Mr Coyle calls the shots,' I said. 'If he wants me to go to Thailand, that's where I'll go.'

'When I told him we might have to detain your Cambodian friend, he became quite upset.'

'I don't blame him,' I said. 'Kam's the key to our negotiations. Without him, they're not going to work. He speaks all the languages that I don't.'

The inspector reached into the pocket of his coat and took out Kam's throwing star. It looked like the rowel of a spur. It was clean and bright and shone under the cabin lights.

'This is an unusual piece of equipment for a negotiator, don't you think?'

'Part of Kam's job is to act as my bodyguard,' I said.

'Most people who do that kind of work carry a gun. He doesn't like loud noises, so he carries that.'

'And a saw,' the inspector said. 'And a knife.'

'Yes.'

'You must expect these negotiations of yours to be quite difficult.'

'I've had an exciting first day,' I said.

'Your military record is most distinguished, Colonel.'

'Thanks,' I said. 'Sometimes I get the idea it's been published in the paper.'

'As a matter of routine, we requested to be briefed on it while you were still in the air. As you may know, it is stored by Deutsche Coyle in their central computer in Bonn.'

'Yes,' I said. 'I've seen that printout. All my bona fides are there.'

'That is true,' the inspector said. 'But as for your Cambodian friend, we can find very little. Only that he came to the United States as a refugee earlier this year and since then has been living in Texas.'

'When a man's country goes down the tubes,' I said, 'it's pretty hard for him to keep his records together. He was a captain in the Cambodian Army who served as a forward air controller during the time I was attached to the embassy in Phnom Penh. He saved my life there more than once, and now he's done it again.'

'Is he fluent in English?'

'No.'

'I gathered as much. When we ask him a question, he merely smiles and says that his name is Kam Trak and that he is Cambodian.'

'He'll talk if I ask him to,' I said. 'Otherwise he won't. You can try pulling his fingernails. Others have. It didn't work.'

The inspector sucked on his pipe. I thought he was trying to decide whether or not to let Kam go, but when

he finally spoke, it was to return to a matter we had already touched.

'It's the motive that puzzles me,' he said. 'Why the girl tried to scuttle this particular flight.'

'I can't give you an answer,' I said. 'Coyle Enterprises is one of the biggest conglomerates around. They've got deals going all over the world. And like most big operations, I suppose they've got enemies: people they've stepped on, people they've ruined. It really doesn't surprise me that someone decided to get even, if that's what happened.'

'If,' the Inspector said.

'Have you got a better theory?'

'No. Not really. I do ask myself what the result would have been if the scheme had worked. The plane would have crashed. We would have investigated the wreckage. We are quite thorough about that. We would, in all likelihood, have found that the crew had been murdered.'

'And you'd come back to why.'

'Yes.'

'Like I say, I really can't help you with that.'

'Of course.'

'Am I free to go?'

'Yes. One of my men will drive you to the clinic. Your son and his nurse have already left.'

I stood up, relieved to hear that. The inspector stood too.

'What about Kam?' I said.

'I'm afraid we will have to detain him.'

'For how long?'

'Perhaps until we have the answer to our question.'

'Mr Coyle won't like that,' I said.

The inspector shrugged. 'I do not work for Mr Coyle,' he said.

# 10

If I had had reservations about going any further with the business at hand, they were quickly dispelled by my first view of the Franki Clinic. It had been built high on the side of an Alp above the village of Bergheim, a collection of single-storey structures that looked as if they had been hewn out of giant redwood trees and were as modern in their effect as Coyle's estate was traditional.

It was dark when I arrived. The facades of the clinic were floodlit. My police driver and I had first seen them from the valley floor eight kilometres away, and as we had wound our way up the tortuous mountain road, they had beaconed to me like an emblem of hope.

Here, Brian would have his chance. And there was something in the very architecture of the place, with its bold angles, its cascading roofs and cantilevered decks and great expanses of glass that looked out over the extraordinary beauty of the Swiss countryside, that seemed to assure me his chance would be good.

Dr Franki himself met me at the door. I had expected the impatient, robotic sort of specialist to whom a patient is little more than a complex of tissue and nerve and bone. I could not have been more wrong. Franki was a kind, bespectacled, white-haired man who wore a white smock and whose head bobbed up and down almost continuously as if to add his own assurances to those of his buildings. I left my bag in the lobby and we walked through a long corridor, talking easily to each other, as though we were old friends. It was several moments

before I realized that we were walking through the mountain itself.

'As you saw,' the good doctor said, 'we are high on an alpine ridge. Several of our buildings have been constructed by tunneling through the ridge. In this way we are above any avalanche danger, and our patients can enjoy the view from either side.'

'I'm impressed,' I said.

'Your son's case is most interesting. I hope you don't object to my putting it that way.'

'I don't mind,' I said. 'I understand you think he has a chance to get better.'

'I do indeed.'

I felt a tightening in my throat. Except for Wilma and Kam, no one acquainted with Brian's condition had ever told me that.

'How long do you think it will take before we see some improvement?' I asked.

'That's difficult to say. I don't wish to promise miracles. It may take quite a while. Now that we have him with us, we will do our own complete workup. Once we have the results from that, we will outline a course of treatment. I should think within six months we will have a much better picture of what we are dealing with. As for the rest, well, as I say, it will take time.'

Brian's room was small, but lovely. The walls were painted a soft lemon yellow with a pattern of sunbursts. The bed linen and curtains were powder blue. The window looked on to a small balcony and, the doctor assured me, an incomparable view. Except for the unavoidable counter-effect of the life-support systems of blinking lights and stainless steel, and the inert presence of Brian himself, the room could not have been more cheerful. I was about to tell Dr Franki this when Wilma bustled in.

She had changed into a fresh uniform and had

somehow managed to find time to wash and dry her hair.

'Hello, Tiger,' she said. 'The kid's tougher than he has a right to be. His temperature shot up for a while, but it's down now. All the other essential signs are reading A-okay.'

'That's great,' I said.

Dr Franki smiled. 'We are delighted to have Major O'Neill,' he said. 'I have put her in charge of the younger staff. Some of them have been complaining that I work them too hard. They are all very able and bright, but like so many of this new generation, they are inclined to be soft on themselves. Major O'Neill should provide an excellent tonic for that.'

'What do you think, Whiskey?' I said. 'Can you shape up the troops?'

'They'll either shape up,' she growled, 'or I'll have them in full field gear doing ten miles before breakfast.'

Dr Franki nodded and chuckled at that. He said I should feel free to call or visit the clinic anytime and that he would send weekly reports to the box I still kept at the Pentagon. After he went out, I went to stand for a moment by Brian's bed.

'It seems like I'm always saying good-bye,' I told him. 'But I guess you're as used to that as anybody could be. Your mother used to say it was amazing that you were able to recognize me, I was off and away so much. Well, I'll tell you something. One of these days I'm going to find a place I like and I'm going to buy it and settle down. I think it's going to be somewhere in that northern Virginia countryside that you and your mother liked so much.

'I'm going to get one of those old brick farmhouses with some outbuildings and maybe fifty acres of land. Rundown, probably, but rock-solid. I'll have plenty of work to do bringing it back.

'You'll be there, and by then you'll be able to help. I'll want Whiskey there too. And Kam, if he'll come.'

For an instant I thought I saw Brian's lips move, as if he were trying to answer me. But it was only the trick of Wilma's shadow as she went quietly out the door. Then, except for the machines that sustained him, my son and I were alone.

'I love you, Brian,' I said. 'I love you very much.'

In the hall outside the room, when I finally came out, I found Wilma crying. She looked angry that I had seen her this way, and she barked something about releasing her tensions, and then we hung on to each other and said our good-byes.

'Your friend Coyle is on the phone,' she said, pulling herself together. 'You can take it in Dr Franki's office.'

'Thanks,' I said.

'You better go,' she said. 'He's calling long distance from Virginia. He says it's important. He's been on for a while. I told him you were busy and he should call back. He said he'd wait.'

'I can take some pleasure in that,' I said.

'How long do you think he would have to hold before he went broke?'

'Two or three lifetimes, I guess.'

She smiled. 'Good-bye, Tiger,' she said. 'Be careful.'

'I will,' I said.

Dr Franki's office was just off the foyer where I had left my bag. His secretary handed me the phone and with well-practiced discretion busied herself at a file cabinet across the room.

'Matt Eberhart,' I said. A voice told me to hold for Mr Coyle. I thought I recognized it as Jassick's. Then the man himself came on.

'Hello, Matthew. I hope the clinic meets with your approval?'

'The clinic's fine,' I said. 'But I've got a whole ration of things that aren't.'

'Yes. I know. I've been told what happened on the plane. I owe you a debt of gratitude.'

'No,' I said. 'You owe me an explanation.'

'I told you when you visited White Oaks there were others who want the diamonds just as badly as I.'

'I don't buy it,' I said. 'They're going to too much trouble. There's something else at stake. I want to know what it is.'

Coyle was silent. I could hear him breathing.

I shifted the receiver to my other hand. 'Let me put it this way,' I said. 'If you don't tell me I don't go.'

'It would be impossible over this phone.'

'Figure out a way that suits you.'

'I have a car waiting for you outside . . .'

'I don't trust your cars,' I said.

'You can trust this one, and I strongly advise you to do so. There may be another attempt.'

'Goddammit!' I said. 'Stop playing games!'

'This is no game, Matthew. Believe me. We are quite sure there will be another attempt. You should leave the clinic at once.'

'For where?'

He paused. 'You'll be taken to an hotel in Zurich,' he said. 'The arrangements have been made. You'll have all the necessary protection.'

'I don't think you're listening,' I said. 'Whoever these people are, they've got you wired. They know when you get up in the morning and what you have for breakfast and when you go to bed. They're professionals. They're as good as any I've seen. They started with a warning, and when that didn't work, they went on to Plan B without blinking an eye. They had Monica in place for over a year. Your operation is rotten from the inside, and

I think you know who's making it that way. Before I leave Zurich, I'm going to know too.'

'All right. I agree.'

'The Swiss police have Kam. I want him back.'

'We have very little influence there.'

'Crank some up.'

'Matthew, he admits that he killed the woman. Of course there are mitigating circumstances, but the Swiss are fussy about these things. They go by the book. It gets into areas of jurisdiction, international law—'

'I don't give a damn what it gets into. I want him back. I told you from square one I wouldn't go without him.'

'We'll work on it.'

'I want some security here for Brian, too.'

'I've already taken care of that.'

'Good. Fine. I'm red-eyed-tired and short of everything but temper. I'm going to get some sleep. I'll hire my own car and pick my own hotel. When I'm caught up, I'll be in touch.'

'I'd really rather you didn't do that, Matthew.'

'Tough,' I said.

When I hung up, I was shaking. I fished for my cigarettes, found them, popped one out of the pack. I had just stuck the filter between my teeth when I heard the snap of a lighter behind my ear. I turned. The lighter was familiar: a Siemens electric. So was the man who held it. Dieter Hoefel.

'Good evening, Colonel,' he said.

Big Karl was there too. He wore a new hat, and there were no splinters in his lapel.

Dieter smiled.

'The car is waiting,' he said. 'Shall we go?'

I didn't have to ask him if he was carrying his gun.

# 11

The black Mercedes with the German BN plates was parked just outside the entrance to the clinic. I threw my bag in the back seat and got in. Dieter Hoefel got in with me.

'We observed your landing of the aeroplane, Colonel,' he said. 'Considering the circumstances, it looked to be skilfully done.'

'I'm glad you liked it,' I said.

'We were to have picked you up then, but the police seemed to have matters in hand. We monitored their calls. Quite interesting. We are ready, Karl. Be careful on this road.'

Big Karl started us down. I could see the lights of Bergheim below. The lights looked like fireflies winking at the bottom of a deep well.

'I'd like to know where we're going,' I said.

'Karl and I have instructions to take you to an address in Zurich. Someone will be waiting for you there.'

'Like who?'

'I am sorry, Colonel. We do not have that information.'

'Coyle told me on the phone just now he had arranged an hotel.'

'It is what one would say if he was afraid to be overheard.'

'That's the trouble when you find a bad apple,' I said. 'You start looking at the whole bunch. He knows he's got people inside he can't trust. Why does he think he can trust you?'

'He has little choice. In Europe, his operations are directed from Bonn. Karl and I have been with him for many years. He is a very shrewd, very intelligent man. I suspect at this point we are the only ones who have had direct communication from him. He left White Oaks to call us from a public telephone. That in itself is singular. If Karl and I are the only ones who know the address in Zurich, and something should go wrong there, then Karl and I will not have our futures with Deutsche Coyle.'

'A future is a nice thing to have,' I said. I cranked my head back, tried to get a glimpse of the clinic as we wound our way down the long series of switchbacks that led to the valley floor.

Dieter looked at me. He kept one hand in the pocket of his trench coat. 'Are you concerned about your son?' he asked.

'Yes.'

'He is in excellent hands now.'

'Somebody wants me dead,' I said. 'That makes him vulnerable.'

Dieter started to say something, but caught himself before he did. I knew very well what it was: *You really shouldn't worry, Colonel. After all, your son can feel no pain. You could probe him with very long, very sharp needles, and at best you might trigger a reflexive convulsion to which he would remain oblivious. He requires intensive care, so to kidnap him would be a logistical nightmare. And to kill him would only make you madder than you are.*

*So. Sit back and relax. You are the one they want. If they could reach you by reaching him, almost certainly they would try. But they cannot reach him. No one can.*

So I sat back for a while and tried to rest. Dieter, watching me, fiddled with the *Blaupunkt* control system. This close to the mountain, there was a lot of static. He finally managed to bring in some Edith Piaf on Zurich FM.

'You will enjoy this?' he asked.

'Not really,' I said. 'It reminds me of somebody I knew once. It's not a good memory.'

'Then I will switch it off.'

He did. We were coming into the village now. It looked like a nice place to live. I folded my arms across my chest. I was about as relaxed as two cats in a sack.

'We're being followed,' I said finally.

Dieter had been watching me with his green eyes, one hand in his pocket. When I spoke, he did not look away. I was beginning to admire him. We had just passed through the village and were motoring toward Zurich.

'Karl?'

'It is true.'

'One car?'

'Yes.'

'Then we will follow our procedure.'

'Yes.'

'Are we armor-plated?' I asked.

'Yes,' Dieter said.

From my place on the backseat I had picked up a tail in Karl's rearview mirror. Now I squinted back through the rear window. The car had followed us out of the village and was staying two hundred meters back. I could see it in the light of the moon.

'It's a blue Fiat,' I said. 'It was parked in front of the rathskeller. I got a glimpse of it as we went by. Karl should be able to eat it up.'

Dieter smiled. 'Help yourself to a drink, Colonel,' he said. 'It should take less than an hour to Zurich.'

I opened the bar, poured myself a brandy. Big Karl sped up for a while, and so did the Fiat. Then he slowed down for a while, and the Fiat did that too. If this was the procedure Dieter had mentioned, I wasn't too impressed. We dawdled our way into Zurich.

It is a city I have always liked. It is neat and clean as

a pin. The people are well dressed. They look happy and healthy and well fed. They obey the laws. There aren't any old cars in Zurich. There aren't any bums in the gutter. Nobody tries to pick your pocket. I suppose it could get dull after a while, but when you've got a case of despair over what's happened to the cities in the United States, Zurich can be a fine tonic. Like putting Nurse Whiskey in charge of your troops.

We drove east past the Hotel Zurich, where Diana and I had once stayed, then south over the Bahnhofbrucke past the big Swissair terminal. The Fiat followed along. I was used to some pretty exciting car chases from watching my TV. This one was a bore. Karl began driving into streets that were narrow and involved some intricate turns, but he almost seemed to wait until the Fiat had a chance to catch up. I wanted to hit the drawbridge at sixty mph just as it was going up. That sort of thing.

We wound ourselves tighter and tighter into a maze of narrow streets. The streets were cobbled and the buildings rose abruptly from the kerb. The windows were casements, closed now against the November chill. The office windows were dark. The windows of the restaurants and private dwellings were lighted. I saw candle lanterns, bright red-and-white-checked table-cloths, a luster of wood, a child combing her hair.

'We will take the next two corners quickly, Colonel,' Dieter Hoefel said. 'Then Karl will stop briefly and you and I will get out. The timing is important.'

'All right,' I said.

Karl did his manoeuvre. He shot suddenly up one block, hung a right on two wheels, then down that block and hung a left. When he stopped it was abrupt and with very little screeching of tires. Dieter and I got out one door. Two men who might have passed for us got in the other. The transfer took about five seconds. Big Karl pulled away.

The Fiat contained three men. It had Swiss plates. Dieter and I watched it go by from the courtyard of an adjacent building. It went by quickly. The driver was hunched over the wheel. One of his passengers, a bulky, round-faced man who looked vaguely familiar to me, was pointing up the street where the taillights of the Mercedes showed like beacons.

'Not bad,' I said.

Dieter was jotting the licence into a notebook. 'We expected to be followed,' he said. 'We took precautions.'

'Who were the two who took our places?'

He laughed. 'Clerks from the bank in this city that handles our accounts,' he said. 'Our accounts are sizable. They were most happy to help. We minimized the risk.'

'That Fiat looked like a rental.'

'It was. Probably from the airport.'

'How come they didn't hit us? They had plenty of time.'

'They would assume we were armed. Once you were at your hotel, it would have been easier for them. Now they will go for a very long drive. Come along, Colonel. We will walk for a while.'

I recognized nothing until we came out on the Quaibrucke, the bridge that crosses the water where the Zurichsee narrows to the Limmat River. The air was cold and damp off the water. We crossed the bridge, dodged some traffic, plodded along the Limmatquai towards the wharf where the dance boats docked. Before we reached it, Dieter stopped.

'Well, Colonel,' he said. 'I have once again delivered you safely.' We were in front of a small office building, timber and stone, mansard roof, lots of grillwork around the windows. There were no lights visible on the ground floor. Two lights shone from the second storey. The sign over the door was the old-fashioned kind that hung by

two hooks from a wrought-iron brace extending over the sidewalk. It proclaimed 'LLOYD'S OF LONDON' in an understated yet elegant script.

'I could use the insurance,' I said. 'But the way things have been going, I doubt if I'll get any bids.'

Dieter Hoefel laughed again. 'You are expected, Colonel,' he said. 'First floor, last door to your left at the end of the corridor.'

He turned and walked away. He wore his hat with the häer feather in the band and was whistling a passage I thought I recognized from one of the later symphonies of Beethoven. The Sixth, I think it was. Or maybe the Seventh. I watched him fall in with the other pedestrians. He looked as if he belonged.

I carried my suitcase down the unlighted corridor to the last door on the left. There was an opaque glass panel with the name 'GREGORY HOWARD' lettered across it in gilt. The ceiling lights were on in the room. I didn't know any Gregory Howard.

I knocked.

I heard the squeak of a chair.

Then the door opened, and Campbell Cooke stood in the frame.

# 12

No one is required to like his father-in-law, but I have always liked mine. He is by nature a gentle man who when called upon can be as hard as any man I know. He is tall, long-boned, and lean. His hair is black. His features are angular, almost Lincolnesque. His eyes are blue. When he shakes hands, his hand advances quickly and grasps you and pulls you out of your space and into his. He is fifty-five now. I have seen him take on men half his age in handball and tennis and run them into the ground.

Diana always wanted me to call him 'Dad.' For a long while I called him 'Sir' and then 'Mr Cooke.' Finally, he took me aside one day and said if we were going to get along I would have to call him 'Campbell.' He wanted me to practice it right there and then. I did, but it cost me an enormous effort. I respected him that much.

Now he wore a grey three-piece suit with a pocket watch and chain. His hand reached out, grasped mine, and brought me to him. His voice was deep and reassuring, cultivated but without pretension.

'Matt,' he said. 'It's good to see you. You look tired but well. I'm up-to-date on that business at the airport. Thank God it wasn't worse.'

'I didn't know you were with Lloyd's,' I said.

'It's damn good cover. We can go anywhere, call anywhere, see anybody we want. All in the usual run of business.'

'Are you Gregory Howard?'

104

'No, no. He's off on a trip to New Zealand. I'm filling in.'

I glanced around. 'The place doesn't look very secure,' I said.

'We try not to be conspicuous about that, but we do look out for ourselves. For example, you arrived with Herr Hoefel several minutes ago. He wore a belted trench coat similar to your own. His hat was wool. When he left, he had his hands in his pockets and appeared to be whistling.'

'Can you name the tune?'

Campbell smiled. He had clean white teeth and healthy gums.

'We have safe houses in this city where the answer to that would be yes,' he said. 'Here all we get on the monitor is a picture.'

'Who's upstairs?'

'Nobody. We leave the lights on in hopes of drawing any moths to the flame. Let me get my coat and we'll be on our way. I know you're wondering how I fit into this Coyle business.'

'Yes, sir, I am,' I said.

We went from Campbell's office to an attached garage. He had an Opel sedan that was so ordinary-looking I couldn't place the year. We drove up into the Zurichberg area, northwest from the Limmatquai. Nobody followed. As we drove, we talked about Brian and other family matters. Campbell's wife, Midge, had come down with mild arthritis. The doctor said it was simply part of the ageing process. Campbell disagreed. He thought if his wife would exercise on a regular basis the arthritis would go away.

We pulled into the drive, finally, of a fine estate house tucked in a secluded lane just off Bannholz Strasse. Campbell said there were six levels in all, four above ground, two below. The facade was white stucco with dark wood trim, black slate roof, copper flashing and

drains. The two-acre lot was bordered with hedge. Iron gates secured the drive.

'Fine-looking place,' I said.

'The KGB know about it, of course,' he said. 'That goes without saying. Swiss Intel. One or two others. But given the way things are these days, Matt, it's as secure as a safe house can be. Gregory Howard inherited it from his grandfather on his mother's side. They were old Swiss money. The family has been here for years. Greg's father was English, also with Lloyd's. Greg was CIA. After his father died, Greg took over. He keeps a domestic staff. They come in during the day. They run the place just as they would the private residence of any well-to-do man. We keep the antennae in the attic and the rest of the clandestine stuff in the two basements. Come on. Let me show you.'

We entered the house through a side door, went through one kitchen and into another, and from there down a rickety set of stairs into what looked to be an ordinary cellar. The cellar was lit by naked bulbs hanging from frayed black wire. It was damp, and filled with the usual material a family collects and can't use and won't throw away – wicker-shot chairs, glass bottles, rusty tools, a headless hobbyhorse, half-empty cans of solidified paint and varnish.

Campbell took out what looked to be a cigarette lighter but was actually a small transmitter of the kind that can be used to open garage doors without leaving the car. In this case it opened a concealed door at one end of the cellar. We went through and the door closed electronically behind us. As it did, a bank of fluorescent lights flashed on and I felt as if I had been taken suddenly into some future world. I blinked and stared.

'This is level one,' Campbell said. 'As you see, it consists of a fully self-contained apartment. Kitchen, bedroom, bath, wardrobe, sitting room, and office. I could put you here tonight and you could stay for thirty

days without being resupplied. You would have complete communications, television, telephone, intercom to the rest of the house, the works. There are three ways out. We just came through one. Another is through a storm sewer accessible from the bath. A third is through an exit tunnel out of the subcellar. Come on. Watch your step.'

There was a trapdoor under one of the rugs in the sitting room of the apartment. Campbell pulled it open and I followed him down a set of steep circular stairs into what must have been the wine cellar of the old estate. The cellar had been converted into a fully equipped gymnasium. The walls were mirrored and the floor covered with green wall-to-wall carpet. There was a Universal machine, a light and heavy bag, exercycles, and a set of graded dumbbells that went from ten to a hundred pounds.

'The bath in the apartment converts to a sauna,' Campbell said. 'Everything's soundproof.'

'What do you do about taps?' I said.

He smiled as if he had hoped I was going to ask. He took out his transmitter again and pointed it at one of the glass-panelled walls. A section of mirror slid open.

'After you,' he said.

The room we entered was as large as the gym. It had bare concrete walls and floor. There was no furniture, no decorations of any kind. The overhead lights were fluorescent. At the centre of this room, a smaller room had been constructed out of clear Plexiglas. The cube was covered on all four sides, top and bottom, with pure copper screening. We entered through a door that had been cut out of the cube once the cube and screening were in place. Inside there were two moulded Plexiglas chairs facing a small Plexiglas table. We sat down. Like a screen porch, we were bugproof.

'We've arranged some special security for Brian at the clinic,' Campbell said.

'Good,' I said.

'I don't think there'll be any problem there, but he's all we have left of Diana . . .'

'I agree.'

'What did Bob tell you this was all about?' my father-in-law asked. He was the only person I knew who called Coyle by his first name.

'He said just before Cambodia fell his people had been negotiating with members of the Lon Nol government to receive rubber shipments from the Chupp plantation. The *riel* was unstable, so they worked out a deal whereby the rubber would be paid for with diamonds.

'They did their business at Sihanouk's hotel. Their courier, a man named Capps, would go there, check into a specially equipped suite, arrange a shipment, and deliver the diamonds. He kept the diamonds in a concealed wall safe along with the records of his transactions. Capps was at the hotel when Kampong Som was overrun by the Khmer Rouge on April 17. He never got out.

'Coyle told me the diamonds are still there. He said his last appraisal put their worth at just under two million. He said he wanted the diamonds back along with the papers in the pouch. He said he had made one attempt but it had failed. The Khmer Rouge caught his guy and hacked him to death with their hoes. He was a Chinese.'

'And Bob claimed this Chinese had been hired by Coyle Enterprises?'

'Yes. Wasn't he?'

'No.'

I leaned back in my Plexiglas chair. The copper screen gleamed in the clinical light of the overhead.

'Dieter and Karl rousted me out of the BOQ in Wiesbaden some thirty-six hours ago,' I said. 'Since then I've been waltzed and danced by everybody from Coyle

108

to the pretty assassin on his plane. I need some straight talk, Campbell. What the hell's going on?'

'I wish I could tell you with much more certainty than I can. A lot of what I have is speculation – a piece here, a piece there . . .'

'I'll settle for whatever you can give me. Go ahead.'

Campbell was tall and his chair was short. With his feet flat on the floor and sitting erect, his knees were above his belt.

'When Bob asked me for your complete military records, he told me about the diamonds and what he was prepared to do for Brian if he decided you were the right man for the job and you agreed to go. If you had been more together at the time, I would have let you know, Matt. I might even have tried to talk you out of it. But as it was . . .'

'When they rousted me yesterday morning, I was in bed with a woman I didn't recognize and whose name I still can't remember,' I said. 'That's how it was.'

'I know. And to speak frankly, I thought what Bob was suggesting, no matter how risky, was better than that.'

'I agree.'

'*But*, I had no idea at the time that there would be anything more involved than your going in and getting the pouch and bringing it out. I knew you were experienced enough to do that, at least to have a good chance of doing it.'

'And now there's more involved.'

'Yes. A lot more. Does the name Manfred Von Regen ring a bell?'

'Sure. He's the German industrialist. Armaments. Chemicals. Shipping. Sort of a Prussian counterpart of Coyle.'

'Exactly. Did you know they were roommates at Harvard in the late thirties?'

'No. I didn't know that.'

'They were very tight then. Same clubs. Same friends.

Same political persuasion. Bob was against our entering the war. Like Lindbergh, Joe Kennedy, and the others, he thought we were making a serious mistake taking England's side against Hitler.'

'I didn't know that either.'

'He's kept it very quiet, for obvious reasons. By the time he joined up, he was as patriotic as the rest of us.'

'Did Von Regen work for the Nazis?'

'Never directly. But after the war there were rumours that he had shared in the Nazi treasure and was part of the web that protected the ex-Nazis in Argentina and elsewhere. Nothing was ever proved, but the rumours were ugly and they persisted long enough to damage Von Regen's reputation.'

'Okay, so how does all this fit with Coyle and the diamonds?'

'As I say, we don't have enough yet to be sure. We learned just recently from our sources in Thailand that the murdered Chinese Bob told you about was actually employed by Von Regen.'

'Which means he wants the pouch too?'

'Yes.'

'Badly enough to kill for it?'

'Apparently.'

'Why?'

'His son Horst is running for chancellor in the next election. Unlike his father, Horst is Mr Clean. He's a big, blond, likable giant. The people love him. He's been married to the same woman for years. They have the beautiful home, the beautiful children. In West Germany today, he's the dream candidate. Few voters will hold his father's past against Horst. He has an enormous appeal to the postwar middle class. The hardworking, decent Germans who want a hardworking, decent chancellor.

'Horst represented the Von Regen interests in the Far East during Vietnam. We know he visited Sihanouk's

110

hotel on more than one occasion. Bob's courier, Capps, was there. Young Von Regen knew Capps and may have been doing business with him.'

'On the rubber deal?'

'Possibly. Horst was in a good position to arrange the shipping.'

'And you think there's something in the pouch that could compromise him?'

'That would be my best guess.'

'Any idea what it is?'

'No. But whatever it is, it's got to be dynamite. Proof of fraud. Illegal transactions. Something that if made public in West Germany would destroy the candidacy of this Mr Clean forever.'

I looked up. 'I get the feeling that wouldn't bother you, Campbell,' I said.

'The President doesn't want him in. He sees him as a front for his father. He thinks his may be one of the powers behind the Neo-Nazi movement. The Agency agrees.'

'What do you want me to do?'

'Let us have a look at the pouch before you deliver it to Bob.'

'Okay.'

'We'll have to arrange it in Bangkok. As soon as you've recrossed the border. I'll set it up.'

'If you're right about Von Regen, I can see why he might go to any length to get the pouch. But what's the burr under Coyle's saddle? Do you know?'

'Bob told me in confidence that there were aspects of the rubber deal that could be embarrassing to him. My guess would be that there were payoffs involved. Talbot, the senior senator from Virginia, is itching to get Coyle Enterprises under the light of his Economic subcommittee. He's primed and ready. That's why Bob began working out a way to interest you in going after the pouch. He wanted to omit a potential problem.'

'And then he heard about Von Regen's attempt to get the pouch and he panicked?'

'I think so. That's why he had you picked up the way he did. If the pouch holds anything that can embarrass Coyle Enterprises, he knows very well Von Regen will use it.'

'What caused them to fall out all those years ago? The war?'

'Probably.'

'And now Coyle knows Von Regen's got him penetrated.'

'Yes. Bob came to me as if on his knees. I've never heard him sound the way he did. Scared. He was calling from a public phone. He begged me to take a hand in the matter, to meet you here and get you into a safe place. I had already helped with your records and Kam's American passport, but that was before the panic had set in.'

'Does Coyle know the Agency has an interest in this?'

'No. He thinks I'm doing it as a favour. I'm an old friend, you know.'

'Where do we stand with Kam?'

'The Swiss are being stubborn. I think they know something is going on and they want to know what. We'll get him out. It's going to take some time.'

'I need to sleep,' I said.

'The apartment is yours.'

I snapped my fingers. 'Ingrid,' I said.

'Ingrid?'

'That was her name. The girl I woke up with at the BOQ. I picked her up at the Arms Bar. We got to talking about the war. Her father had been a pilot in the Luftwaffe. We drank a lot.'

Campbell nodded. 'I think you're getting better,' he said. 'I think you're coming back.'

hotel on more than one occasion. Bob's courier, Capps, was there. Young Von Regen knew Capps and may have been doing business with him.'

'On the rubber deal?'

'Possibly. Horst was in a good position to arrange the shipping.'

'And you think there's something in the pouch that could compromise him?'

'That would be my best guess.'

'Any idea what it is?'

'No. But whatever it is, it's got to be dynamite. Proof of fraud. Illegal transactions. Something that if made public in West Germany would destroy the candidacy of this Mr Clean forever.'

I looked up. 'I get the feeling that wouldn't bother you, Campbell,' I said.

'The President doesn't want him in. He sees him as a front for his father. He thinks his may be one of the powers behind the Neo-Nazi movement. The Agency agrees.'

'What do you want me to do?'

'Let us have a look at the pouch before you deliver it to Bob.'

'Okay.'

'We'll have to arrange it in Bangkok. As soon as you've recrossed the border. I'll set it up.'

'If you're right about Von Regen, I can see why he might go to any length to get the pouch. But what's the burr under Coyle's saddle? Do you know?'

'Bob told me in confidence that there were aspects of the rubber deal that could be embarrassing to him. My guess would be that there were payoffs involved. Talbot, the senior senator from Virginia, is itching to get Coyle Enterprises under the light of his Economic subcommittee. He's primed and ready. That's why Bob began working out a way to interest you in going after the pouch. He wanted to omit a potential problem.'

'And then he heard about Von Regen's attempt to get the pouch and he panicked?'

'I think so. That's why he had you picked up the way he did. If the pouch holds anything that can embarrass Coyle Enterprises, he knows very well Von Regen will use it.'

'What caused them to fall out all those years ago? The war?'

'Probably.'

'And now Coyle knows Von Regen's got him penetrated.'

'Yes. Bob came to me as if on his knees. I've never heard him sound the way he did. Scared. He was calling from a public phone. He begged me to take a hand in the matter, to meet you here and get you into a safe place. I had already helped with your records and Kam's American passport, but that was before the panic had set in.'

'Does Coyle know the Agency has an interest in this?'

'No. He thinks I'm doing it as a favour. I'm an old friend, you know.'

'Where do we stand with Kam?'

'The Swiss are being stubborn. I think they know something is going on and they want to know what. We'll get him out. It's going to take some time.'

'I need to sleep,' I said.

'The apartment is yours.'

I snapped my fingers. 'Ingrid,' I said.

'Ingrid?'

'That was her name. The girl I woke up with at the BOQ. I picked her up at the Arms Bar. We got to talking about the war. Her father had been a pilot in the Luftwaffe. We drank a lot.'

Campbell nodded. 'I think you're getting better,' he said. 'I think you're coming back.'

# 13

For a while it was a waiting game. With the situation the way it was at White Oaks, Coyle had decided to leave all the arrangements to my father-in-law. We could reasonably assume that Von Regen's assassins were following Karl on a cold trail. Campbell would want to make certain we kept it that way.

He left me at ten o'clock that night. I slept until ten the next morning. I shaved and showered. I fried some eggs and bacon, made a pot of coffee, began to feel like a human being again.

At noon I went down into the gymnasium and worked out on the Universal machine. I went around the machine twice, making use of each of the stations. I used very light weight. My joints felt as if they needed oil. My back ached. When I tried some sit-ups on the incline board, I grunted like a pig.

Wages of sin, Eberhart.

I got on the exercycle and pedalled for a while, easing the tension off on the wheel. I gave the light bag a decent flurry and whopped the heavy bag a left and a right.

Oh, yeah. As Campbell had said, I was coming back.

I converted the bath to a sauna. When I sat on the small wooden bench and looked down, I saw the belly of the whale. I sucked it in. Some of it went away, some of it didn't. I had the advantage of hair: a thicket of it that ran from pubes to pectorals. The hair covered the flesh. I was grateful.

I let the sauna cook me for thirty minutes. Then I exhausted away the steam and let the cold shower cool

me down. There were slacks and a shirt in the well-stocked wardrobe that fit me. I put them on.

There are times when I like to be alone. Times when I don't want anybody to call me or knock on my door or stumble around in my space. This was one of them. I enjoyed Campbell's hideaway that entire afternoon. I listened to *The Mikado* on Zurich FM. I sipped grapefruit juice. I thought about Brian and Diana: not the bad stuff, the good stuff. The way it had been in the years before the war. It was as if I held those years in my hands like bubbles, and through the translucent film could see the three of us sitting at the table with our hands joined and heads bowed, playing football in the yard, running and laughing in the rain.

No, the bubbles didn't burst. They were simply there for a while, and then they were gone.

And then Campbell joined me for supper.

'Hard day at the office?' I asked.

He had taken off his suit coat and put on an apron. He was broiling two steaks.

'Busy, not hard,' he said. 'I missed connections with Dieter Hoefel. He was going to update me on the situation at White Oaks. It was to be one of those pay-phone-to-pay-phone operations. I hung around my booth as long as I could, but never got the call.'

'Any news on Kam?'

Campbell peppered the steaks. 'Not really,' he said. 'I've got some good contacts with Swiss Intel. They're working on it. According to them the inspector in charge is jealous of his prerogatives. He can't be pushed, but he can be persuaded. We'll have to keep our fingers crossed.'

'How freely can we talk?'

'I think we should be conservative.'

He jotted some notes on a single sheet of ruled paper, handed the paper to me. He had printed in large block letters:

114

YOU WILL LEAVE TOMORROW BY CAR FOR MILAN. YOU
WILL FLY COMPANY CHARTER MILAN TO ROME, THEN
COMMERCIAL ROME TO BANGKOK. YOUR ETD OUT OF
ROME IS TWENTY-ONE HUNDRED TOMORROW. KAM IS
TICKETED SAME. ADUNE EXPECTS YOU, BUT WILL NOT
HAVE YOUR DETAILS. ONCE YOU HAVE ESTABLISHED
COVER IN BANGKOK YOU WILL HAVE TO CONTACT HIM.

I read the note, then burned it in one of the ashtrays. We
sat down to eat. The steaks were lean. Campbell had his
well done. I had mine rare. I skipped the rolls and salad
dressing. I drank one glass of wine. When Campbell
asked me if I were going to smoke, I clamped my jaws
shut and shook my head. He smiled.

'Good,' he said. 'I've gotten so I can't stand the smell
of them. I'm delighted to see you this way, Matt. I really
am. You don't know how worried I was.'

'I know.'

'It seemed to me that ever since you retired, you'd
been determined to self-destruct. I had reports on you
from Paris, Copenhagen, Amsterdam, God knows
where. They were not good. The night you called me in
New York from Brussels. You were higher than a
kite.'

'I remember,' I said. 'That was to tell you I was off
to Oman to fly Hunters for their air force. It fell through
at the last moment.'

'Yes, didn't it,' Campbell said. 'I had our man tell the
Brit in charge you were unsuitable.'

I looked up, surprised. 'Well, their losses were high,
I suppose that's why I wanted to join them.'

'How well I know,' Campbell said. 'Then you understand why I decided this mission of Bob's, even with its
hazards, was more desirable than that?'

'Yes.'

He paused, as if he wanted to broach a subject that
might be delicate.

115

'Jillion Leggett is still in Bangkok,' he said finally. 'I take it you knew.'

'I wasn't sure.'

'Will you be seeing her?'

'I suppose I will.'

'She's an able and attractive woman. Very tough, too. Of the copy that came out during the war, I would rate hers close to the top. Clear, cool, professional. No ax to grind.' He poured himself his second glass of wine. 'I always thought,' he said, 'that if it hadn't been for Diana, you and Jillion ... well, might have made a fine couple.'

'I'm not sure about that,' I said. 'Diana was one kind of woman. Jillion was another.'

'Of course. I agree. Do you mind talking about it?'

'No.'

'I brought it up for a reason. I think if you don't find Jillion in Bangkok, she's liable to find you. She'll want to know why you're there. You two will clap each other on the back and drink to some old times ...'

'You're telling me to be careful.'

'Yes.'

'I'll try. With Jillion it won't be easy.'

'It's not a matter of trust. I know you trust her implicitly. But she is a reporter. One of the best. And the story you have, if we're right about Von Regen, could be the most spectacular of the year. I don't think you could fairly ask any good journalist to keep it in her hat.'

'You're right. There never was anything between us, by the way. Not until after Diana was killed. I hope you believe that.'

'Of course I do. I remember when the six of us had supper in the Swiss Room of the Erawan Hotel in Bangkok. You, Diana and Brian, Jillion and Kam. That was in the early spring of '74. I was on my way home from Australia.'

'It was the first time we let Brian have some wine. He got a little tiddly, didn't he?'

'Yes! He stood up on his chair and sang "There Are No Fighter Pilots Down in Hell." We all joined him.'

We laughed at that memory, then Campbell took out his watch. It was a Patek Philippe on a gold chain.

'Turn on the television for me, will you?' he said. 'Channel 14 on the UHF.'

I did. When the picture came on it was of the front door of the house. It was in colour, very sharp. I could read the initials GH on the big brass knocker.

'What's up?' I asked.

'I'm expecting someone.'

'Anybody I know?'

'I think you will know her before the night's over.'

I looked at him. He smiled what was very close to a wicked smile.

'Oh, hey, look,' I said. 'I really appreciate the thought, sir, but I'm still dragging ass . . .'

'There's nothing to worry about. Her name is Erika. We've used her for years. She's completely reliable, a licensed masseuse.'

'I'll bet.'

He pointed at the screen. A woman stood now on the stoop. She wore red spike heels, fishnet stockings, what looked to be a burgundy soft suede dress, and a short fur coat. Her hat was one of those wide-brimmed floppy jobs that were beginning to come back into vogue. I could see her hair where it fell below the brim. Long. Dark. She banged the knocker once. Campbell went to the television set, activated the intercom that had been run through it.

'Be with you in a minute, darling,' he said.

'Wow,' I said.

'You do promise never to tell Midge,' he said.

'Okay,' I said. So, Erika wasn't for me.

When he came back with Erika on his arm, I couldn't

117

decide whether I was happy or sad. I stood up for the introduction.

'Hi,' I said.

Erika scowled, and threw her hat on the floor.

I looked at her again. It was Kam.

'I do think I will ask for more pay,' he said. He looked very unhappy about his disguise.

Campbell Cooke was already laughing. His laugh rose up like the scale on a contrabassoon. Kam kicked off the heels, tore off the fur coat. He struggled out of the burgundy dress, all arms and elbows and spare parts. Then he stood there in his sleeveless undershirt and shorts, glaring at me.

'Don't forget the stockings,' I said. 'And the wig.' There were tears in my eyes from laughing.

'I will not forget, *Sakpram*,' he said. 'I will require more pay.'

'*Sakpram*' was Khmer for 'Colonel.' When Kam called me that, I knew he was mad.

I made him some tea while he found a pair of slacks and a sweater in the wardrobe. Then the three of us sat at the table while he drank. The tea seemed to settle him down.

'It's good to see you, old friend,' I said. 'Do you have any news?'

'Yes,' he said. 'I do.'

He told us two bodies had been pulled out of the Limmat less than an hour ago. They were both males. Their throats had been cut. He had not caught the last names, only the first.

One was Dieter.

The other was Karl.

'It was the first time we let Brian have some wine. He got a little tiddly, didn't he?'

'Yes! He stood up on his chair and sang "There Are No Fighter Pilots Down in Hell." We all joined him.'

We laughed at that memory, then Campbell took out his watch. It was a Patek Philippe on a gold chain.

'Turn on the television for me, will you?' he said. 'Channel 14 on the UHF.'

I did. When the picture came on it was of the front door of the house. It was in colour, very sharp. I could read the initials GH on the big brass knocker.

'What's up?' I asked.

'I'm expecting someone.'

'Anybody I know?'

'I think you will know her before the night's over.'

I looked at him. He smiled what was very close to a wicked smile.

'Oh, hey, look,' I said. 'I really appreciate the thought, sir, but I'm still dragging ass . . .'

'There's nothing to worry about. Her name is Erika. We've used her for years. She's completely reliable, a licensed masseuse.'

'I'll bet.'

He pointed at the screen. A woman stood now on the stoop. She wore red spike heels, fishnet stockings, what looked to be a burgundy soft suede dress, and a short fur coat. Her hat was one of those wide-brimmed floppy jobs that were beginning to come back into vogue. I could see her hair where it fell below the brim. Long. Dark. She banged the knocker once. Campbell went to the television set, activated the intercom that had been run through it.

'Be with you in a minute, darling,' he said.

'Wow,' I said.

'You do promise never to tell Midge,' he said.

'Okay,' I said. So, Erika wasn't for me.

When he came back with Erika on his arm, I couldn't

decide whether I was happy or sad. I stood up for the introduction.

'Hi,' I said.

Erika scowled, and threw her hat on the floor.

I looked at her again. It was Kam.

'I do think I will ask for more pay,' he said. He looked very unhappy about his disguise.

Campbell Cooke was already laughing. His laugh rose up like the scale on a contrabassoon. Kam kicked off the heels, tore off the fur coat. He struggled out of the burgundy dress, all arms and elbows and spare parts. Then he stood there in his sleeveless undershirt and shorts, glaring at me.

'Don't forget the stockings,' I said. 'And the wig.' There were tears in my eyes from laughing.

'I will not forget, *Sakpram*,' he said. 'I will require more pay.'

'*Sakpram*' was Khmer for 'Colonel.' When Kam called me that, I knew he was mad.

I made him some tea while he found a pair of slacks and a sweater in the wardrobe. Then the three of us sat at the table while he drank. The tea seemed to settle him down.

'It's good to see you, old friend,' I said. 'Do you have any news?'

'Yes,' he said. 'I do.'

He told us two bodies had been pulled out of the Limmat less than an hour ago. They were both males. Their throats had been cut. He had not caught the last names, only the first.

One was Dieter.

The other was Karl.

# 14

We were silent for a while. Finally, I stood up from the table and began to pace. Kam watched me.

'You be very nervous now, *Lōk*,' he said.

'You're right about that,' I said. 'Who gave you the information about Dieter and Karl?'

'The chief of inspectors. The same who has asked you many questions on the big plane. He take me to pagoda building: so, so tall with two big stupas on each side; but here now there is no Buddha, no place to pray or burn incense – only many doors and rooms, and halls of five meters.'

'That's the Polizei Kommando des Canton Zurich,' Campbell explained. 'It's the main building for the office of criminal affairs. The inspector's name is Selinger. He's in charge of their foreign stuff.'

'I don't get it,' I said. 'Why would the bad guys dirty their hands with small fry like Dieter and Karl?'

'I was wondering that too,' Campbell admitted. 'Everything up until now has been imaginative and professional: the two warnings you got on your flight from Frankfurt, the really lethal business with Monica on Bob's plane. Now, all of a sudden, it looks as if the amateurs have taken over. I didn't think the tail with the Fiat was very impressive. And to murder a couple of relatively small fish in a city as well policed as Zurich is just plain stupid.'

Kam, who had been listening patiently to all this, asked us just who these men were who had been killed. I told him as much as I knew about Dieter and Karl. He

119

thought the matter over for a while, sipping his tea. Finally he said, 'Other side angry now, *Lōk*. We very much make them look foolish. Also maybe they in trouble now from top – feel much heat. So when they not find two fish they want, they kill two fish at hand.'

Campbell smiled. 'I like it,' he said. 'It's as good as anything we've got.'

'Who set up the phone contact between you and Dieter?' I asked.

'Swiss Intel. Bob must have put Dieter in touch with one of my contacts there. The way things are, he wouldn't want any more direct communication.'

'Suppose somebody followed Kam when he left the inspector's office in that hooker's rig of his?'

'I don't think Selinger would let that happen.'

'Maybe not,' I said. 'But I'd be a lot happier right now if we had somebody outside the house.'

Campbell thought for a moment, weighing the merits of what I had said.

'You may be right,' he replied. 'I'll arrange something before I turn in.' He picked up the bottle of wine he had opened for supper. It was a Wente Pinot Noir. 'You know, Matt,' he said, 'I've come to prefer the California wines. I have them sent over by the case. This particular variety of grape is grown in the Arroyo Seco Canyon, not far from the Pacific. The days there are consistently warm, the nights cool. The result is splendid. Will you have some?'

'No, thanks,' I said. 'I'd like to keep my head clear.'

'Kam?'

'Will now only drink tea,' Kam said.

Campbell poured himself a glass, held it briefly to the light, drank it. Then he stood. 'We leave first thing in the morning,' he said quietly. 'I'll get you up at 0500.'

'I know you like to keep your cards close to the vest,' I said, 'but do you mind telling me how you managed to spring Kam from the inspector?'

He smiled. 'It was a matter that required a good deal of delicacy and a certain amount of grease. The idea for the disguise was Selinger's, actually. He'd used it once before on another case. He'll want a full report on how successful it was.'

'Erika,' I muttered.

'Now, there really *is* an Erika,' he said. 'I'll have to introduce you to her one of these days.'

He boomed his laugh and went out, the electronic door whisking shut behind him. Kam was yawning now, and very quiet. I puttered around, cleaning up the supper dishes, sighing some restless sighs. The apartment was nicely appointed, but I felt I had been shut up in it for too long.

When I had the dishes racked in the drainer, I poured myself another coffee and sat at the table again, across from my friend. I guessed he hadn't slept much during the last several days. He looked bushed, his black eyes blinking slowly.

'Now I must sleep, *Lōk*,' he said.

'You've done a great job,' I said. 'You always do. And this time you'll make some money for a change.'

He looked away, silent for a while. When he finally spoke, it was in a low voice. 'Money is useless to me. What I do? Get house? Get car? You keep the money, *Lōk*. Make Brian well. I am here only because you are my brother.'

'And I yours,' I said.

'When we go to Cambodia,' he said, 'I maybe not come back.'

'Do you feel you might be killed?' I asked, aware he believed in premonitions.

'No,' he said. 'I know how long my time to go. But the ashes of my people lie in the soil of my country. In Texas I am as a dead man. I walk in mud. My arms and legs are heavy.'

I told him I thought I understood the feeling he was

trying to convey, the deep depression he felt over the loss of his family and home. I had felt something similar during the past year in Germany, Turkey, Greece. Like swimming in molasses.

'You're going to be fine,' I said. 'You won't be able to stay in Cambodia, not as long as that bloodthirsty regime is in power, but you could stay in Thailand. With the money you'll earn, you could stay there very well.'

'Then you find money-house for me in Bangkok,' he said. 'For now, I will sleep.'

I showed him to the bedroom, told him good night.

'If trouble comes, *Lŏk*, you wake me quick,' he said.

'Only if it's big trouble,' I said. 'Sleep well.'

# 15

It was nearly 0200 by my watch and I was still roaming around the apartment. I had looked through all *The Reader's Digests* on the table in the sitting room, had rummaged through the empty desk in the office. I was so bored, my fingers had started to itch.

I snapped on Channel 14 to have a look at the door where Kam had first appeared as Erika. The stoop was empty now, the brass knocker gleaming as before. I found a rotor control and swivelled the outside camera. It allowed me to scan the grounds in front of the house, the drive, the street, and the sidewalk beyond the wrought-iron fence.

It was the only show in town. I settled into a TV slump, mesmerized by the screen.

At the end of a half-hour I had seen exactly one Volkswagen bus, and a man in a hat, walking a dog.

By then I would have killed for a Carson rerun even if Pat Boone had been the guest host.

'Take a hot shower,' I told myself. 'Try to induce some drowsiness.'

I padded into the bath and looked around for some fresh towels. I opened the door to a linen closet, and as if by magic, there they were. Who says you don't have to be smart to be a fighter pilot. I was about to shut the door when I noticed an unnatural outline in the tile that made up the floor of the closet.

Remembering what Campbell had told me about the tunnels that led out of the house, I reached down and began to press and fiddle. In minutes I had removed a

two-foot-square section of the floor and was peering down at what I was sure was the iron hatch cover of a shaft that would eventually lead to the storm sewer Campbell had mentioned.

I took the cover by its ring, hoisted it up, set it aside. Then, on my knees now, I looked down into the shaft. It was lined with old brick. A narrow rusting ladder, bolted to the brick, disappeared into an ink-black void below. I felt around for a light switch, found one, flipped it on. An eerie glow illuminated the bottom of the shaft, apparently reflecting from the tunnel itself.

What the hell, I thought. Let's have a look.

I lowered myself into the shaft, climbed a dozen feet down the vertical ladder. The air was dank and smelled like green cheese. As I had expected, the tunnel opened out from the bottom of the shaft. It was narrow, maybe three feet wide, five feet high. A black wire ran the length of the passage, with low-watt bulbs every ten feet or so. The passage looked to be about a hundred feet long. It slanted down. There was a tap in the shaft, with a garden hose attached. The hose, like the black wire, ran the length of the tunnel.

I got into a crouch and began to walk. My shoes crunched in the grit of the tunnel floor. At first as I approached the end I could see no obvious way out. The passage looked as if it had been bricked up. The garden hose fed into a spill pipe that went through the wall. The light was dimmer here.

I ran my fingers around the brick, found a couple of bolts, threw them, saw a centre panel in the wall start to swing inward. Then I realized what the hose was for. It put enough water through the spill pipe to look like a standard drain from the house to the main sewer line.

So, I thought. In for a penny, in for a pound.

I shut down the hose valve, let the centre panel open, stuck my head and shoulders through. From the glow of the last bulb behind me, I could see the sewer. It was

124

about eight feet high by six feet wide. Water ran along the bottom. Across from me, to my right, another iron ladder led up to a grate.

I pulled myself through the opening, crossed to the grate, looked up into the crisp night sky. Except for a dry rustling of wind-scattered leaves, I could hear no sound. Tentatively I put my hand on the ladder. The rungs were nubbly with rust, cold, about the thickness of reinforcing rods. I tightened my grip on one, sighing one of my restless sighs.

It seemed a long way back now, through the tunnel, and for me the tunnel had been claustrophobic. Except for the cockpits of fighter planes, I've never felt comfortable in confined spaces. The air coming through the grate above was fresh. Beautifully, even spectacularly so.

I began to climb the ladder.

I assured myself there was no possibility of danger here. Surely, I thought, the tunnel would exit into some secure or innocuous place. Campbell or Gregory Howard would have made certain of that.

With the grate just above my head, I touched its bars with the tips of my fingers and exerted a gentle upward pressure. The grate rose silently and more easily than I had expected. I moved it carefully to one side, poked my head above the level of the ground.

At once my ears tingled in the chill night air; my breath clouded in front of me.

I had come out just at the edge of what looked to be a small municipal park that bordered the rear of the safe house. Behind me, I could see the house itself, rising in massive silhouette. A single light was visible on the third floor: Campbell, no doubt, unable to sleep, reading a novel at this late hour, or maybe writing a letter to Midge. I gave his window a casual salute.

*Request permission to jog once around the park, sir.*
*Permission denied, Eberhart.*

*Figured you'd see it that way, sir.*

I turned to look in front of me again. The pathways of the park were illuminated by gas lamps. Dry leaves scattered past me like scraps of paper in the wind. The grass was frost-blighted, the flowerbeds picked clean and turned under for the approaching winter. About fifty yards away I could see a duck pond with a skin of ice around its edges and a small bridge arched over its centre. There was a man standing on the bridge.

I was in shadow. He was in light. He stood with his gloved hands clasped behind him, the collar of his trench coat up, a heavyset, rumpled-looking man, mid-thirties, maybe older, thin hair combed flat on his head. Several times as I watched him he looked in the direction of the safe house, head cocked up, as if he were curious about the light that burned from Campbell's room.

Moths to the flame, I thought idly, remembering Campbell's words to me in his office in Zurich.

The man on the bridge had turned now to face the pond again, and I realized he had begun to whistle. It was a soft whistle, off-key at times, as if he were at least partially tone deaf. For a long minute I studied him, listening to his tune. I didn't recognize it, but there was something vaguely familiar about the sour notes he was hitting, all in the lower register.

Then it came to me, as bright as the light in Campbell's room.

I climbed up through the sewer exit and slipped through the shadows towards him, angling in a wide half-circle to my right to avoid his line of sight. When I reached the bridge abutment, I crouched behind it for a moment, checking the shadows around me, trying one last time to make certain he was alone. My breath was coming hard now, my adrenaline pumping. No one in sight except for my whistler, etched above me in the light of the moon. I stepped up on to the bridge.

'*Wie ist die Aussicht von der Brucke?*' I said.

He stopped in mid-whistle, slipped his gloved hand into the pocket of his trench coat.

'Don't try it,' I said. 'I'll break your back if you do.'

Slowly he withdrew his hand, stood motionless while I patted him down from behind. There was a pack of cigarettes in the pocket he had reached for. Also a small switch-blade knife. I took the knife, worked the spring mechanism that released the blade. The sound was ominous.

'*Wie heissen Sie*?' I said.

'*Ich heisse Hornbeck*,' he replied. '*Ernst Hornbeck*.'

'*Sprechen Sie Englisch*?'

'I do. Yes.'

'A couple of days ago,' I said, 'you were on my flight from Frankfurt to Dulles. You were playing the piano in the upstairs lounge right after a charge of black powder went off in the ashtray of my assigned seat.' I spun him around. '*Haben Sie alles verstanden*?' I said.

He smiled. His teeth were prominent in his plump face, stained above the lip line. His eyes were grey-blue, the left clear, the right milky, as if he might have injured it once as a boy. He glanced at the knife I held blade-up and low in one hand.

'I understand you very well, Herr Colonel,' he said. As he spoke, his breath clouded in front of him. His voice was bubbly, like soda out of a siphon.

'You've got a pretty guttural accent there,' I said. 'It raises bloody hell with your French. "*N'allez pas à White Oaks sous peine de mort*."'

He shrugged, as if to say he had done his best with that.

'I saw you again,' I said. 'Last night in a rented Fiat. You and two of your goons were following me and two good Krauts named Dieter and Karl. They're dead now. Somebody cut their throats.'

Again he shrugged. '*Das Leben ist kurz, Herr Colonel*,' he said. 'Life is short.'

'Keep that in mind,' I said, 'while you start walking. Walk very quietly towards the house where the light just went out in the upstairs window.'

'As you wish.'

'If you're as smart as I think you are,' I said, 'you've got one of your men watching the front of the place. We won't be going in that way, so I'm not worried about him. Where's the other one?'

We were in the shadows now, not far from the tunnel exit. Hornbeck paused. 'If he heard my radio signal, Colonel,' he said, 'he should be just behind you.'

It took me a half-second to react, then I wheeled, knife in hand. It was too late. I felt something explode along the side of my head, and then all of my own lights were out, even before I hit the ground.

# 16

When I finally came to, I was twisting slowly in an agony of pain. Blue lightning ran up the back of my neck, into my skull, exploded a Roman-candle shower in my head. The pain was so persuasive, so consuming, so mind-numbing and jolting, I couldn't begin to tell where it came from or what was causing it. I felt a rush of air expel from my lungs, heard a chuffing drawn-out rasp through my throat. I was flicking in and out of consciousness. Voices seemed to whisper close to me and then recede. When I tried to open my eyes, all I could see were bright white flashes on a crimson field.

Then the voices near me suddenly grew louder.

'*Wissen Sie, wann er kommt?*'

'*Baron Von Regen?*'

'*Ja.*'

'*Ich glaube, er kommt morgen.*'

'*Ja, ja . . .*'

I started to scream. It was a half-choking scream which I tried to bite off, almost punching my teeth through my lip, tasting blood. There were two voices. I heard them again. One was asking if he should relieve the guard at the gate. The other said no, he should go do the cooking. Then the one voice went away, and the other spoke my name.

'Colonel Eberhart?'

I don't know if I answered, or even tried to answer. I seemed to hang suspended in a barnlike room that revolved in a half-circle around me; first to the left, then to the right. Light brightened, dimmed, brightened again.

A lantern on a cluttered workbench turned slowly by, as if caught in the currents of a deep sea.

*For God's sake, cut me down!*

The words screamed silently in my brain. Though the air around me was cold, I poured sweat as I tried to identify the specific areas of the excruciating pain. Chest first. Then shoulders. Chest feeling as if at any moment it would split down the middle and my bones would pierce my skin from neck to belly. Shoulders stretching towards some terrible dislocation.

'Colonel Eberhart?'

The voice was bubbly, familiar.

'Cut me down,' I croaked as I revolved towards it.

'You are awake now,' the voice said. 'That is good.'

There was blood in my nose, blood in my mouth. When he finally came into focus, standing just below me with the collar of his trench coat up and hands clasped behind him, I choked and spat between his feet. He stepped back, a flicker of rage evident on the otherwise *gemütlich* expression of his face.

'I have done my best to carry out my orders,' he said. 'But each time, you have humiliated me.'

He seemed to be speaking with genuine regret, as if he were truly sorry things had worked out this way. As I listened to him – only half-listening through my pain – I began to realize for the first time with any clarity exactly what it was he had done to me.

The awareness came like a nightmare from the war – not my personal nightmare, but that of the US pilots who had been captured by Hanoi. It was an old and brutal technique, used with particular relish by the North Vietnamese.

The prisoner's arms were forced behind his back. Then his arms were tied at the biceps. A makeshift turnbuckle was used to apply additional pressure until his clavicles came together. Then he was strung up until he hung from the same rope that bound his arms, twisting

130

slowly from side to side with his shoulders half pulled from the sockets and his sternum threatening to split through his skin. During every mission I had flown over the North, I had wondered whether I could stand that much pain if I were captured. In the depth of my heart, I had always been afraid I could not.

'Bastard,' I croaked.

'You have humiliated me, Colonel,' he said quietly.

'You have caused me to lose the trust of the people for whom I have worked for many years. You have brought about the death of one of our most valued agents: Fräulein Eklund, for whom the younger Von Regen felt a special affection. Now his father, the count, is on his way here to see for himself that you will no longer be a problem. It humiliates me even further that he feels required to do this.'

'You better tell your count all you've got is one man,' I grunted. 'The others will keep going. They don't need me.'

'Regretfully, we disagree, Colonel,' he said. 'Without you, the mission will end, for there is no one else available to your employer who has sufficient motives to assume such a risk.'

He glanced at his watch, angling it towards the lantern.

'Already after five,' he said. 'Soon it will be dawn. One of my men has gone to the house to prepare breakfast. Feel free to cry out if you wish. We are several miles from the main road. No one will hear you.'

He started to walk away, then paused to gaze up at me again, his one eye clear, the other like spilled milk.

'Dieter Hoefel told us about the Lloyd's office,' he said. 'From there it was a reasonably simple matter to locate Mr Howard's estate. But there was no way to be certain you were there, and no safe way to force you out

if you were. You made our job very easy for us. For this we thank you.'

He took out his cigarettes, held up the pack for me to see.

'It contains a simple radio signalling device,' he said. 'If you had been more thorough you would have discovered it.'

He watched me for a moment, looking disappointed when I failed to react.

'Dieter Hoefel was frightened when he died,' he said finally. 'Are you frightened, Colonel?'

I tried to lash out at him with my bound feet, the rope squeaking on the crossbeam above. He caught me easily by the ankles, held me motionless in a firm but gentle grip.

'It is appropriate, is it not?' he said. 'This method, I mean?'

Suddenly he jerked down on my feet. I screamed in agony, trying not to, screaming all the same.

He waited until I had finished. 'Good-bye for now, Colonel,' he said.

And he left.

# 17

I grunted and chuffed and twisted and sobbed, my efforts as useless as those of a beef hanging in a slaughterhouse. My pain had begun to dull now, receding into a vast numbness, as if my arms, shoulders, and chest had been pumped full of Novocain. For that much, at least, I was grateful.

Because of the way I was hanging, it was almost impossible to raise my head, but I forced myself to do that, cranking it back, trying to scan the dusky interior of the barn for something, anything, that might do me some good. A rusty hand sickle, stuck into a post, was well out of reach, the hook of its shadow sharp on the wall. A three-tine pitchfork stood by the open barn door; a small tractor with a side-bar cutter was backed into one of the stalls.

Nothing I could use.

The nearest thing to my feet was the floor, which I couldn't begin to reach. Next was the workbench where the lantern burned. Sweat was splashing from me, though I had begun to shake from the cold. I knew if I didn't have a goal, no matter how hopeless the goal might be, I was going to give up.

So I made the bench my goal.

I swung my bound legs towards it, pendulumed away, swung towards it again. The rope squeaked like a rat on the beam above. Motes of dust filled the air.

Do it, I thought.

Set up a rhythm.

Swing, *squeak*, swing, *squeak* . . .

I kept it up for a long time. At first I was missing the bench by over a foot. Then, gradually, the distance narrowed to half a foot, then to inches. Either the rope was stretching or my efforts were moving it along the beam. Not much, but enough. And I thought maybe if I could stretch it some more, or move it along the beam far enough, or maybe even weaken it by the friction I was creating...

But I knew all this was useless speculation, and I narrowed my focus to the rhythm of what I was doing.

Swing, *squeak* ...

Swing, *squeak* ...

After what seemed like days, but might have been half an hour, I finally managed to graze the edge of the bench with my shoe. It was a small victory, under the circumstances, but it gave me the glimmer of hope I needed.

Now I began to swing with everything I had. My feet thunked on the bench, skidded off. I swung again. This time, they held. I flopped and crabbed my way as far as I could, inch by inch, on to the bench. Tools clattered on to the floor. The exertion was terrible. I felt like I was going to vomit. My breath was coming in cruel spasms. But the rope was definitely sliding with me now, along the beam, and at last I had my knees on the bench, and I clenched my teeth and rolled up until I had my weight off my arms.

And then I realized Hornbeck was watching me.

He said nothing, his face as expressionless as a bowl of pork. I knelt on the bench, still sobbing for breath, my head resting on my knees, my arms still tied behind me.

'From the beginning,' he said at last, in his siphon-bubbly voice, 'I have made the mistake of underestimating you. I will not make such a mistake again.'

He took hold of my arms, pulled me off the bench. As I fell against the rope, lights exploded through my skull.

I felt as if everything in me had broken. I thought I was going to black out; I prayed for that. But the pain was so intense, instead of dulling my awareness, it sharpened it.

Hornbeck reached into the pocket of his coat, brought out his knife. He worked the mechanism that released the blade. As I watched the lantern light gleam along its razor edge, I felt something I had never felt before: resignation in the face of death.

I hope he does it quick, I thought. I hope he goes for the heart.

And then through my pain I saw Master Sergeant Maul appear in the open doorway of the barn, his flintstone bulk wrapped in a leather coat and cap, his gravelly voice unmistakable. 'Drop the knife,' he growled.

Hornbeck spun towards the door. In a blur of motion I saw him take the knife by the point of its blade, cock his arm, and throw. It pierced the thick fabric of Maul's coat just below the left shoulder. Maul, eyes red with anger, paid no attention to the knife. He picked up the pitchfork propped by the barn door, hefted it once, and hurled it like a javelin. It hit Hornbeck in the chest. I could see him trying to grip the handle as he dropped to his knees and slumped over. All three tines had come through the back of his coat.

I felt no relief that the man who had tortured me was dead, or pleasure that Maul had saved my life. All I felt was excruciating pain.

'Cut me down,' I grunted. 'I hurt.'

# 18

Maul plucked the knife from his coat. There was no blood. He hurried to me, put his arms around my legs, lifted me easily back on to the bench.

'Better step on it,' I grunted. 'He's got troops.'

'How many's he got?' Maul said. He was on the bench with me now, sawing at the ropes with Hornbeck's knife.

'Two, I think. One at the house. Another guarding a gate somewhere...'

'I took care of the one on the gate,' Maul said. 'Soon as I get you clear, I can take care of the one at the house.'

'It's getting light,' I said. 'Their boss is due in from Germany sometime this morning, and he could be bringing a division. I think we better get out of here. Have you got wheels?'

'There's a VW bus outside. Keys are in it.'

As soon as Maul had cut me free from the ropes, I eased myself down from the bench. My hands, arms, and shoulders were as numb as if they had been frozen. Maul watched. I knew he wanted to help me, but wouldn't unless I asked.

'I'm okay,' I said. 'Let's go.'

The air outside was cold. The main farmhouse was a hundred yards up a dirt drive. Smoke rose from the chimney into a wintry sky. The bus Maul had spoken of was parked just in front of the barn. It was the same bus I had seen the night before when I had been watching the monitor at the safe house.

Maul opened the door for me and I lugged myself into the passenger seat, front. Then he got in behind the wheel and cranked up the engine. It was tinny-sounding, but well muffled.

'You ready?' he said.

'Ready,' I said. 'Let's roll.'

He floored the bus and we fishtailed away from the barn and down the dirt drive. By the time we reached the house, we were already doing forty-five. Hornbeck's man saw us go by. He had run out on the porch, waving his hands. He had an apron on. That seemed like some kind of final straw for Maul.

'Asshole,' he growled as we sped by.

I started to laugh, but the pain in my chest cut me off.

'Some kind of hurt, I guess,' Maul said.

'Yes,' I said. 'Some kind.'

It was three miles to the property gate. Maul drove, hunched over the wheel. I sat scanning the woods and pastures on either side as we went. Neither one of us would be interested in talking further until we knew we were out of danger.

When we finally got to the property gate, it was open. I saw a man propped inside it, bound and gagged. He glared at us as Maul drove through, peeling rubber, on to the main road.

'It looks like you treated that one okay,' I said.

'I didn't know what the situation was,' Maul said. 'Nobody told me. I had to work things out.'

He said that Coyle had sent him to Zurich to provide some extra security for Brian at the clinic. By the time he got there, the Swiss police had taken over the job and he didn't have much to do. He hung around, trying to keep out of Whiskey's way, which, he said, was like trying to keep out of the way of a mortar barrage.

Finally, late last night, Campbell had called the clinic and asked to speak with Maul. Maul had done some

Green Beret work for Campbell and the CIA in the Laotian White Star project. It had been Campbell who had got Maul his job at White Oaks after he had retired from the Army. They knew and respected each other. Campbell asked Maul if, as a personal favour, he would mind coming into Zurich for the night to keep an eye on the safe house.

From that point on, nothing had gone well for Maul. He had driven from Bergheim to Zurich in a battered Renault, lent to him by one of the orderlies at the clinic. He had found the safe house, had driven around the block a couple of times, and had finally parked at the kerb.

'I was so tired by then I couldn't walk straight,' he said. 'I guess I crapped out right there in the car. First thing I know, this bus pulls up by the park entrance, and I see two guys loading you into it, and another guy behind the wheel.'

He said he knew he couldn't take the three men without putting me in jeopardy, so he decided to follow the bus, hoping sooner or later his chances would improve. For twenty miles, he drove with his lights off, keeping well back, coaxing the Renault along. When the bus dropped one man off at the gate to a private drive, Maul left the Renault up a dirt road and set out on foot.

'Like I say,' he explained, speaking in his slow and deliberate way, 'I didn't know what the situation was, so I slipped up behind this guy at the gate and put a hammerlock on him. I asked him some questions, and all I got back was Kraut.'

Maul had not been looking at me while he talked. The feeling was starting to come back into my hands, and so was the pain. Every time the bus hit a bump in the road, I winced. There was traffic now, most of it heading for the city.

'So I tie up the Kraut,' Maul said. 'He's got some kind

138

of elephant gun, which I take, and move out through the woods alongside the road. I don't want to stay in the road because I figure the bus could come back anytime, and I want the advantage there, but then the terrain turns to shit and I wind up in some kind of swamp. The rifle's weighing about forty pounds now, so I stash it in some weeds. After that, I come out where I can see the house, and the bus parked in front of the barn.'

'Right about then I'll bet you wished you had a weapon,' I said.

'I did have one,' he said.

Disgusted, he reached into the pocket of his leather coat and brought out one of the smallest automatics I had ever seen. It looked like a chrome-plated toy in his knuckly paw.

'It's twenty-five-calibre,' he said. 'It's some kind of lady's gun. The Swiss police issued it to me.'

'Jesus,' I said, 'a gun's a gun. How come you didn't use it back there at the barn?'

'Because,' he growled, 'I can't get my finger through the trigger guard.'

I grinned, and then, in spite of my pain, began to laugh.

'Master Sergeant Maul,' I said, 'I've got something to tell you.'

'Yeah, what,' he said.

'You're a goddamn jewel,' I said.

He tugged at his cap. 'Yeah,' he said. 'I know.'


At the first gas station with a phone, Maul stopped to check in with Campbell. The message he brought back to me was short and direct.

Campbell was relieved to hear I was all right. So was Kam.

As soon as I got back to Zurich, the three of us would be on our way to Milan.

# 19

We rendezvoused at the safe house at 0700 hours. I took a long warm bath. As I did, Campbell and Kam listened to my story of what had happened. Neither of them commented about my having left the house to explore the exit tunnel. They could see from the ugly look of my upper arms what that indiscretion had cost.

An hour later, we were in Campbell's Opel, on our way to Italy. Maul had been left behind. He would personally brief Inspector Selinger as to the circumstances leading up to Hornbeck's death, but not until the rest of us were out of the country. There was little doubt in our minds that Von Regen had been warned away from the farmhouse by the two men we had left there alive.

Campbell did the driving. Kam and I were travelling light: no suitcases, no shave kits. We wore Dacron leisure suits with short-sleeved open-throat shirts and crepe-soled shoes. We carried our passports in our money belts. Kam's weapons had been confiscated by the Swiss police. He said he felt undressed without them.

We drove through a drizzling overcast that obscured the splendour of the Alps. The windshield wipers on the Opel squeaked back and forth in a slow, halting rhythm that lulled me to sleep in spite of my discomfort. Curled up on the backseat, I didn't wake until we were passing through Andermatt. I heard Campbell telling Kam that some of the earliest inhabitants of Switzerland lived on apples and acorns and nuts; later, he said, they switched to millet-gruel and frogs.

The weather improved on the other side of the mountains. The sun shone through a haze over Lugano, then brightly in Como and on to Milan.

'I think we've shaken your bad guys,' Campbell said. 'At least for a while.'

'I hope so,' I said.

'We'll rendezvous in Bangkok. I'll arrange it with Adune.'

'Can we trust him?'

'Yes.'

'I was beginning to like Dieter and Karl,' I said. 'I liked Flahaven too. And Sandy Johnson.'

'You're looking back,' Campbell said. 'Don't do it.'

'If you were Von Regen,' I said, 'what would your next move be?'

'Assuming I'd lost track of you?'

'Yes.'

'I'd put my people in the places you'd most likely turn up. Bangkok would be one. Malaysia. Singapore.'

'Try to nail me before I launched?'

'Definitely.'

'I got the idea this Hornbeck might have been their top gun,' I said.

'Maybe so,' Campbell replied. 'But if I were you, I wouldn't get complacent.'

We were on E13 now, travelling west out of Milan towards Brescia. Campbell looked enormous over the wheel.

'Where do we pick up the company charter?' I asked.

'On a private strip off the road to Monza,' he said. 'The flight to Rome is an easy one. You'll get there in time to see some of the sights.'

'I will see the fountain?' Kam said. 'Where into the water one throws coins?'

'Absolutely,' Campbell said. 'And I'll give you the

141

name of a small restaurant near the Spanish Steps that may serve the finest veal scallopini in the world.'

We bade our farewells to my father-in-law. We flew to Rome. Kam threw a coin in the fountain. We ate the veal, which was as fine as Campbell had promised. At nine p.m. we boarded our Qantas 747 to Thailand. We rode cabin class and sat aft. The trip would take twelve hours: eleven in the air, one on the ground in New Delhi. I looked at Kam. Kam looked at me.

'Nothing for it,' I said. 'It's a bloody long flight.'

'You will teach me the trick of playing cards,' he said. 'It will be good for your soreness.' He produced a deck from the pocket of his suit.

'Okay,' I said. 'But it'll cost you to learn. The name of the game is gin rummy. We'll play for a penny a point.'

By the time we reached New Delhi, he had lost three hundred and fifty dollars. Before we reached Thailand, he had won it back.

Landing at Don Muang, the big international airport north of Bangkok, is an experience most pilots would prefer to do without. Though not as hairy as Hong Kong, it has its own peculiar hazards. During the dry season, visibility is reduced by the smoke from burning rice fields. Flights of Thai fighters can join the pattern at any time without warning. The Royal Thai Air Force has its own runway on the military side of the airport, and as far as the control tower is concerned, the activity there should be of no concern to civilians.

As we made our approach, I stared out my window at the smouldering rice fields below, waiting for a flight of F-5's to appear out of the murk. During all my time in Southeast Asia, I had piloted many aeroplanes in and out of Don Muang and I knew midafternoon was the time when all the Thai fighter jocks returned to base. It was

midafternoon now. Our pilot would be landing on two-one right. I squinted into the haze, tried to pick out the khlong intersection where he would turn. Kam, who had been sleeping, roused himself.

'We land soon?'

'In about ten minutes.'

'You know, *Lōk*, Bangkok city built on water. Was also once in Khmer empire. Too many roads now.'

'And too many cars,' I said. The plane gave a quick wing-up, wing-down, obviously not turbulence. Probably a flight of F-5's turning on to initial approach just in front of our pilot.

After twelve hours on board, some sleep, no booze, several half-eaten servings of plastic food, I felt as grungy as a gym sock. My mouth was gummy and sour. My eyelids felt heavy with grit. I wanted a room and a bath. And I wanted Jillion. Campbell had guessed it. There was no way we could be in the same city and not wind up together.

'Where we stay tonight?' Kam asked as the 747 taxied to the terminal.

'Have you got any friends in town?' I replied.

He pondered for a moment. When Kam ponders matters that are not military, he looks as slack as he walks: head tilted down, eyes tilted up, mouth slightly open.

'All in refugee camps except my cousin's brother of his wife. He is a *chau vay*, what you say top bell jump at Siam Intercontinental.'

'That's bellhop,' I said. 'Are you sure he's still there?'

'No. Only partly sure.'

We remained seated after the captain stopped the big jet and cut engines. The Thai officials came on board to exchange papers with the crew. Then one of them advanced down the long aisle with a spray can of

143

pesticide. Paying no attention to standing, yawning, stretching passengers, he gave desultory poofs of spray every six feet or so. Once properly fumigated, we could deplane.

'I hate the smell of that stuff,' I said as we went down the ramp.

Kam wrinkled his nose. '*Kan yao* is worse to me,' he said. 'It is a fruit that smells of the sewer. My nose remembers it well from my time here in refugee camp. It was a time that was bad for me.'

Kam would say no more than this. There was no need. I knew his story as well as anyone could who hadn't lived it himself. After his wife and two children had been murdered by the Khmer Rouge, he had escaped Cambodia through the jungles to the northwest. Skirting Poipet, he had crossed the border at the Thai village of Arangphathet, where he was put into a Cambodian refugee camp. The Rustic Foundation, a volunteer group of USAF types formed in the early 1970's, heard of Kam's plight and paid his way to the States.

'You're right about the *kan yao*,' I said. 'It has the stink of a latrine.'

We rode the seatless cattle car from the plane to the main terminal. Still undergoing renovations after four years, the terminal was all concrete floors, portable customs tables, partitioning curtains, wayfarer signs in Thai, Chinese, English, German, and French. It was truly the international airport: Japanese businessmen in dark suits, American tourists in luau shirts, earnest Thai travellers in black pants and long-sleeved white shirts open at the throat, Germans in garb more suited to Munich in November, the ever-present young, male and female, knapsacks and jeans and shoulder-length hair. The inside temperature was ninety-plus. Outside, it would be eighty or so. We were in the dry season, which runs from October to April and is usually quite comfortable.

144

We lined up for customs and passport control. Since we were carrying nothing, customs was a wave of a hand. At passport control, however, the agent behind the desk fired some rapid Thai at Kam as he thumbed through his American passport. Kam looked bewildered, shook his head, and loudly declared, 'Hey, man, I speak no Thai. You talk English to me.'

The agent tried Khmer, then Chinese.

Kam turned to me and said, faster and louder than before, 'Hell, damn, what he want to know anyhow? I cannot wait all day. I got to go!'

'He doesn't realize you're a big-league ball player from Minneapolis with a bone spur and a backache and a contract that runs to six figures,' I said. I said it as quickly as I could, and now it was the agent who looked bewildered. He stamped Kam's passport and gave it back. Kam stomped away. The irate American. A Cambodian Rod Carew.

At the money booth I exchanged six hundred dollars in green for over eleven thousand *baht* at just under twenty for the dollar. I gave Kam five thousand.

'Rate is better in town,' he said.

'I know,' I said. 'But I think we should spread our purchases around. Not be too conspicuous.'

'I am watching with care,' Kam said. 'I have seen no one suspicious.'

'There's a young Chinese outside,' I said. 'Baby face with bangs, tight pants, white shirt, and tie. I noticed him when we first came into the terminal. He was watching us while you argued with passport control. He fooled with the gum machine while we made our change. Now he's hanging around the taxi pool. You see him?'

Kam took a look. 'Yes,' he said.

'I'd say he's too obvious to be one of Von Regen's boys. He could work for Coyle, or maybe Adune. Let's keep an eye on him.'

'We will take taxi?'

'No,' I said. 'Bus.'

We went out separately and queued up: me, just a foreigner short on his cash; Kam, just another Thai, close enough in general features to pass. The bus was packed. Every seat was taken. People crowded in the aisles. When the baby-faced Chinese finally made his way on board, he had to stand in the step well.

The highway was a moving sea of Fiats, Toyotas, motorbikes, taxis, and trucks. Our bus was big and red. Our driver used its size to steamroll into the traffic stream. We dodged, weaved, darted, won every game of chicken, to the happy applause of the passengers. I sat at the rear of the bus, trying to protect my arms. Kam sat towards the front. The boy with the bangs watched us. He was certainly no pro.

We passed Timland, Thailand in Miniature: a collection of all the tourist sights rolled into one. Here you could see pottery made, Thai silk woven, elephants at work, jewels polished, Thai boxing, and Thai ballet.

'You an American, yes?' asked the neatly dressed young gentleman who sat next to me.

'*Excusez-moi*,' I said. '*Je ne parle pas anglais.*'

He looked away.

We were approaching Bangkok from the north. Through the open windows of the bus I watched as we paralleled the train tracks leading into the city. An electric engine, pulling seven passenger cars, slowly drew even, then passed us. Each car had its complement of workers returning home from outlying factories. Commuters, just like Connecticut. It had been over a year since I had traveled this road. Diana had been with me then, two weeks before she was killed. With Phnom Penh surrounded by the Khmer Rouge, the only way to reach Bangkok was by air. Occasionally my embassy business would take me there. Whenever it did, I would fly a C-47, the venerable Goony Bird, from Phnom Penh

146

to the military strip at Don Muang, then take a staff car or taxi into town.

Diana loved to join me on these trips (though she was never too thrilled about flying). She liked to shop at the commissary or PX during the afternoons, and dine with me at Nick's Number One each night. Nick, an enigmatic man, had a fighter-pilot son-in-law. This gave us a bond in common. Whenever we arrived, no matter how busy he was at the time, he would welcome us with a special courtesy and carefully reserved wit. I had always felt a fondness for Thailand. The country. The people.

Our bus careened to a halt by the Thai War Memorial on Rajavithi Road. I motioned to Kam and we got off. The tall spire of the memorial cast its shadow from the lowering sun as we looked for a taxi.

'Chinese boy got off too,' Kam said.

'I see him.'

'You want me to remove?'

'No. Not yet. Let's see if we can get him to take some bait.'

I flagged a Toyota Crown taxi and told the driver to take us to an address one block from the Dusithani Hotel. The boy with the bangs hopped a cab behind us. Kam and I rode in silence. When we reached the address I had given the driver, I paid him off and we got out. A half-block away, the Chinese boy did the same. Kam looked as if he didn't approve.

'Okay,' I said. 'We'll check in separately at the Dusithani. Get yourself a single room in your own name. Pay cash in advance for one night. I'll meet you in one hour at the bar. Then we'll cut out. Have you got the number of the Siam Intercontinental?'

'I can find.'

'Good. Before you check in here, find a public phone and give that *chau vay* cousin of yours a call. If he's still there, see if he can work something out to put us up tonight. I don't want to be seen in the lobby, and I don't

want either of us to register there in our own names. Have you got it?'

'I got it, *Lŏk*,' Kam said. He smiled, happier now. I watched as he ambled across the street, straight through the raging traffic.

The doorman at the Dusithani wore bloomers. They were traditional. He wore them to catch the Saviour after the child was born of man. Because I had arrived on foot and was casually dressed, he made no attempt to open the door. I went in, secured a single room, waved the bellhop away, took the elevator to the fourth floor.

I don't know why I felt angry, but I did. Maybe it was the accumulation of all that had happened in recent days. Whatever it was, I took it out on my friend the young Chinese.

He had followed me into the lobby. While I was busy at the desk, he loitered around the newsstand. When I went into the elevator, he headed for the stairs. When I reached my floor, I waited for him. He came up, huffing and puffing. I stepped out and took him by the tie. He was a good deal shorter than I was and I put enough upward pressure on the tie to force him to tiptoe along as we headed for my room.

'*Gargh*!' he hissed. '*Geech*!' He tried to pummel me, but he had no leverage and his blows fell harmlessly against my sides. I opened the door to my room with one hand, waltzed him in with the other.

'Assume the position, please,' I said. 'Hands against the wall. Feet apart.'

I patted him down. He smelled of cologne and carried something that looked like a knitting needle in a slit pocket along one seam of his trousers. I took it, broke it in half, dropped it in a wicker basket by the chest of drawers.

'Have a seat,' I said.

The knot in his necktie was now the size of a peach pit. He tried to loosen it, sitting on the edge of the bed. His

to the military strip at Don Muang, then take a staff car or taxi into town.

Diana loved to join me on these trips (though she was never too thrilled about flying). She liked to shop at the commissary or PX during the afternoons, and dine with me at Nick's Number One each night. Nick, an enigmatic man, had a fighter-pilot son-in-law. This gave us a bond in common. Whenever we arrived, no matter how busy he was at the time, he would welcome us with a special courtesy and carefully reserved wit. I had always felt a fondness for Thailand. The country. The people.

Our bus careened to a halt by the Thai War Memorial on Rajavithi Road. I motioned to Kam and we got off. The tall spire of the memorial cast its shadow from the lowering sun as we looked for a taxi.

'Chinese boy got off too,' Kam said.

'I see him.'

'You want me to remove?'

'No. Not yet. Let's see if we can get him to take some bait.'

I flagged a Toyota Crown taxi and told the driver to take us to an address one block from the Dusithani Hotel. The boy with the bangs hopped a cab behind us. Kam and I rode in silence. When we reached the address I had given the driver, I paid him off and we got out. A half-block away, the Chinese boy did the same. Kam looked as if he didn't approve.

'Okay,' I said. 'We'll check in separately at the Dusithani. Get yourself a single room in your own name. Pay cash in advance for one night. I'll meet you in one hour at the bar. Then we'll cut out. Have you got the number of the Siam Intercontinental?'

'I can find.'

'Good. Before you check in here, find a public phone and give that *chau vay* cousin of yours a call. If he's still there, see if he can work something out to put us up tonight. I don't want to be seen in the lobby, and I don't

want either of us to register there in our own names. Have you got it?'

'I got it, *Lōk*,' Kam said. He smiled, happier now. I watched as he ambled across the street, straight through the raging traffic.

The doorman at the Dusithani wore bloomers. They were traditional. He wore them to catch the Saviour after the child was born of man. Because I had arrived on foot and was casually dressed, he made no attempt to open the door. I went in, secured a single room, waved the bellhop away, took the elevator to the fourth floor.

I don't know why I felt angry, but I did. Maybe it was the accumulation of all that had happened in recent days. Whatever it was, I took it out on my friend the young Chinese.

He had followed me into the lobby. While I was busy at the desk, he loitered around the newsstand. When I went into the elevator, he headed for the stairs. When I reached my floor, I waited for him. He came up, huffing and puffing. I stepped out and took him by the tie. He was a good deal shorter than I was and I put enough upward pressure on the tie to force him to tiptoe along as we headed for my room.

'*Gargh*!' he hissed. '*Geech*!' He tried to pummel me, but he had no leverage and his blows fell harmlessly against my sides. I opened the door to my room with one hand, waltzed him in with the other.

'Assume the position, please,' I said. 'Hands against the wall. Feet apart.'

I patted him down. He smelled of cologne and carried something that looked like a knitting needle in a slit pocket along one seam of his trousers. I took it, broke it in half, dropped it in a wicker basket by the chest of drawers.

'Have a seat,' I said.

The knot in his necktie was now the size of a peach pit. He tried to loosen it, sitting on the edge of the bed. His

148

face was puffed up and pretty in the babyish way they use to sell soup.

'Who do you work for?' I said.

'I will tell you nothing,' he hissed.

I looked at my watch.

'My friend will be back soon,' I said. 'His name is Kam Trak. He's Cambodian. His wife and two children were killed in the war. They were tortured to death by the Khmer Rouge. Kam escaped by crossing the border into Thailand near the village of Arangphathet, where he was put in a refugee camp.'

The boy had finally managed to loosen his tie. He looked at me venomously.

'Kam is very sweet,' I said. 'Until he gets angry. Then he likes to cut off people's heads. He carries a wire saw for that purpose. It has silicone teeth that are sharp enough to slice through a one-inch tempered-steel bar in just over a minute. Heads take less. I hope you're getting all this.'

He shook his head, mumbled something in Chinese. I glanced at my watch again.

'When Kam comes in, I go out,' I said. 'You can deal with me or you can deal with him. It's up to you.'

'I do not speak English,' he said.

'I think you speak it very well. If you want to run that number, you better get rid of your frat pin. Where did you go to college?'

He looked resigned. 'VPI,' he said.

'Virginia Tech?'

'Yes.'

'What's your name?'

'Chin.'

'Coyle likes to recruit people from VPI. Do you work for him?'

'Yes. I help handle his affairs with Mr Adune. I am an accountant.'

'Was it Mr Adune who had you follow me?'

'No. I was told to do so by Mr Coyle's man at White Oaks.'

'Which man was that?'

'His name is Jassick.'

I stepped to the window and looked down at the turmoil of traffic below. The window was closed, the room stuffy. There was a muted clamor of horns and bells.

Jassick. I remembered him. Patches of hair that looked glued on. A mouth the size of a dime. I wondered if he was the one who had betrayed Coyle from inside.

'I want to think well of you, Chin,' I said. 'I want to believe you weren't coming up here to slip that needle of yours between my ribs.'

'I would not do such a thing,' Chin said. 'I was to watch the airport and if you and Mr Trak arrived I was to follow you to your hotel. I was to make sure of the room and then telephone my report.'

'Have you ever followed anybody before?'

'Oh, yes indeed. Two or three times before.'

'You're lousy at it,' I said.

He looked crestfallen.

'Really awful,' I said. 'You should stick to accounting.'

There was a moment of silence between us.

'What will we do now?' he asked finally.

'We will tear the sheet in half and tie you up,' I said. 'Then we will put you in the closet and see how much of the pillowcase you can eat. If you stay very quiet in there, you'll hear me go out. I'm a big clod, and floors tend to squeak under me when I walk. Now, Kam, on the other hand, glides like a snake. You won't hear him when he comes in. He's tired and he'll probably curl up by the door and fall asleep.'

Chin looked worried. 'He will open the closet first?' he said.

150

'I don't think so. The only clothes he has are the ones on his back.'

'But what if I make a noise that is inadvertent?'

'Then he will find you,' I said. 'And he will cut off your head.'

# 20

When I squeaked out of the room twenty minutes later and hung the DO NOT DISTURB sign on the door, there wasn't a sound from the closet. I rendezvoused with Kam and we taxied through the rush hour to a side street of Rama I Road. The driver had been imaginative, and Kam tipped him an extra ten *baht*.

'All fixed, *Lōk*,' he said as the taxi sped away. 'Siam Intercontinental.'

We stood alongside the vast acreage behind the hotel. The main hotel building was one storey with a four-sided sloping roof that looked like a coolie hat someone had sat on. There were two parallel wings, each two stories high, with the coolie hat connecting them. Between the wings nestled a large swimming pool and outdoor bar. There were rows of palm trees and hurang bushes; the lawn was lush and green.

'There is a zoo maintained for guests,' Kam said. 'We will walk that way.'

The zoo was at the far edge of the grounds, facing the parallel wings of the hotel. Kam led and I followed. A full-grown peacock, alert to our approach, raised his tail, spread his feathers into a fan, and rattled them at us from his giant cage. The radius of the fan was about eight feet, the dark green feathers covered with the pattern of a thousand eyes. Meeting one unexpectedly can send you straight up.

We entered a room at the far end of one of the wings of the hotel. We were not observed. Kam, who had not

been happy with my gentle handling of the Chinese, now seemed pleased.

'Okay, *Lōk*,' he said. 'I tell you how it is. Bunya still here and has assigned us this room. No write on books. I pay him sure. He give me clothes so I be waiter *boy* and can move around. You will stay here, *Lōk*. I will bring food just like *boy*. Okay room here, I do think. Two doors, ground floor.'

'Perfect,' I said. 'I need one more favour. Would you go to the API office and tell Jillion I'm here?'

He was silent. I knew he liked Jillion, but was thinking we should be getting in touch with Mr Adune.

'We'll go to work in the morning,' I said. 'We've earned a night off.'

'You no go out,' he said. 'You no call. Okay, *Lōk*?'

'Okay,' I said.

I showered after Kam had left. I did alternate sets of some slow and painful push-ups and leg raises, and when I couldn't stand doing that anymore, I stood up and ran in place for a while. I had my skivvies on. I've tried running without them and it's a pretty funny show. When someone knocked on the door at seven-thirty, I was drenched with sweat, had muscles that quivered and ached, and a heart that pounded.

It was Jillion.

She stands five-ten, weighs a hundred and thirty, has thick tawny hair that falls below her shoulders. Her mouth is generous and wide. Her eyes are brown, so dark that in soft light they appear to be black.

She stood before me now in her standard garb: Levi's and an olive-drab combat blouse. The lower blouse pockets were filled with notebooks, micro recorder, Minox camera, pencils and pens. The upper blouse pockets were amply filled with herself.

She came in. I rebolted the door. She eyed me critically. 'Do you always greet your guests in sweaty skivvies?' she asked. She has a very low, quiet voice.

There are times when you have to strain to hear it. I have seen men topple out of their chairs, leaning forward, trying to hear what Jillion Leggett had to say.

I smiled. 'Only those I love, my love.'

She looked at the bruises on my biceps. They resembled purple armbands. 'My God,' she said. 'What happened?'

I hesitated. 'A couple of Turks with truncheons taught me some manners,' I said, 'in the old marketplace in Istanbul.'

She stood in front of me, ran her fingers over my arms. We looked at each other expectantly, waiting. We had been through too much together to waste words. I put my hand up and cupped her chin. She put her arms around my waist. I kissed her softly. She moved her hands up. We sighed and clutched each other and kissed. We moaned. Gradually everything disappeared around us. I felt her flesh, earthy and warm. We fumbled and stumbled towards the bed.

'Oh, God, Matt,' she breathed. I held her waist with one arm, tore the bedspread, blanket, and top sheet from the bed. I flung them away so hard they wound up draped over the desk by the wall, knocking over a lamp, teetering a chair.

Then we were locked together, rolling, tossing, tasting, panting, her hair all around me, our bodies grinding in a mingle of sweat and need.

When it was over, we surveyed each other from the wreckage. We were lying collapsed, side by side, heads down, crosswise on the mattress, resting on the bed frame, which had given way. The bottom sheet was in a wet, sweaty pile somewhere behind the headboard. The top covers and broken lamp were off to one side of our heads. The telephone *peep-peeped* sadly in a sprawl on the floor. I hung it up.

154

'Ah, tell me,' Jillion said, still gulping for breath, 'what do we do for an encore? Tear down the Eiffel Tower?'

'Why not?' I said.

'It's good to see you, Matt.'

'And you. It always is.'

We lay quietly for a while, then stumbled to our feet and went into the bath. We took the coed shower, twenty minutes under a gentle spray. We drank all the ice water in the two-quart thermos the hotel kindly provided for its guests. Then we flopped in two chairs overlooking the patio.

'So,' Jillion said. 'Why are you here? Besides servicing horny correspondents, I mean. And how's Brian?'

'He's fine.'

'Still at Walter Reed?'

'Right,' I said. 'I needed some R and R. Bangkok is good for that. And I wanted to see you.'

'So why all the secrecy? Kam had me swearing on Scripture I wouldn't tell anyone you were here.'

'We've got a deal going. It's nothing big, but I could blow it if I show myself too soon.'

'Ah, so.'

'Remind you of the good old days?'

'Yes. And, oh, by the way, you need a shave.' She rummaged through her clothes, still scattered on the floor, found a Gillette Kam had bought for me. I went into the bath. Jillion leaned against the door.

'Nothing big, huh? How come no luggage? Not even a razor.'

'My bag got lost in the shuffle out of Germany,' I said. 'You look beautiful in a towel.'

'You told me once you thought I was overendowed.'

'That couldn't have been my word.'

'It was.'

I smiled, and tweaked her nose with lather. 'Jillion,' I said. 'I hear a knocking at the door.'

When Kam came in, he came in tall and erect, bearing

a heavily laden tray. He was dressed in a waiter's uniform: black slacks and shoes, white shirt with a black bow tie, wine-coloured cummerbund. He even had a towel draped over one arm. He looked askance at the room. 'Here I do believe there has been a typhoon,' he said.

'An invasion of Mongols,' I said. 'You've arrived in the nick of time.'

I scooped up Jillion's clothes and tossed them to her through the bathroom door. Kam pretended not to notice. He was busily setting out champagne glasses, putting a champagne bottle on the table, and opening several packages he had brought. One contained the standard brown two-piece safari suit from Sin Do the Tailor. Another had socks and fresh underwear, a gold neckerchief, and a belt.

'Now, *Lŏk*,' he said. 'I tell you what I have done. *Muoy*, I pay Bunya and make all operations. *Pir*, I get you clothes. *Bei*, I get all new weapons me. *Buon*, I locate office of Mr Adune.'

I listened to Kam's recitation as I put on the safari suit. When he starts putting in more Cambodian words, then I know he is thinking more of his beloved country. I once heard him swearing in Russian while clearing a jammed Kalashnikof rifle. He uses language to suit the occasion and his mood.

Jillion came out of the bath barefoot, wearing her Levi's and jungle blouse. She went to Kam and they embraced.

'*Chum rip seour*,' she said.

'*Chum rip seour*,' he replied.

I felt good. I wanted to lie back for a while.

'We'll need another bottle of champagne,' I said. 'And some *Kao chae* and shrimp bits while you're at it.'

Kam looked at me soberly as he went out the door.

Jillion eased off the champagne cork: Piper Heidsieck, extra brut, undated. We drank it while we tidied the

156

room. By the time we had finished, Kam was back with bottle two and the hors d'oeuvres.

'You should join us for a drink,' Jillion said.

'*Tay*. No. I go now, stand guard,' Kam replied. 'You have little party.'

'Could you bring us a dish of . . . no, make it two dishes of *pat priew wan nua*?' I asked. That was sweet-and-sour beef. Kam nodded. When he went out, I thought the door shut a trifle sharply.

Jillion refilled our glasses. It was nearly ten o'clock in the evening, cool, dark blue outside. We opened the sliding door to the patio. I hadn't realized how stuffy the room had become until the sweet breeze silked in around us. We sat in our chairs, looking out. Jillion told me about her Australian diplomat, and how she had loved him in many ways, and how, finally, it hadn't worked out.

'I'll bet he wanted you to wear dresses,' I said. 'Go to diplomatic functions. Not ask questions. Be the charming, dull wife of an Aussie chargé.'

'Yes.'

'And you couldn't because you're like me. You've got a wild hair.'

'Yes.'

We sat silently then, gazing into the tropical night. I wondered if the peacock was watching us with its thousand eyes.

Diana and I had been at one of those rollicking Aussie functions at the Phnom Hotel, Anzac Day I think, when I had first seen Jillion. Superficially, she and Diana looked alike. They were both tall, both blonde. But there the resemblance ended. While Diana was willowy, Jillion was sinewy. Wellesley v. the University of New South Wales. Diplomatic drawing rooms v. triple-canopied jungle. Dedicated mother v. swamp-slogging correspondent with the troops.

'We could have had a life together,' I said.

'No,' she said. 'We're too much alike.'

'Things went sour for me after I left.'

'And for me.'

I shivered. The scars on my back had begun to pulse. Too many memories. Too many, too sad. Jillion touched me with her hand. She murmured a phrase in a language I had never heard.

'That's Maori,' she said. 'It means we've a long time to walk together, brother of my very soul.'

A soft rap on the door broke the spell. Hand in hand, like a couple of kids, we sprang to the door and let Kam in. My head felt light from the champagne.

'You no check on door banger, *Lōk*. Bad business.'

He came in, looking stern, with a laden tray. Jillion and I giggled. I draped my arm around Kam's shoulder and said, 'My good friend, we are going out tonight, tear the roof off the town. Garden Café, Cat's Eye, the An-An Room. We'll hit 'em all!'

Kam stiffened. He moved out from under my arm and placed the food tray on the desk. The little table between the chairs was too loaded with junk.

'If the *Sakpram* please, he *no* go out tonight.'

There he was. Calling me the Colonel again.

'Now listen, my friend,' I said. 'This is our last night before we're locked in with Adune. Let's move it!' I had been bending over, inspecting the sweet-and-sour beef. There were no noodles and as I mentioned this I felt a slight movement behind me and then a draft.

'What the hell!' I yelled, straightening.

Kam faced me, looking innocent as he shrugged something up his sleeve. Jillion started to guffaw. I grabbed my backside with both hands and felt skin. I turned to get a look at myself in the mirror.

Kam had very delicately and quickly made a surgeon's slice in my pants from hip pocket to hip pocket, skivvies

158

included, so the two pieces of cloth hung down like the flaps on a pair of long johns.

He nodded happily as I looked in the mirror.

I was mooning myself.

# 21

It was fair to say that Kam had made his point. He promised to bring me a new pair of pants, but not before morning. I called him a conniving *preyet* and a poor man's Gunga Din. He bowed and asked would the *Sakpram* care for anything else. I said yes, goddammit, I wanted two more bottles of champagne. He assured me the bar had closed. When I tried to dial room service, I found the line had been cut. When I looked for something to throw, Kam ducked out the door.

'You're not really mad at him, are you?' Jillion asked.

'I guess not. *No*,' I said.

'I think all he wants is for you to be safe and sound for your meeting with Mr Adune.'

I looked at her, warning bells clanging.

'You're some kind of reporter,' I said.

She shrugged. 'Adune isn't a name I would miss. He's Mr Big in Thailand,' she said. 'He's got a beef ranch southeast of the city that runs all the way to Cambodia. He's not only known for his fabulous wealth, but also for his religious devotion. He was appointed this year again by the king to be lord of the Ploughing Festival as a reward for his zeal.'

'Okay,' I said.

'You don't have to tell me a thing,' she said. 'And if you do, it can be off the record. You know that.'

'Okay,' I said. 'I've got a contract to check out the training programme Adune runs for his ranch hands. The

whole operation is insured by Lloyd's through an agent who's a friend of mine. Like I said, it's nothing big.'

Jillion eyed me sceptically.

'Tell you what,' I said. 'We can't go into town with my butt hanging out, but we can slip into the pool and go for a swim. Are you up to it?'

She glanced at the phone wire Kam had cut. 'Lloyd's, you say?'

'Right.'

'Of London?'

'Right. Friend's name is Gregory Howard. He operates out of Zurich.'

Jillion smiled. It was a slack, sad smile. She eyed my bruises. 'Matt,' she said. 'You're a terrible liar.'

She was right. I was as bad at it as Chin was at being a gumshoe. I put my hands in her hair. 'Will you go swimming with me?' I said.

'Can I call Howard?'

'Sure,' I said. 'His first name's Gregory.'

I kissed her. For a half-moment she seemed annoyed, but then she kissed me back. We undressed each other.

'You're not overendowed,' I said. 'You're beautiful.'

We went out, slipping past the Nipa Hut bar, and dived into the pool, side by side in clean deep dives.

The pool lights were off. We swam underwater to the far side and slowly let ourselves float up flat against the pool wall, arms upraised to break the surface first.

The water had the same warm and silky quality of the night breeze.

We faced each other, immersed to our shoulders. Jillion's eyes were dark. I kissed her again, tasting the sweet water of the pool. Then we made love, with her hair floating around us like grass in the sea.

She called the bureau first thing in the morning, was told

she had to cover a proclamation by the king. She wished me luck and kissed me good-bye. I was worried. The night with her had been beautiful, one I would treasure. But when I thought of Campbell's warning, I found myself gritting my teeth.

'We go now,' Kam said after she had left. 'It is arranged to see Mr Adune.'

We went by taxi to the river. The markets were open. The streets were crowded with schoolchildren, all dressed in white and blue. Their mothers bought fruit from the open stalls, yards of bright flowered cloth, joss sticks for Buddha.

We walked the last two blocks to our rendezvous point, making our way past bustling dock workers in cotton shorts and rubber zoris, their calf and shoulder muscles ropy and oiled under their parchment-brown skin. The smell of the river was staggering. Alternate whiffs of human waste, rotting fish, decaying vegetation, diesel fumes, and muck. In the Orient, culture shock begins at the tip of the nose.

We took a table under the striped awning of the Krathong Café. The awning was faded from too many years in the sun. The table was tin. The café had been named for the small leaf cup that the Thais set adrift on their rivers and canals, tiny candles burning in them to mark the lunar month in October.

'What do you want, Lòk?' Kam asked.

'Get me a couple of Singha beers,' I said.

'They will be warm,' Kam said. 'They will attract flies.'

'I know, my brother,' I said. 'But humour me, will you please? I've got a head from that champagne.'

Kam clucked his tongue.

'Hair of dog,' he said. 'It is an expression I have learned in Texas.'

The river was called the Chao Phya. It flowed south

162

into what used to be called the Gulf of Siam when the country had that name. It was crowded with small boats, fishing junks, sampans, and barges. I had just finished the first of my beers when a covered launch drew up to the double-plank dock just below the café. The helmsman waved us down.

'His name is Photra,' Kam said. 'Mr Adune told me he would be here. He is Cambodian. I know and trust him.'

'Okay,' I said. 'Let's go.'

We went on board. The launch was about twenty feet long. It rocked under our weight. The helmsman added throttle and we pulled away from the dock at a leisurely pace, engine chortling. Kam sat on one of the deck benches. I lifted the canvas curtain and entered the shadowy interior of the covered section. A Buddhist monk in saffron robes sat at the far end of a narrow table running its length.

'Welcome, Colonel Eberhart,' he said. His voice was smooth, almost hypnotic in its effect. 'Please be seated. I am Adune.'

I slipped out of my shoes, took my seat across from him.

Adune appeared to be in his mid-fifties, which meant he was probably over seventy. Beneath his shaven skull and eyebrows, he had a serene, unlined face. His accents were cultured, pleasantly modulated, with only a trace of the watered R.

'You are, perhaps, surprised at my robes, and . . .' He bent towards me, touching his shaven head. 'As you know,' he continued, 'one can increase one's karma by taking impermanent monastic vows. I served my vassa years ago as a youth.'

He was silent for a moment. I could hear water gurgling as we rocked in the wash from another boat. I felt cool and calm in the presence of this tranquil man, as if we were in a temple.

'I see by the fact you have removed your shoes that you are aware of our traditions,' he said.

'And respectful of them,' I said.

'*Kob koon*,' he said, thanking me.

'*Kob koon, mahk, krop*,' I replied.

He was silent for a long moment. Then his demeanor began to change. Lines appeared along his brow. His eyes became narrow, his voice sharper in timbre.

'We will not go to my office,' he said. 'We will conduct our business here. I understand from our friend Mr Coyle that I am to provide you with whatever you need in order to retrieve the diamonds from the hotel at Kampong Som. How do you propose to proceed?'

I slipped back into my shoes. 'I'll go in by boat at night with a small squad of men,' I said. 'Minimum six, eight at the most. The boat will lie offshore. We'll go from there by rubber raft. Two teams. We'll grab the pouch and be out before dawn.'

'Why, with your background, will you not use a plane?'

'Since the *Mayaguez* affair, their air-defence system has been beefed up. Their coastal patrol, on the other hand, is a lot more careful these days about who they intercept.'

'Excellent. Where will you enlist your men, and where will you train?'

'Kam will do the recruiting at the refugee camp at Arangphathet. He'll need a van. As for the training, I'd like to use some suitable part of your ranch.'

'This will be arranged. You have prepared a list of the necessary equipment?'

'I jotted one down in the cab on our way here,' I said. 'It's fairly detailed.'

I handed it to him. He read it carefully.

'I see no problem except with the boat,' he said. 'You must be more specific.'

'She'll have to cruise easily at thirty knots,' I said. 'Be

into what used to be called the Gulf of Siam when the country had that name. It was crowded with small boats, fishing junks, sampans, and barges. I had just finished the first of my beers when a covered launch drew up to the double-plank dock just below the café. The helmsman waved us down.

'His name is Photra,' Kam said. 'Mr Adune told me he would be here. He is Cambodian. I know and trust him.'

'Okay,' I said. 'Let's go.'

We went on board. The launch was about twenty feet long. It rocked under our weight. The helmsman added throttle and we pulled away from the dock at a leisurely pace, engine chortling. Kam sat on one of the deck benches. I lifted the canvas curtain and entered the shadowy interior of the covered section. A Buddhist monk in saffron robes sat at the far end of a narrow table running its length.

'Welcome, Colonel Eberhart,' he said. His voice was smooth, almost hypnotic in its effect. 'Please be seated. I am Adune.'

I slipped out of my shoes, took my seat across from him.

Adune appeared to be in his mid-fifties, which meant he was probably over seventy. Beneath his shaven skull and eyebrows, he had a serene, unlined face. His accents were cultured, pleasantly modulated, with only a trace of the watered R.

'You are, perhaps, surprised at my robes, and . . .' He bent towards me, touching his shaven head. 'As you know,' he continued, 'one can increase one's karma by taking impermanent monastic vows. I served my vassa years ago as a youth.'

He was silent for a moment. I could hear water gurgling as we rocked in the wash from another boat. I felt cool and calm in the presence of this tranquil man, as if we were in a temple.

'I see by the fact you have removed your shoes that you are aware of our traditions,' he said.

'And respectful of them,' I said.

'*Kob koon,*' he said, thanking me.

'*Kob koon, mahk, krop,*' I replied.

He was silent for a long moment. Then his demeanor began to change. Lines appeared along his brow. His eyes became narrow, his voice sharper in timbre.

'We will not go to my office,' he said. 'We will conduct our business here. I understand from our friend Mr Coyle that I am to provide you with whatever you need in order to retrieve the diamonds from the hotel at Kampong Som. How do you propose to proceed?'

I slipped back into my shoes. 'I'll go in by boat at night with a small squad of men,' I said. 'Minimum six, eight at the most. The boat will lie offshore. We'll go from there by rubber raft. Two teams. We'll grab the pouch and be out before dawn.'

'Why, with your background, will you not use a plane?'

'Since the *Mayaguez* affair, their air-defence system has been beefed up. Their coastal patrol, on the other hand, is a lot more careful these days about who they intercept.'

'Excellent. Where will you enlist your men, and where will you train?'

'Kam will do the recruiting at the refugee camp at Arangphathet. He'll need a van. As for the training, I'd like to use some suitable part of your ranch.'

'This will be arranged. You have prepared a list of the necessary equipment?'

'I jotted one down in the cab on our way here,' I said. 'It's fairly detailed.'

I handed it to him. He read it carefully.

'I see no problem except with the boat,' he said. 'You must be more specific.'

'She'll have to cruise easily at thirty knots,' I said. 'Be

capable of carrying some armament, but I'd prefer plywood to a metal hull.'

'To avoid radar.'

'Yes.'

'I know of a converted motor torpedo boat that meets your specifications. It may take a day or more for me to acquire it.'

'I'll need at least that much time at your ranch,' I said. 'Going into Kampong Som won't be a picnic.'

'There is much brutality in Cambodia now. The blood of innocent people runs like water in the Chao. I am a peaceful man, but there are times when even my religion . . .'

He stopped. Abruptly. I could feel the vibration of the boat's engine through the hull.

'I'll need transportation to the ranch,' I said.

'You will be flown there by one of my pilots. I keep two planes at Don Muang.'

'I appreciate your help,' I said.

Mr Adune stood up. 'This message arrived for you this morning at my office,' he said.

He handed me a piece of paper. In spite of the humidity over the river, it felt crisp. I unfolded it. It was from Campbell. 'MATT,' it said, 'MOVE WITH EXTREME CAUTION. RENE DUBOIS HAS BEEN GIVEN YOUR CONTRACT.'

# 22

Mr Adune got out of his robe and into a suit coat and tie. 'I know this Rene Dubois,' he said. 'He is a mercenary who worked for the opium dealers in Laos before they were driven out by the Americans. He has a small number of men, Corsicans, ex-Legionnaires. They have operated in this country by hiring out to gem smugglers and arms traders.'

'Do they come high?' I asked.

'Dubois would peel the skin from his mother for a half-million *baht*. That may sound like a substantial sum. In your currency, it is no more than twenty-five thousand.'

'That's penny-ante,' I said.

'The people who wish you dead could afford more?'

'Much.'

'Then perhaps it was a matter of convenience. Dubois is well known here. If one were in a hurry, he would be a logical choice.'

'Is he capable of laying siege to your ranch?'

Mr Adune laughed. It was a good-natured laugh, as if I had asked an amusing question. 'I believe we are prepared to handle the likes of Mr Dubois,' he said. 'On that point, Colonel, you should not worry.'

'Then I'll be glad to get there,' I said.

'Photra, our helmsman, has access to a van. He will drive Mr Trak to the village of Arangphathet, where men will be recruited for your mission.'

'What can you tell me about him?' I asked.

'Photra?'

'Yes.'

'Only that he is a Cambodian who was captured by the Khmer Rouge when his country fell. He underwent the usual torture before managing to escape. I have used him before. When I mentioned his name to Mr Trak, Mr Trak said that he knew of Photra and was willing to trust him. Do you have a particular reason for asking?'

'Not really,' I said. 'We've got some people behind us who apparently won't stop at anything to keep me out of that hotel at Kampong Som. We left seven dead in Switzerland. I guess I'm getting a little jumpy.'

Mr Adune smiled. 'It is for these reasons,' he said, 'that I have met with you here instead of in the comfort of my office. I know your father-in-law and hold him in the highest esteem. We have worked together before. He is not a man who would raise an unnecessary alarm.'

'No.'

'I must ask you to wait on board this launch until I can make the necessary arrangements to have you picked up and taken to my private hangar off the military field at Don Muang.'

'How long?'

'That is difficult to say. This launch is inconspicuous. I will have my people watch over it from the wharf. No harm will come to you here. When we have determined that the way to Don Muang is clear, I will send a man named Chai to pick you up. He is one of my ranch foremen. He will accompany you to the plantation. Please be patient, Colonel. These arrangements will take time. Use the hours to meditate upon the great truths of Gautama.'

Adune told Photra to land at a public dock two miles upriver from the Krathong Café. He spoke his instructions in Thai quietly through the canvas curtain. When he left, he was carrying a briefcase. I parted the curtain a crack to watch him go. The launch tipped noticeably under his weight. The sun shone brightly from his head

as he walked away. I motioned to Kam, showed him Campbell's message about Dubois. He read it, nodded once, and left with Photra.

Five hours later, I was airborne in one of Adune's twin-engine light transports out of Don Muang. The transport was a Britain-Norman Islander. Chai, the ranch foreman, accompanied me. Short and stocky, he reminded me in some ways of Coyle's man Maul. He told me he had served as a sergeant chief in the Thai Black Panther Brigade in Vietnam. He was barefoot and wore a tattered sarong, a costume that had allowed him to mingle freely with the workers on the docks as he had come to meet me.

'I prefer the clothes of a cowboy as in the movies from your country,' he said over the racket of the engines. 'I do not like these clothes.'

'Your feet give you away,' I said.

He grinned. His large toes were, like my own, parallel and not separated from the rest. This would not have been true of a genuine Thai labourer, whose large toes would be permanently separated from a lifetime of wearing sandals with thongs.

'Do you have knowledge of the plantation?' he asked.

'I've tasted your beef in Bangkok,' I said. 'It's as good as Kobe.'

'Yes,' he said. 'And better than Australian, is this not also true?'

'No question,' I said.

He smiled. 'The ranch lies one hundred fifty miles southeast of Bangkok,' he said. 'Its border is common with Cambodia against the Cardemonnes Mountains. It is in ninety sections measuring fifty-eight thousand acres. There are now twenty thousand cattle, Brahman and Simmental. There are four hundred employees. Many are ranch hands like myself. Others are farmers.

168

We plant ten sections of soybeans, three sections of rice, rotating and alternating our crops. Compared to the King Ranch in Texas, we are small. They have two thousand sections to our ninety. But we have many cobras to contend with, and also the Khmer Rouge.'

'They steal your cattle?'

'Yes. They slip from the mountains at night on to our range. Mr Adune has developed a force of men to patrol the border. Our guard camp is in the valley by Khao Wah. It is to Khao Wah that I have been instructed to bring you. We have three gunships and two AU-24's with cannon. Mr Adune is a fine tactician. He fought with General Wingate against the Japanese.'

We were nearing the plantation now. I could see the fishing port of Trat, which lay just to the southwest, the blue-gold Gulf of Thailand, the islands of Ko Chang and Ko Kut.

In minutes Chai said, 'Now you will see below us the main house and airstrip. To the west are the bunkhouses, grain silos, and shipping pens. To the east, the rice and feed acres. Beyond these, north to the mountains, lies our range.'

The pilot turned to the northeast. We were now cruising at a thousand feet. Below us I could see mile upon mile of lush acreage crossed by a network of drainage canals and dotted here and there with individual palms and brakes of cane. Beyond all this, shimmering like a mirage, lay the five-thousand-foot peaks of the Cardemonnes.

As we approached, Chai pointed out one of the lesser mountains. 'That is Khao Wah,' he said. 'It is where you and your men will meet and train.'

The sunsets in Asia during the dry season are among the most spectacular I have seen. Haze in the air combined with distant high cirrus provides a spectrum of light colours similar to those of the desert canyons in Arizona

and Utah. The sun lowers towards a distant line of trees. The wind dies. Everything becomes still except for the flick of swallows darting in search of food.

The Islander touched down into this stillness at a speed of fifty knots. The pilot turned off the five-hundred-yard sod strip in less than a thousand feet. A light dust trail hung over our landing roll.

We taxied to a corrugated metal roof supported on poles. Inside were two helicopter gunships and one AU-24. The choppers were Hueys, the same as we had used during the war. The AU-24 was a Pilatus high-wing, fixed-gear aircraft. It looked like any other light plane you might see on a civilian flight line except for the rocket pod under each wing and the open port side with its 20mm swivel-mounted cannon. I smiled. When Mr Adune went after rustlers, he didn't mess around. As an open Jeep dusted up to the Islander, a Thai driver in tiger suit and beret, I had the distinct impression I was back at one of our forward operating bases in Laos or Vietnam.

The guard camp at Khao Wah consisted of a dozen thatch-roofed huts set on poles in a compound a half-mile from the airstrip. Chai rode with me in the Jeep to the hut that had been assigned to me. It had screened windows, hardwood floors, measured about twenty by thirty. It was divided into two sections. The smaller contained two bunks and a desk, the larger ten bunks and no desk. The bunks had straw-ticking mattresses and T-bars with rolls of mosquito netting. At the foot of each rested a battered footlocker. Kerosene lanterns, lighted now, hung from the rafters.

'You will have the small room,' Chai said. 'Your men will have the rest. Behind this hut there is another with latrines and washbasins. The largest hut is the dining hall. You will be comfortable here.'

'We're going to need tetanus shots,' I said. 'Routine physicals, malaria pills...'

'Mr Adune has arranged for a physician to visit this camp in the morning. It is then that the equipment you have ordered will also arrive.'

I thanked Chai for his help, told him I was hungry and tired. He brought me a plate of spiced beef with rice from the mess hall. I ate alone in my new quarters. The camp was filled with Adune's men and their families. Through the thin walls of the hut I could hear the snap of their fires, murmuring voices in a language I liked but had never been able to master, the calling and crying of children.

When I had finished eating, I put out the lantern in the room and lay back under the netting of my cot. The mosquitoes serenaded me for a while and then from somewhere distant in the camp a solitary flute played in the gentle manner of the Thais, the notes sounding like the repeat in Ravel's *Bolero*.

I hope Kam's all right, I thought.

We had been lucky with Von Regen's assassins, and I knew there was a chance our luck wouldn't hold. But as I drifted towards a restless sleep that night under the shelter of my straw roof and a star-bright sky, I found it wasn't Von Regen or Rene Dubois who worried me. It was Photra, the helmsman.

And the funny thing is, I couldn't have told anybody why. It was a pure gut feeling, nothing more.

I didn't like him.

Just before dawn, I was awakened by a familiar voice.

'Time, *Lōk*. Time.'

I sat up quickly. Kam stood in the door, visible in the lantern light that spilled from the room behind him. He still wore the travelling clothes he had got from Campbell's safe house in Zurich. They looked now as if they had been powdered with dry cement.

'Any trouble on the road?' I asked.

'No trouble. Photra has quick van. We all drive and sleep, drive and sleep. Ready to start now.'

I got up and went into the larger room. Photra was there along with the five Cambodians Kam had managed to recruit from the refugee centre. They wore tattered army uniforms and battered bush hats with chin straps. Two had faded red-white-and-blue Mike Force scarves around their necks. They were all slender dark-haired men with dusky skins. Not one of them was as tall as Kam. I towered over them, feeling as conspicuous in their presence as a modern-day Gulliver. Each of them looked hungry. Each was smiling.

'All good,' Kam said. 'All with names too long for you, *Lŏk*, so I will call Alpha, Bravo, Charlie, Delta, Echo.'

Alpha was ex-artillery. I would remember him by the way he cocked his head when someone spoke, as if one of his eardrums might have been shattered during the war. Bravo and Charlie were infantry. They had wire scars on their hands, and eyes that never stopped moving. Delta and Echo wore the scarves. They were Khmer Serei who had fought with the Mike Force in Vietnam, drawing their pay from the US government. They were the most eager of the group. They promised me that once we were in Cambodia they would kill many Khmer Rouge.

'It's not that kind of mission,' I said. 'We're going to go in as quietly as we can and come out the same way.'

They looked disappointed, but only for a moment.

Kam beamed as if they were his children. 'We pay each man twenty dollar a day,' he said. 'We give them clothes and two hundred dollar at end. If they not come back, then money go to families or friends at Arangphatet.'

'They look fine,' I said. 'I wish we had a couple more.'

'Photra wishes to be with us,' Kam said. 'He is our number six. Okay with you?'

Right then I wanted to say no. I don't like his looks, deal him out. But I didn't. Instead, I asked Kam whether or not his helmsman friend spoke English.

'No English,' Kam said. 'I translate. You want to talk?'

Before I could reply, Photra began speaking rapidly in Cambodian, grinning happily, bobbing his head up and down.

'What's he saying?' I asked.

'He say he is a true Cambodian soldier who has been captured by the Khmer Rouge. He say he has left behind in his escape three of his enemy dead.'

'Do you believe him?'

'Yes, I think.'

'All right.'

Kam turned and barked some orders to his troops. They came smartly to attention.

'I take them on long run, see who fall out,' Kam said. 'You come too, *Lŏk?*'

'Yes,' I said. 'I come too.'

We ran through the heat of that day. We took our shots and malaria pills. We ran some more.

# 23

Our equipment had arrived on schedule. It was stacked in crates outside our hut. Kam and I were going over it by lantern light after supper when Adune's foreman, Chai, showed up. He was wearing his cowboy rig: boots, chaps, shirt, vest, neckerchief, and Stetson hat. The fabrics were faded, the leather scarred. There was a salt ring around the crown of the hat. Except for his nationality and the army-issue .45 he carried on his hip, he looked like the real thing.

Kam took a long look at him, then the two of them began talking quietly in Thai. Finally they laughed and embraced.

'He with Black Panther in Vietnam,' Kam said. 'We meet at Tuy Hoa while I train as FAC. He number-one good man.'

'The equipment looks fine,' I said.

Chai seemed pleased. 'The boat to your specifications,' he said, 'arrives even now at the personal dock of Mr Adune, south of Trat. It will make thirty-five knots for ten hours. We are even now refueling, and removing identification.'

'Is the motorized raft on board?'

'Yes. Also ropes and grappling hook.'

Chai said he had been asked by Adune to stay with us for the remainder of our brief time at Khao Wah. In the morning, he would take us to the target range, where we would practise with our weapons. I asked him if he would like to sit in while I briefed the men on our mission. He said he would.

174

'Today we lose Charlie,' Kam said. 'Doctor find tapeworm. Charlie in latrine now. Very sad.'

We dragged the desk from my room into the larger room of the hut. Adune had provided a Weems Plotter, an E-6B computer, and detailed maps of the strategic area. Sitting at the desk, I spread the maps and measured the 136 nautical miles from the fishing village of Trat across the Gulf of Thailand to the Cambodian port of Kampong Som. The men huddled around me, watching with interest, Alpha cocking his head to hear, Photra pressing so close I could feel his breath on my neck.

'We'll have to skirt Koh Rong,' I said. 'That's the big island here, ten miles west of Kampong Som. The hotel rests on top of a walled promontory a hundred feet above the water. It's accessible by steps from the east. A couple of miles to the north and west is an old gambling casino with a PSP landing strip behind it. There's a road connecting the hotel to the casino and strip, then to the docking facilities at the seaport.'

While Kam translated what I had said, I did a rough sketch of the hotel site and the adjacent coast. To the south, it was rocky and uninhabitable. Trees rose fifty and sixty feet up the promontory. The walls of the hotel towered above, like those of an ancient fort.

'South coast,' Kam said. 'Good place to bring raft. Will be guards around hotel. One post maybe at east side by steps. Another on roof. Maybe on south coast too, not sure.'

'Okay,' I said. 'We'll bring the motor torpedo boat to about three miles offshore southeast of the hotel. From there, we'll take the raft in to the beach. We'll leave Delta on board the MTB with a machine gun to cover our retreat. Once we're ashore, we'll split into two teams. Echo will lead the red team with Alpha and Bravo. Kam will lead the blue team with Photra and myself.

'Red team will follow the coast east and take up a position short of the steps that lead up to the hotel. Blue

175

team will climb the promontory from the south. On a radio signal, red team will start a diversion with small-arms fire and concussion cans. We'll want a first-rate show down there to draw the hotel and wall guards away. While that's going on, our blue team will scale the wall, enter the hotel, retrieve the pouch, and go out the same way we came in.

'We'll rendezvous at the raft on radio signal and return to the MTB. By the time the Khmer Rouge put their pursuit together, we should be in international waters.'

'What is time schedule for us?' Kam asked.

'We'll have the tides with us going in,' I said. 'Figure four hours down in the MTB and four and a half back. Fifteen minutes each way in the raft. Forty minutes on shore. That's nine plus forty. Add another twenty minutes for the unexpected, and we have ten hours. We launch night after tomorrow, eight P.M. Should be back in Trat the next morning at dawn.'

Each team would have a radio and a pair of night binoculars. Each man would carry a K-bar knife, a Browning 9mm automatic with two clips, an Uzi or AK, whichever they preferred, also two clips, and a web belt and single canteen of water. I would need some burnt cork for my face. We would all wear black pyjamas and jungle hats. The mission would be sterile. No identifiable markings on the clothes or gear. No personal belongings, except for the small metal or ivory Buddhas each man wore around his neck on a chain. In times of danger, these icons were slipped into the mouth to ward off harm.

'We will tape our Buddhas, *Lōk*,' Kam said. 'And blacken chains to keep off light.'

'Have you briefed Chai and the others about the threat from Dubois?'

Kam assured me that he had.

'Good,' I said. I got up slowly. I hadn't felt this stiff

since I'd gone through jump training with the Special Forces at Bad Tolz in the fifties.

Kam grinned. 'We clean Cosmoline off weapons now,' he said. 'We sharpen K-bar knives, file points of bullets, grease ammo into clips. We go first-class shipshape.'

I visited the latrine before turning in. Charlie was still there. He looked pallid and gave me a weak wave.

'*Suer sedei*,' I said.

That meant good luck.

Old Charlie was going to need it.


It seemed I had no sooner fallen asleep than Kam was nudging me awake.

'Time, *Lōk*. Time.'

I had to loosen up for ten minutes before I could put on my black pyjamas. Kam had brought me some burnt cork, but I wouldn't be needing that. Not yet.

Our second day was much like the first. A half-hour of calisthenics by lantern light in front of our hut. A two-mile run. A breakfast in the mess hall of eggs and beef. By the time the sky had begun to turn pink over the eastern ridge of Khao Wah, we were already back at the hut, with Kam putting the others through an equipment inspection. I picked up an AK rifle, hung a holstered Browning, canteen, knife, and ammo clips on my webbed belt, caught up with the men as Kam quick-marched them outside. Chai had a small troop carrier waiting. We bounced down a dusty four-mile track, arriving at the target range just as the sun rose over the ridge line.

'How you feel, *Lōk?*' Kam asked.

'I've got the smoke out of my lungs and the booze out of my brain,' I said. 'My arms are feeling better every hour. What kind of reading can you give me on the troops?'

'Alpha okay, but only know big guns. Bravo good

man, but not have discipline. Photra good. Delta and Echo from Mike Force best.'

'How many hours do you want to take with the weapons?'

'Three, maybe four.'

'Okay. Let's get started.'

And so it began, and it was familiar: The *chuk-chuk-chuk* of the AK contrasting sharply with the tearing canvas sound of the Israeli Uzi. Delta and Echo checked out the PRC-90 radios, experienced enough to know they had to keep the antennae up and not angled towards each other as they talked. Bravo exploded a couple of concussion cans. The sound was similar to that of a mortar. Chai helped Alpha set up the heavy machine gun with its bipod mount. The area around the range grew noisy and dusty and hot. I practised with the AK and then with the Browning. I'd always flown with one holstered inside my G suit. The standard issue was a .38-caliber revolver, but I preferred the extra firepower of the automatic and its ease of loading.

We practised firing together from prone, kneeling, and running positions. Then Kam ordered us into full field equipment and took us on a ten-mile forced march. No piss calls. We were sweating so much we didn't need them. We staggered back to the range at four p.m. Chai had some freeze-dried rations soaking in the sun for us. We broke for twenty minutes, then double-timed to a nearby canal for the water training.

'Bravo lack discipline,' Kam said. 'He want to fall out on march, so I have him carry heavy gun now.'

'You're all heart,' I said.

We swam the canal, forded it, kept our weapons dry. Our black pyjamas clung to us like wet wool.

'These men okay,' Kam said. 'We go back to camp now, work with ropes, practise field strip of weapons with blindfold. In morning, we study maps again, repeat mission. Then be ready for tomorrow night.'

# 24

We rolled out of the staging area at Khao Wah late the next afternoon, heading west-southwest towards Trat and the sea. Our vehicle was the same three-quarter-ton Dodge troop carrier we had used the day before. It had no top, and a windshield that folded flat. Chai drove, Stetson cocked back on his head. I sat passenger seat right. Bravo stood between us, gazing over the barrel of the M-60, which he had placed on its bipod on the hood.

Directly behind me, Kam sat on a bench, Alpha at his side. The two of them faced Delta and Echo, who sat on a bench behind Chai. All four held their rifles, butts to floor, muzzles up. Photra squatted behind the tailgate, his rifle levelled back the way we had come.

'I am glad we are started now,' Kam said. Although he sat just behind me, he had to raise his voice over the growl and whine of the Dodge.

'We're really rushing it,' I said. 'I wish we didn't have to. We could have used another week.'

'You have all good men here, *Lŏk*. All used to battle. You will see. Nothing to worry. Dubois, he may guess we are with Adune, but no way for him to know about boat. By time he find out, we are already gone.'

'We'll have to use a different port coming back. Dubois probably hasn't been told about the diamonds, but he'll assume we're going after something valuable.'

'We go get pouch. Choose port on way back. Keep secure that way.'

'Yes,' I said.

179

'Okay, good,' Kam said. 'Nothing to worry.'

It seemed to me that Kam was right. From the start, Adune's security had been impressive. Chai had told me the motor torpedo boat had been purchased through a blind corporation by brokers not ordinarily associated with Adune. The MTB had been on the market for several months and hence was without a crew. The crew we would use would consist of an engine man and the captain from Adune's own Pattiya yacht. They had brought the craft by night to the private facility by an inlet out of Trat. It lay waiting for us now under the tin shelter of a boat shed, its bow pointing towards the gulf, all of its tanks topped off.

So I tried not to worry as we rumbled and lurched down the long dirt road that cut across the plantation to the sea. The road was narrow, and as soon as we came down from Khao Wah it ran straight for many miles, with flat grassy land on either side and only an occasional palm or herd of grey hump-shouldered cattle to break the monotony of the view. We rode with the late sun in front of us, Chai, Bravo, and I squinting through our dark glasses while the rest of the men sat with their rifles steadied by one hand, talking happily to each other as if we were on our way to a Boy Scout jamboree.

We're all nervous as hell, I thought. Asians cover it with levity. I wish I could.

We were ten miles from Trat when Bravo raised his hand suddenly and told Chai to stop the truck. The road here had begun to curve to the right away from a high stand of saw grass and through an abandoned village of thatched huts. In the distance beyond the huts I could see smoke rising from a burning rice field. Bravo was talking rapidly to Kam.

'What is it?' I asked.

'Bravo say road ahead look good for ambush. Would like to go first by foot to check.'

'All right,' I said. 'Send somebody with him.'

Photra jumped out of the truck as if eager to volunteer. He and Bravo began moving slowly down the road, rifles held at the ready. Bravo went first. Photra followed him at a distance of fifty feet. There was no cover between them and the first of the huts except for the saw grass, and it was impenetrable.

'Bravo want to show you he have good discipline,' Kam said. 'So you will think better of him now before mission starts.'

'I do think better of him,' I said. 'He's right about this place.'

One hundred yards from the first hut, Bravo motioned cautiously with his hand, then lay belly-down at the roadside. Photra dropped to one knee, fifty feet behind him, his AK levelled. Bravo was using binoculars. He lay on the road, elbows propped, scanning the abandoned village. I listened. Over the rough idle of the truck I could hear the breeze rustle the tall grass, the singing of insects, the chirp of a sugar bird. I took off my jungle hat, mopped the sweat from my brow. My eyes stung.

'You need haircut, *Lōk*,' Kam said.

'You're right,' I said.

'I give you one free with number-eight knife.'

'You keep that bloody knife to yourself,' I said.

'Very quick haircut, chop-chop. You look like marine . . .'

We saw it first, heard it a split second later, but it was as if we had seen and heard it at the same time. Bravo stood up. The binoculars hung from a leather strap around his neck. He gave us the thumbs-up sign, motioned for Photra to follow him towards the village. Then he held his rifle in the ready position and began to advance. He had not gone six yards when he stepped on the mine.

There was a flash of light, a concussive roar, a geyser of dirt and metal fragments and chunks of flesh that blew

thirty feet into the air. They were still going up when Chai jammed the Dodge into gear.

'Take us into the grass!' I shouted. 'Move it! Move it!'

I tried to snatch the M-60 as we lurched around, but it skittered off the hood. Photra was running towards us. He ran in a zigzag pattern, with a scatter of bullets behind him.

'Get the machine gun!' I shouted.

He tried. He dived for it, missed, rolled by it with the dirt stitched up around him, and then he was on his feet again, scrambling after us into the grass, with Echo leaning over the tailgate and pulling him in and Delta firing steadily back towards the village.

The grass was ten feet high and razor-sharp. We got the windshield up just as we went in. Chai and I ducked behind it. The rest of the men huddled in back.

'Photra has seen one Jeep,' Kam said.

'They'll have at least two,' I said. 'They'll send one after us and use the other to try to cut us off.'

'We can pick up wagon trail, then road to Trat on other side of field,' Chai shouted. He had put the carrier into four-wheel drive. We zigged and zagged through the grass, the big rib tyres leaving a track a child could follow. I pulled my hat over my ears, crouched as low as I could. The grass screeched like nails down a slateboard across the metal sides of the truck. I heard a cry of pain from the back, turned to see Delta hold up his hand. It was gushing blood, had been sliced to the tendons. Echo bound it with his Mike Force scarf.

At least one Jeep was behind us now. We couldn't see it, but we could hear it whining through the grass.

'They may not close,' I said. 'Not until they're sure we're cut off.'

'Mine that killed Bravo was for all of us,' Kam said.

He was right. The charge had been big enough to rip the truck in half – an antitank mine, probably, with a

pressure-sensitive ring detonator. Most of them took at least three hundred pounds of downward force to trigger them, unless the force was supplied to one edge of the detonating ring. Then it took less. Bravo's foot must have come down exactly right.

The truck swerved suddenly, and we were out of the saw grass and on to the wagon trail Chai had mentioned. He pressed the accelerator to the floor and I watched the speedometer needle quiver to fifty as we bounced and swayed towards the wider dirt road that led to Trat. There were burning rice paddies now at our left, across the thickets of grass to our right I could see a plume of dust raised by the intercepting Jeep.

Dubois, I thought. The mercenary who would peel the skin from his mother for twenty-five grand.

'We can't beat them to that intersection,' I said.

'Other Jeep closing now,' Kam said. He was standing just behind me, clutching the seat back with one hand, his rifle with the other. The brim of his bush hat was flat in the wind. Echo and Alpha were on their knees, firing steadily over the tailgate. I could hear the whip of bullets around me, coming through the dust we raised.

'It's no good,' I shouted at Chai. 'Go into the rice.'

He looked at me as if I were crazy.

'Do it!' I shouted.

We careened off the wagon trail into the burning paddies. The area we entered was ash. A half-mile ahead, the fire line lay like an orange rope. The sky overhead was black. I could taste soot, feel the wink of burning cinders on my skin.

'Open the Jerry cans!' I shouted. 'Splash them out behind us! Hurry up!'

The cans were in wells bracketed to either side of the truck. Kam got one open, passed it to Alpha, who began pouring it over the tailgate. Then Echo was doing it too, and I could smell the gas, and feel the heat of the fire as we sped towards it with the Jeep in pursuit and closing,

one of their gunners firing steadily into the rooster tail of ash we raised, bullets spanging off the carrier; and then, just as we reached the fire line, I heard Alpha cry out and saw him stand and topple out into the foot-high fire with the can still gurgling in his arms, and then saw a whoosh of flame as the high-octane trail we had left ignited through the ash and enveloped the Jeep that had closed to fifty yards before its tank exploded.

We fought our way back to the road. The intercept Jeep was nowhere in sight. In my mind's eye I could still see Alpha, engulfed by flames, just prior to carbonization – a seated black silhouette drawn into the defensive position of a boxer.

Well, Coyle, I thought, this is what your money buys. The lives of some good men.

'They quit now,' Kam said. His face was black with soot.

'Maybe,' I said.

'We will soon reach regular road to Trat,' Chai said. 'Will be people and traffic. Should be okay.'

The regular road to Trat was a strip of blacktop six feet wide with dry, well-travelled shoulders. The traffic was a mix of oxcarts, bicycles, motorbikes, and pedestrians. The people glanced at us as we rumbled by. I knew they had seen the likes of us before. We were mercenaries, like Dubois. And while I thought there was some distinction between us and the men who had been paid to kill us, I knew it was not a distinction these poor farmers and fishermen and peasants were likely to make.

'Thailand be invaded someday,' Kam said. 'These people all be refugees. Khmer Rouge, Chinese, North Vietnamese, they will come and country will fall.'

'Maybe not,' I said.

'Yes,' Kam said. 'It will happen. Just as in Cambodia. You remember, *Lōk*, I said so then and you told me I was wrong.'

I did not reply. We picked up speed out of Trat and made our run for Adune's private pier. We ran parallel to the shore now where the Thai fishing boats were beached. They had large eyes painted on the bows. Giant nets, dark brown, hung on drying racks. The sky overhead was streaked with orange. Gulls wheeled and turned.

We boarded the boat without incident. Chai insisted on joining us now that we had lost two men. I said I was happy to have him. The captain slammed the throttles forward and we pulled away.

'Glad to be aboard, sir,' I said. 'Are you briefed on the mission?'

'Yes,' he said. He was Thai. He wore a yachtsman's cap, white ducks and a short-sleeved shirt. 'I will radio Mr Adune. He will have Dubois's men picked up and will see to the burials of the two you have lost. Belowdecks we have a prisoner you may wish to question.'

'Who is it?' I asked.

'Her name is Jillion Leggett,' the captain replied. 'She says she is a reporter for the API.'

# 25

I was shaking as I went below, certain Dubois had followed Jillion to Trat. I found her in the cramped galley, sitting at a table, sipping tea. Her notebooks were spread around her. She had tied back her hair, and her hair was damp where it lay along her brow. The sleeves of her combat blouse were rolled up.

'What are you doing here?' I said.

She looked at me without apology, her eyes belligerent and dark. 'I'm covering a story,' she said.

'Bullshit.'

'It's about a USAF light colonel who used to play by the rules but doesn't anymore . . .'

'I'll tell you what your story's about,' I said. 'It's about two good Cambodians who got killed back there. One was blown to bits and the other burned to death. It wasn't pretty, and it shouldn't have happened.'

'That's your problem, Matt,' she snapped. 'Don't dump it on me. I'm a reporter and I was doing what any good reporter would do. It was you who got drunk and dropped Adune's name and then lied about why you were going to the ranch. Anything Adune does is *news* in this country. I did some checking. I found out one of his dummy corporations had suddenly purchased this boat. Nobody seemed able to tell me why. Nobody had the foggiest notion where it was. I began checking every dock, slip, and pier Adune had ever used. The last one I checked was the one out of Trat.'

'And you led the bad guys *right* to us,' I said.

'I didn't know there *were* bad guys.'

'Oh, yeah,' I said. 'They're behind us, and up ahead, and now you're in the middle.'

'That suits me fine.'

'Well, it doesn't suit me.'

'I don't know what legal right you have to be here with these men, but I know *damn* well I have a right to cover the story, and you know it too. So unless you're prepared to throw me overboard, you better get used to my being around.'

'Don't tempt me,' I said.

She sipped from her tea. Her hand was trembling. The captain had throttled back to a cruising speed of thirty-five knots. I could hear the rush of water along the plywood hull, and the dull throb of the diesels. Under the yellowish cast of the galley lamp, Jillion looked at me.

'You might as well tell me what's going on, Matt,' she said. 'I'm here, and there's nothing you can do about it.'

I wanted to hold my anger, but it was already leaking away. The ambush hadn't been Jillion's fault. If anything, it had been mine for not levelling with her in the first place.

'All right,' I said. 'But we go professional. Everything I'm going to tell you is off the record until you hear otherwise from me or from Campbell. Agreed?'

'Yes.'

I fixed myself a cup of tea, then sat beside her at the table. We were alone in the galley, and I spoke quietly. Now and again I could hear footsteps padding across the deck overhead. Jillion listened to me without interrupting.

'My God,' she said when I had finished.

'That's all I know,' I said. 'The rest of the answers should show up in the pouch. There's something in it that could do young Horst Von Regen out of the chancellorship and put Coyle under indictment to a Senate subcommittee.'

'Any idea what it could be?'

'No.'

'The last time you asked me to quash a story was when you got pinked doing things for the Cambodians that weren't in your charter as air attaché. But Jesus, Matt, this . . .'

'It's as big as they come.'

Jillion was silent. I wondered if she was writing the heads. 'BILLIONAIRE INDUSTRIALIST SPONSORS ILLEGAL RAID ON CAMBODIA. VON REGEN BID FOR CHANCELLOR DOOMED.'

Finally she looked at me. 'Why are you in it?' she asked.

'As I told Whiskey, I'm in it for Brian.'

'Is that it?'

'That's most of it.'

'What's the rest?'

'I like the work.'

'That isn't the impression I got when you first came down here, telling me how one man had been blown to pieces and the other had burned—'

'I said it wasn't pretty, Jillion. I wish it hadn't happened. I wish the world was a neat clean place where we all looked out for each other and nobody got hurt. I *wish* it was.'

'Are you making excuses?'

'I don't know. Maybe I am.'

'Diana told me once she thought you were a born killer. She said it had taken her a long time to think that, but finally that's what she thought. She had come to realize it was essential to combat. She wasn't being critical.'

'Fine,' I said.

'It was her image of you. Not mine.'

'What's yours?'

'More on the order of Larteguy's French officer, I

think. The lieutenant who searches for his lost battalion after Dien Bien Phu.'

'Oh, come on Jillion,' I said.

'Your drinking rampages across Europe made the circuit here. I heard from a mutual friend who had gotten drunk with you in Ankara that just before you passed out you were shouting for Dietz and Jack to form up.'

'Dietz and Jack are dead,' I said. 'They were shot down over Laos.'

'Exactly.'

I didn't remember the incident Jillion had mentioned, but had no doubt it had taken place. Until Diana's death the losses in the war had for me been barely acceptable. After her death they had become intolerable. More than once out of a drunken stupor I had called her name and those of my friends who had not come back.

'I don't think you're here because you like the work,' Jillion said. 'I think you're here because of Brian. If there's anything more to it than that, it has something to do with being a professional. It's like me with the writing. It's the thing you do best.'

'Yes. It is.'

'You really did look angry when you first came down.'

'I was.'

'Are you still?'

I was silent.

'Even if you are,' she said softly, 'I wish you'd put your arms around me.'

I didn't move. I felt cold inside. I didn't like talking about the past. I spent most of my time now trying not to think about it, not to be consumed by it, not to sink into the bitterness that part of me would always feel.

She reached towards me and touched my hand very lightly, as if she were afraid of triggering some reflexive or even brutal response.

'Please, Matt,' she said. 'Don't be like this.'

'I tend to be pretty bad company these days,' I said.

'You weren't in Bangkok.'

'That seems like a long time ago.'

'Only four days. It does seem more like weeks.'

I shook my head. Again, the images tumbled there: of Bravo blown to smithereens and Alpha curled in the flames.

'There are times when I wish I'd never gotten started,' I said. 'Times when I wish I could wind everything back to Montana and start over.'

'I know,' Jillion said. 'I feel that way too. I never used to, but lately I do.'

She stood up and moved behind my chair. I felt an instant prickling of my skin as she bent towards me and put her arms around my shoulders.

'Every time I'm near you,' she whispered, 'it's always the same. Whether I want it to happen or not, it always does.'

'This really isn't the time *or* the place,' I said.

She kissed the back of my hand, my ear; I could feel the warmth of her breasts against my back.

'We've got six people up there who can come through that galley door any minute,' I said.

'There's a latch,' she said. 'We can lock the door.'

She caressed my ear with her tongue, moved her hands from my shoulder to my thighs. I groaned, feeling a mingle of apprehension, irritation, and need.

'It wouldn't have to take long,' she whispered.

I stood up abruptly. She caught her breath and backed away. I took two solid strides to the galley door, threw the latch, and returned. We kissed, openmouthed, so hard I could hear our teeth come together. I fumbled with her blouse, she with my pants. Her bra was damp. I unhooked it, pulled it away, took her breasts in my hands. They were very warm and slippery with sweat. She pressed against me.

'*Hurry*,' she said.

I felt a knee-buckling wave of desire, my head light and buzzing. I half-carried her to a padded bench attached to the bulkhead behind the galley. In seconds, we were naked.

It was awkward. We shoved and squirmed, slipped and lunged. Our sweat ran in rivulets, mingled into pools on the vinyl padding. The engines seemed to roar louder and louder until the sound from them obliterated the noisy slap of water along the hull, and the slap of our own flesh as we held each other tightly and exploded together as silently as we could.

'I love you,' she whispered. I couldn't reply. My bones had turned to rubber, my muscles to string. I kissed her salty cheek, stood up finally, swaying and panting.

'I want to say something dumb,' she said, 'like am I the best you've ever had?'

I smiled.

'Don't answer that,' she said.

I said I thought I had.

'And you're not angry with me anymore?'

'No.'

'Good,' she said. 'I'd like to go on deck now. I need some air.'

Kam, Chai, and the others had eaten lunches the captain had laid in from Trat. The men were sprawled on the afterdeck, smoking cigarettes, murmuring quietly to each other. The sky was a dark azure from horizon to horizon, sieved with a million stars. Jillion and I went into the deckhouse, where the captain stood at the helm. I told him he could speak freely in front of her.

He referred us to his charts. 'I will take you inside the twelve-mile limit,' he said, 'here to a point three miles off the peninsula and the hotel. Once we are in Cambodian waters, we will extinguish all lights and proceed at slow cruise. Here, between these two small

islands, we will anchor in ten fathoms and you and your men will proceed by raft. I will wait until precisely one hour before dawn. If you have not returned by then, I will have to withdraw to international waters. If necessary, I will make a second attempt to pick you up after dark on the following night.'

Photra had joined us. I could see him by the light of the binnacle, peering at the charts, which, I assumed, made little sense to him.

'We should be able to drop anchor in less than two hours,' the captain said.

'We'll have radio contact with you from the shore?' I asked.

'Yes.'

'I'd like to use your galley to brief my men,' I said. 'I've got some reassigning to do.'

'Please help yourself.'

'Do you mind if I sit in?' Jillion asked.

'Not so long as it stays off the record.'

'It will.'

Our session lasted more than an hour. I decided Chai should remain on board the MTB to handle communications and cover our retreat. He argued that his experience as a Black Panther should make him one of the most qualified to go ashore. I agreed, but said it was essential to have an absolutely dependable man on the boat, one who could manage a radio, a variety of weapons, and would not panic if things turned sour. I put Photra with Delta on the diversion. I said Kam, Echo, and I would be the ones to go into the hotel. Kam translated as I talked. Delta and Echo looked disappointed when they learned I had split them up. They were close friends, and in the tradition of male Cambodians who were close, when they walked together they did so with two fingers entwined.

'I'd like to go with you and Kam,' Jillion said.

'No,' I said.

'I've been in the field before. I know what it's like to be under fire. I've also been to the hotel. And if I've understood you correctly, you've lost two men and only gained one. That means there should be room in the raft.'

'The answer is no,' I said.

'Can you give me one decent reason?'

'Yes,' I said. 'In order to gain access to the hotel, we're going to have to go hand over hand up a rope. You're not strong enough for that.'

'You'd be surprised how strong I am, Colonel Eberhart,' she said.

Kam smiled. For a moment I thought he was going to take Jillion's side, but he didn't.

'Okay,' I said. 'That's it.'

# 26

We readied our equipment on deck. Jillion smeared my face with cork. She seemed to take pleasure in that. We were well inside Cambodian waters now, with our engines throttled back and lights out, slipping quietly towards the distant coast. The men were excited. I could sense it in their movements, in the hushed, eager quality of their voices. It was more than a mission to them. They were coming home.

'Like old times, *Lŏk*,' Kam whispered. He put his arm across my shoulders while Jillion finished with the cork.

'Now for some cup grease,' she said. 'So the black won't come off when you sweat.'

'There must be easier ways to make money,' I said.

'Actually, ducks,' she said, 'I think this is an improvement. Now you've got a face that matches your pajamas.'

Suddenly the engines stopped. I looked for the two small islands the captain had mentioned, but they weren't there. Already the boat had begun to lose headway. I could feel it rocking in the gradual swells.

'Something's wrong,' Jillion said.

I went into the deckhouse. The captain stood at the helm. He was looking through a night scope, which he handed to me as I came up.

'Two patrol boats,' he said. 'Off the starboard bow.'

'Khmer Rouge?'

'Yes.'

I found them with the scope. Their images were blurry

and green in the light-amplifying device. They appeared to be cruising at moderate speed on a course that would intercept ours were we to continue.

'We will have to wait until they pass,' the captain said. 'We are low in the water and dark. They will not have night viewing devices as sophisticated as this. They should pass four to five hundred meters off the bow. Please tell your men to remain perfectly silent.'

I did that. Then Jillion and I lay on the starboard decking amidships, peering across the night sea, trying to make out the dusky shapes of the two boats, unable to do that, but hearing them finally, the distant chortle of their exhausts.

Jillion squeezed my hand. We held our breaths. Our own boat was silent except for the slight ticking sounds of the diesels as they cooled and the gurgle of water against the hull.

We're going to be all right, I thought. They're going to pass well off.

Then I heard a sharp cracking sound from our afterdeck and saw three flares go up, one after another, trailing sparks. I whipped around in a bright bath of red light, to see a figure dive into the water from the stern, and then another; and I was on my feet, and the captain was shouting commands into the voice tube, and I heard the electric whine of the starting motors.

'Where's Kam?' I shouted.

'He's gone,' Jillion said.

'What in Christ Jesus . . . ?'

The engines of the distant patrol boats had gunned from cruise to a high-pitched growl. Searchlights had snapped on, picking up the last of the falling flares. I jumped aft, where Delta and Echo were frantically unwrapping the waterproofing from our weapons. One of the searchlights had picked us up. I heard the boom of a 20mm cannon. That would be the warning shot over our bow.

'Open fire on those lights!' I shouted. 'Get them out!'

The first shell landed beyond us as one of our engines rumbled to life. We were completely illuminated now in the twin-beam glare from the rapidly approaching boats. Delta and Echo had begun firing steadily, over the roof of the deckhouse. I saw Chai bent at the starboard rail, helping someone on board just as we pulled away. It was Kam. He had his knife in his teeth. The patrol boats had closed to six hundred feet.

'The captain can't get the other engine started,' Jillion said. Her voice was steady, but she looked scared. I handed her one of the AK's. 'Go for the lights,' I said. 'Keep squeezing them off.' She joined Delta and Echo. A clip of five 20mm's went off on the port side. The patrol boats continued to close. I saw one of the searchlights blow as double muzzle flashes lit up the deck. Shells were exploding in and around the stern. Kam joined me at the rail amidships.

'Was it Photra?' I said.

'Yes. I make him talk. He say he work for Khmer Rouge as small-fry undercover in Bangkok. He would gain favour by betraying us.'

'I hope the son of a bitch is dead,' I said.

'Head removed from body,' Kam said. 'In this manner, he will not continue wheel of life.'

We were both firing now, kneeling at the rail. The afterdeck was a shambles. Spikes of wood stuck up where the shells had exploded. I saw the Very pistol Photra had used to send up the flares. We were twisting and swerving in a vain attempt to shake the pursuing boats. Then shells started exploding along the deckhouse, and I saw the captain slump over the helm. The sounds of our own firing were sharp in the noise of the shells. The boats were coming into a decent range now. I saw a figure topple overboard from the deck of the second boat just as its searchlight blew. Then there was

196

a dull boom and ball of flame and the first boat half lifted out of the water and fell back as if cut in two. Then we were in the midst of a firestorm of hot metal and wood splinters and I heard Echo give a bubbling sigh and fall back from his AK. Our boat was veering in an aimless circle. The remaining patrol boat had closed to two hundred feet.

'No good, *Lōk!*' Kam shouted.

I went for the raft pack. The motor was riddled, but the raft itself looked all right. I heaved it as far as I could over the rail. Delta had his arm around Echo's bloody chest. He was dragging him towards me.

'Go ahead!' I shouted. 'Get him overboard!' They were gone in an instant. I slapped Jillion on the shoulder. 'You next!' I said. She emptied her pockets into the water, got out of her boots, tied the laces together so she could carry them around her neck. 'Kam! Chai!' I shouted. 'Bail out!' The boat was on fire. Jillion was gone. I saw Kam leap by me into the sea.

'You go!' Chai shouted. 'I will cover!'

I hesitated, then dived as long and deep as I could away from the burning boat. The water felt cool at first, then warm. I swam under until my lungs felt as if they would burst, then bobbed to the surface not far from the raft pack, where Jillion already held on. Delta was still making his way, bringing the wounded Echo in a cross-chest carry. The fire glare was bright on the water. I could smell the stink of diesel fuel. Kam trod water next to me, panting for breath.

'Chai stayed behind,' I said. 'I shouldn't have let him.'

Kam shook his head. 'Engine boy dead. Captain too.'

'Look,' Jillion said. 'The patrol is going to board.'

The remaining boat had throttled back and was riding its wake up to the stern of the burning MTB. Two men stood on the deck with boat hooks. Two others, their

197

automatic rifles trained on what was left of our craft, were poised and ready to jump aboard as soon as the boats were joined.

'They will look for prisoners before tanks explode,' Kam said.

'Then they'll come after us.'

'Yes. Too bright now to hide.'

I trod water, watching helplessly as the men with the hooks grappled our boat and the men with the rifles jumped on board. Then I saw Chai. He seemed to step out of the flames themselves, a familiar silhouette in a Stetson hat. He held his AK-47 in both hands at hip level, firing fully automatic from a thirty-round clip. I could see him work to hold the muzzle down, could see him aim, not at the men who were firing back, but into the fuel area of the enemy boat. Then he was falling forward, and there was a flicker of flame, and then a terrific blast as the boat went up.

Instinctively we gulped for air and dropped below the surface. The concussion from the explosion, travelling through the incompressible water, punched our guts and hammered our chests. When we surfaced, both boats were awash with flame. Hot bits of metal chunked and hissed around us. The boats went down, first one, then the other. Burning fuel was sucked into the whirlpools they made. Our faces were hot until the fires flickered out and we were left to tread water in a dark sea.

'How far offshore do you think we are?' I asked Kam.

'Eight, maybe six miles.' He pointed towards Kampong Som, its lights so distant on the horizon they tended to disappear behind the gentle waves. 'Current with us now,' Kam said. 'We use paddles, work hard. Get to shore before sun comes up.'

'They'll be sending other boats.'

'They will come from far side of peninsula. We go straight from here. Little luck, be okay.'

198

We pulled the raft pack over. I found the lanyard and gave it a yank. I heard two pops sound deep in the pack, then, like a giant blossoming flower, the black raft unfolded and enlarged upon itself. We pulled ourselves aboard, thrashing and kicking. Delta slid Echo in. I touched the tips of my fingers to the wounded man's neck, then looked at Kam.

'He is dead,' Kam said. 'Now we will take him home.'

# 27

We established a rhythm of paddling across a current that wanted to take us east of the hotel. Jillion, Kam, Delta, and I each took a corner of the six-man raft. Echo's body lay lengthwise down the middle. Kam and I had the rear corners. Other patrol boats were speeding now towards the area where our original encounter had taken place. They would pass well to the west of us.

Kam had inventoried our equipment. We had four web belts, two K-bar knives, Kam's Morseth, one sidearm, and two clips of ammunition. Jillion and I had managed to save our boots. Kam and Delta had lost their sandals, but their feet were so calloused this would not matter. Jillion now wore Echo's web belt and carried the canteen. I carried one of the K-bars and the sidearm.

'We have enough still, *Lŏk*, to go get pouch,' Kam said. 'We find Khmer Rouge. Take weapons from them.'

'I agree.'

'Then what?' Jillion asked.

'We go through jungle to Thailand. Take long time. We cross border over Cardemonnes. Come out by Adune plantation.'

I sensed that Kam was trying to sound more confident than he was. Even if we were able to avoid the Khmer Rouge, our chances of surviving a trek that would take weeks through the jungle were poor. I knew that. So did Jillion.

'This is rotten hard work,' she said. 'I'll be glad when

it's over.' She straightened her shoulders and resumed paddling. Her hair was ropy and wet.

'So will I,' I said.

We landed a mile southeast of the hotel two hours before dawn. We came ashore at a point where jungle vegetation grew to the water line. We could hear combers breaking on the beach to the west.

'Best to sink raft here,' Kam said. 'Cover with stones. You do that. Delta and I fix grave.'

A quarter-inch line had been doubled through grommets around the perimeter of the raft. Jillion and I worked for ten minutes, loosening the knots. Once we had them, I pulled the line free and formed it into a coil, which I looped across my shoulders. I estimated its total length at fifty feet. It was synthetic – nylon, I guessed, by the feel of it – that had been dyed black.

'Anything else we can use?' I asked. Jillion was on her knees, rummaging through the gear pockets that had been sewn along the insides of the raft.

'Some survival rations,' she said. 'First-aid kit.'

'We'll take them,' I said.

We deflated the raft and sank it with stones in four feet of water. Then we joined Kam and Delta.

Using their knives, they had managed to hack a shallow grave out of the rocky and root-matted soil of a thicket fifty feet in from the shore. As we came up, they were chanting softly, '*Arahan, Arahan.*' They had placed a palm leaf between Echo's fingers, a strip from his clothes around his legs, a Mike Force scarf around his neck. Now Delta sprinkled water on his dead friend's face. These preparations were all that could be done, under the circumstances, to allow Echo to enter his next life cycle with a minimum of difficulty. Ideally, he would have been cremated. But at least he had been brought to lie in his native soil and would now continue in the wheel of life.

Photra would not.

When the ceremony and burial were finished, we set up our movement towards the hotel. Delta volunteered to take the point. He would break trail and flush out any Khmer Rouge. I would follow at about five meters. Jillion would follow me. Kam would be our rear guard.

For an hour we made our way through the tangle of vine and thicket that lay between the coast and the thicker canopy of the jungle itself. We moved by starlight in dusky shadow, travelling as much by sound as by sight, the soft splash of water to our left, the rustle of palms to our right, the thump of surf on sand in the gloom ahead, growing louder and louder as we went.

When we finally reached the beach itself, we lay down just inside the last of the vegetation. The beach was two hundred feet long. The sand was white and seemed to glow like phosphorus. There was a sea wall along its length. At the far end, a road sloped up the eastern escarpment to the hotel. Stairs had been cut parallel to the road to provide access to the beach.

'Be patrols on road,' Kam said. 'Maybe one, two guards on stairs. Delta say command post on roof, maybe four men. Could be more inside. He not sure.'

'The road and stairs are too risky,' I said. 'We'll stick to our game plan. We'll cross the beach and climb the escarpment to the southwest wall. We'll scale the wall, slip into the hotel, and grab the pouch. Then we'll find a place to hole up.'

'Be daylight soon,' Kam said.

'Let's move it, then.'

We made our way together to the close end of the sea wall. The base of the wall was in shadow. Delta was the first to cross the sand. He put his Buddha in his mouth, drew his knife, sprinted barefoot into the gloom. The diminishing squeak of the sand sounded like a shutter moving in the breeze. We waited until we saw his slight form emerge from the sea-wall shadow and dart into the cover on the far hill. There was silence. We waited. At

last he popped out, gave a wave, and disappeared again.

I took out my automatic, looked at Jillion. 'Let's you and me go together,' I said.

'Bet I can beat you,' she said.

We took off sprinting across the sand. We were halfway when we heard the noise of a vehicle up the road in the direction of the hotel. It was coming our way. We hit the sand, pressing ourselves as tightly as we could into the protective shadow of the wall. I slipped the safety off the automatic, let the pistol lie along my thigh. I was gulping for breath. The vehicle was coming closer. It sounded like a Jeep. I could see the rake of its lights sweeping over the wall. Then it was directly above us, so close we could smell the exhaust and hear the voices of the Khmer Rouge, and then it was gone on its way towards the casino at Kampong Som.

For a few seconds we lay together, holding each other, pressing each other.

'Oh Jesus, Matt,' she whispered.

I could smell her sweat, remembered our time on the boat.

'I want you,' I said. 'When this is over I want you all day and night for a week . . .'

Then we were up and running again, sprinting past the last hundred feet of the sea wall, diving towards Delta into the underbrush, flopping on the ground and panting for air. Kam had joined us before we caught our breath. Now the escarpment rose steeply above us to the retaining wall of the hotel. We went up on a diagonal towards the southwest corner. Dawn had begun to pink the sky, so we went together now, clawing our way through the dense vegetation of the slope, hearing the peep of the tree toads diminish around us, hearing the snapping of dry vines and the scurrying away of small animals and lizards as we forced our ascent to the base of the wall.

The wall was a crumble of mortar and stone, forty feet high. Vines grew partway up from the bottom and hung partway down from the top. Kam took hold of one of the bottom vines and gave it a yank. It came loose in his hand.

'Top vines be stronger,' he said. 'We give Delta big boost. He climb up, take rope, lower from top. We be okay.'

Delta held up his hand. It was still wrapped with the Mike Force scarf, bloody and filthy now. I had forgotten it. So had Kam.

'The next lightest person is me,' Jillion said.

'Kam will do it,' I said.

'Has he ever climbed rock?'

'Not that I know of.'

'Well, I have,' she said. 'I've climbed in Wales and in the Dolomites. I'm good. Give me the rope.'

I wanted to argue, but she was already on the wall, picking her holds, stepping up. I tossed her the coil. She looped it across her shoulders. We stood and watched as she climbed. She moved quickly and with fine precision, dislodging bits of mortar and small pebbles, leaning out occasionally to peer up, choosing her route with the eye of a practised mountaineer. Soon she was in the blank section of wall between the last tendrils of the bottom vines and the first of the top.

'She climb like fly,' Kam whispered.

'A few more feet,' I said, 'and she should be able to use those upper vines.'

She was moving more slowly now, stretching and reaching towards the first coiling tendrils above. In the distance I could hear the horn of a freighter. The sea was beginning to colour now, pink in the false dawn.

'Can see lights on road,' Kam said. 'Maybe too late to go into hotel now.'

'She's almost up,' I said.

Jillion had reached the vines. She was using them now

204

as she went, clutching two and three at a time, pulling and kicking her way towards the top. I could hear the thudding sounds her boots made. As I watched her, the palms of my hands grew wet. She was thirty-five feet up when one of the vines broke suddenly and I saw her peel away from the wall, swinging from the grip of one hand, clutching with the other, scrabbling and fighting her way back and up. And then she was there. Perched high above us. Anchoring the rope in a clot of vines, tossing the free end down.

'Like you say, good show,' Kam said. 'Now we go quick.'

We tied the rope around Delta's waist. Jillion kept tension on it as he fumbled his way up. Kam went next. I followed. The wall had been set deep into the escarpment. On the far side, it was an easy jump from the top to the ground. We lay panting in the shadows. All the stars had gone from the sky. Fifteen feet away, the southwest corner of the hotel rose six storeys to the Sihanouk penthouse that capped the building, with its incomparable view of the sea. According to Coyle, the room we wanted was on the sixth floor, directly above us. There were no lights anywhere apparent. The once manicured lawn had gone to seed. We heard no noise.

'It's still beautiful,' Jillion said. 'But sad too, to see it empty like this and overgrown.'

'I guess it was too decadent for the Khmer Rouge,' I said.

A tiny pinwheel of light arced from the roof above and fell on the ground between us and the hotel. It scattered sparks when it hit.

'Command post on top,' Kam whispered.

'All right,' I said. 'We'll go in through the side door to the ballroom.'

'Be too much daylight soon,' Kam said.

'We'll hole up inside. Go out after dark.'

'You know good place?'

'Yes,' I said.

The ballroom was at the rear of the hotel. It had been designed with French windows to give dancers a view of the sea. A single door of wrought iron and glass provided access to the grounds. We darted there, going one at a time across the exposed section of lawn. Kam jimmied the lock with his Morseth. When he began to open the door, its hinges squealed from disuse. Delta and I slipped our fingers under the butt and lifted the door enough to ease its weight. Once in, we closed it behind us.

The ballroom was a vast empty space of dusty parquet, broken here and there by octagonal supporting columns that rose from floor to ceiling. Jillion and I had laughed about them once. They had always seemed to get in the way of our dancing. Now, quietly, we crossed the floor under a half-dozen crystal chandeliers that already reflected the first light of day. We went through the kitchen and up the concrete stairs that had been used by the servants when the hotel had been open. We went up on the balls of our feet, and at every landing we paused to listen. We could hear nothing except our own quickened breath and the crowing of roosters from somewhere outside.

'Where did Coyle's man stay?' Jillion asked.

'He had the corner room on the sixth floor,' I said. 'The safe is under the parquet in the closet.'

'Did Coyle give you the combination?'

'Yes.'

'I've been thinking about that crawl space we found above the Sihanouk suite . . .'

'I have too,' I said. 'We can hole up there.'

We went into the room that had been used by Dennis Capps. I used my K-bar knife to pry the parquet loose from the closet floor. The safe was small but it had been cemented into place and I had to work the combination on my knees. The dial was hard to see. I had memorized

the combination Coyle had given me, but it didn't seem to work.

'Delta say men approaching front of hotel,' Kam said.

'I can't get the son of a bitch open,' I said. It was stuffy and warm in the closet. I could hear muffled footsteps from somewhere distant in the building, the sound of men's voices. Drops of my sweat splattered the safe.

'Better leave now, Lōk. Come back later . . .'

'I've got it,' I said. The door of the safe was removable. It was the size and shape of a saucer, felt like it weighed about five pounds. I lifted it away and reached in.

'Hurry,' Jillion said. 'It sounds like those men are coming the same way we did.'

'I've got the pouch,' I said. 'Let's go.'

## 28

It was six a.m. and the command post on the roof was changing the guard. We ran up the last flight of stairs and ducked into the Sihanouk suite, with the sounds of approaching feet heavy behind us. I took the safety off the automatic. Kam and Delta had their knives ready. I could feel Jillion's hand clutching mine.

The Khmer Rouge went by the door so close we could hear them breathe. They went down a long corridor and climbed the iron ladder that would take them to the roof. Their boots clanged noisily against the rungs. We heard voices and laughter, and then the guards who had been relieved came by the door and one of them started to open it and there was more laughter and then the laughter and footsteps faded away.

'They could come in here anytime,' I said. 'It looks like plenty of people have.'

The room was still furnished, but was now in disarray. There were empty wine bottles on the floor, woven containers that had once held food, cigarette butts, candle stubs. Kam picked up one of the bottles, looked at the label. 'Rice wine,' he said. '*Chen*. Chinese.'

He sounded disgusted, but Delta prowled the suite in awe. Sihanouk had once been the god-king of Cambodia, a direct descendant of the royal family of Norodom. He had voluntarily abandoned his throne in 1955 to assume the role of chief of state. Subsequently overthrown, he had for a while been a virtual prisoner in Peking and now was under palace arrest in Phnom Penh. This `once

opulent suite had been his playground. Kampong Som had once been called Sihanoukville.

When I had convalesced here that drunken week with Jillion and Kam, the hotel had been less than one-third full. There were no tourists in those days, and transportation for the rest of us had been sporadic at best between Phnom Penh and the deep-sea port. Jillion and I had taken to exploring the hotel late at night. We prowled the floors, slipped once into the Sihanouk suite itself. The furniture was Queen Anne-style, upholstered in green and red stripes. Jillion had struck sensuous poses. We had made love on the prince's own bed.

And then we had found the crawl space that had been constructed between the suite and the hotel roof. Apparently it had been intended for air-conditioning ducts never installed. We had climbed into it from a walk-in closet.

Now we climbed into it again: Jillion first, then Delta and Kam, then me. The space was less than four feet high. Otherwise its dimensions were the same as the suite below. A fine powder of dust covered all of its surfaces. Small ventilating louvers, six inches square, had been placed at intervals along the outside walls. A single large vent had been cut into the ceiling over each room. The vents had been covered with screens of wire mesh. Daylight seeped through the louvers, brightly along the east wall.

It was a cramped, uncomfortable place, already much too warm; but I felt an enormous sense of relief as I wriggled into it and slid the closet panel back into place. It took a moment for my eyes to adjust. Then, with the others behind me, I crawled to one of the east louvers and opened the pouch.

It was made of kidskin and had been rolled into a tubular shape about a foot long, tied once in the middle with a leather cord. The diamonds were in four velvet

pouches. I asked Jillion to put them into the pockets of her combat blouse.

'A girl's best friend,' she said.

'Better keep them in the pouches,' I said. 'They're strictly on loan.'

'Worse luck,' she said.

'Check this,' I said. I held up a shiny piece of paper about the size of a playing card. It was white on one side, black on the other.

'It looks like the back strip from a Polaroid picture,' she said.

'There are ten of them here,' I said. 'They were in the safe next to the pouch.'

'Can you make anything out?'

I held one to the light, thought I saw the silhouettes of two figures, but couldn't be sure.

'I'll bet you half the diamonds this is what Von Regen didn't want us to see,' I said. 'They should print up nicely.'

'I'll do it at the bureau as soon as we get back.'

Kam pointed up. We could hear muffled steps on the roof above. They passed over the place where we were and went on.

'*If* we get back,' Jillion said.

'We will,' I said.

'I'll bet those pictures are nasty,' she said.

'I'll bet,' I said.

The rest was a sheaf of foolscap, each page divided down the middle by a thin red line. To the left of the line were columns of figures, to the right meticulous notations in French. Dennis Capps had been a very careful, very thorough man. At the bottom of each page Horst Von Regen's signature was scrawled in black.

'Is it what you expected?' Jillion asked.

'I'm not finding the word for "rubber,"' I said. 'Your French is better than mine. Take a look.'

I handed her the sheets of foolscap and she scanned each one, slowing down as she went.

'The word for rubber is *caoutchouc*,' she said. 'It's not here. I don't see the word *latex*, either.'

'Any mention of the Chupp plantation?'

'No. All I see is a record of transactions between Coyle Enterprises and two Cambodian generals. App Reng and Po Sot. For *des obus de cuivre jaune* . . .' She looked at me. '*Pour les diamants*,' she said.

'Brass for diamonds,' I said.

'Yes.'

I felt the dull flame of the scars on my back. Anger at Coyle for using me. Anger at myself for letting him. I had heard of the black-market trade in brass, and had once met the Cambodian generals mentioned by Capps in his ledger. The brass came from empty shells smuggled from artillery positions on the battlefronts. A single 105mm shell weighed nearly four pounds and could bring as much as two dollars in the marketplace. The transactions were in violation of the US Munitions Control Act and were strictly illegal in Cambodia.

'Does it look as if Von Regen was handling the shipping?' I asked.

'Yes,' Jillion said.

I shook my head. 'Senator Talbot could skin Coyle alive with this.'

'What a story,' Jillion said. 'Jesus, what a story.'

It was one long, hot, miserable day in that crawl space. The only way I could sit up was in a half-slouch with my head cocked to one side and the concrete roof pressing against me. Every time one of us moved, a powder of dust would rise. We chewed on the rations Jillion had found in the raft. They tasted like sawdust flavoured with chocolate. We sipped the warm water from the canteen. As the hours passed, the atmosphere became more and more like that of a sauna. We wrung the sweat

211

from our clothes. We crouched by the louvers on the north side of the building, peering through the small slits seven storeys down to the curving drive at the front of the hotel. Now and then we would see guards of the Khmer Rouge patrolling the grounds. They walked in pairs, with rifles slung over their shoulders. They flipped their cigarettes into the swimming pool which was half-empty now and filled with debris. They walked across the overgrown lawn, through what had been a miniature golf course and a children's play area with statues of gargoyles.

Then we would crawl on our bellies to the mesh screen that looked down into the Sihanouk suite, where the air was a few degrees cooler, and we would lie there for a while and try to breathe.

'We should have brought some pillows up here,' Jillion said.

'Better we didn't. Someone could have noticed they were missing.'

'The canteen's almost empty. Couldn't we risk getting some more water?'

'No.'

'Delta's hand looks awful. I did the best I could with the first-aid kit.'

'He'll be stoic about it. He'd be stoic about it if he lost an arm.'

We peered through the screen, into the suite.

'I feel like a voyeur,' Jillion said.

'Not much of a show right now.'

'Remember the one we put on?'

'Yes, my love,' I said. 'I do.'

We decided to sleep during the afternoon. We set up a one-hour rotating watch. I took the first shift, then woke Kam and settled in for my three-hour nap. I lay on my back near one of the louvers by the north wall. I used my boots for a pillow. I thought about Brian and Whisky and

how one way or another I was going to get back to them. I thought how we needed some luck now, enough to see us through whatever it was going to take.

I think I prayed for that luck just before I dozed off. I didn't form the words, but the prayer was there like an image in my mind.

And then Delta was touching my shoulder with his freshly bandaged hand. He had had the fourth shift. The light in the crawl space had diminished. The air was stuffy, but not quite so hot. Jillion and Kam were asleep. Delta was speaking to me in Khmer. He seemed excited and kept pointing at the louver where he had been sitting on watch. I saw that he had forced one of the slats, and I was angry about this, because I knew in order to do it he had risked making some noise. Then Kam was awake.

'What's he saying?' I asked.

Delta spoke rapidly to Kam. I saw Kam's head bob up and down. They spoke to each other for several minutes. Then Kam translated for me. He said Delta had heard an aeroplane fly over the hotel. He had pried the louver slat with his knife so he could look up. He caught a brief glimpse of the plane and thought it might have landed at the old airstrip by the casino.

I didn't doubt the truth of what Delta was saying, but it puzzled me. The Khmer Rouge were rural insurgents. They had no air force and virtually no pilots. Before the country fell, most of the aeroplanes we had lent them had been brought out. Cambodian pilots had filled them with their families and a few possessions and had flown them to Thailand, where the planes had been inventoried by the US government and sent back to the States. The planes that had been abandoned in Cambodia had either been left by the Khmer Rouge to rot on the airstrips or had been salvaged by the Chinese advisers to the insurgency.

With Kam doing the translating, I pressed Delta at

length. By the time I had finished, Jillion was awake and listening. I filled her in. 'He says it was high-wing, singleprop. That means either a T-41 or a U-10. He thought some of the markings had been painted over, but it was too far away to be sure.'

'I thought the airstrip here had been shut down ever since the fall of Kampong Som,' Jillion said.

'So did I.'

'God, Matt, if we could get that plane . . .'

'Car coming, *Lŏk*,' Kam said. 'Up road from casino.'

I crawled to one of the louvers and looked out. A black Citroën staff car was just pulling into the drive in front of the hotel. Gravel crunched under the wheels as it came to a stop. Khmer Rouge guards opened the rear doors. Two men got out. Their uniforms were different in cut and colour from those of the guards.

'Chinese officers,' I said.

'And look who else,' Jillion said. She was kneeling at the louver next to mine. Seven stories below, I saw that a woman had joined the two Chinese. She was Eurasian. Her hair was long and raven black. She wore a blue silk dress. She was middle-aged, but looked as slender as a girl.

'Sanya Tohmi,' Jillion said.

I nodded. 'The Pearl of the Orient,' I said. 'Still working her beat.'

# 29

She had been born in Hanoi of a Vietnamese mother who had been consort to a French colonel. She had been educated in the lycée in Saigon, had quickly become the darling of the Cercle Sportif. By the time she was seventeen, she had started into business for herself, making a fortune in piasters finally by managing the flesh trade during the American construction of the Saigon-Bien Hoa highway.

In the early seventies she had purchased the now defunct casino near the Sihanouk hotel. She was thought to have been for a time the mistress of the prince himself. I had met her just before the fall of Kampong Som. She had told me then she would not leave for the safety of Thailand. 'Each regime is like the next,' she had said. 'The Khmer Rouge will be advised by the Chinese. The Chinese will have money and predictable tastes. Surely, my colonel, you realize this is true.'

We heard the door open to the master bedroom of the Sihanouk suite below. I inched my way to the screen and looked down. Sanya had come into the room. She looked at its disarray with distaste. I could hear voices from the corridor. Then one of the officers came in, a heavyset man wearing a tan uniform with red pips and a Sam Browne belt. He shut and bolted the door behind him. He had a bottle of rice wine which looked to be about half full. He offered the bottle to Sanya. She shook her head. They were standing almost directly below me. He took a long swallow from the wine, set the bottle on the floor. Then he said something to Sanya and she began to

215

unbuckle his Sam Browne belt. She was doing this when he hit her, once, sharply, with the back of his hand. I inched away from the screen.

We gathered at the farthest corner of the crawl space and spoke in whispers. We could hear the footsteps of the guards on the roof above, and Sanya's periodic cries.

'I can't stand this,' Jillion said.

'Take it easy,' I said.

'Why does she do it?'

I shook my head.

'We kill Chinese,' Kam said. 'Go get plane.'

'We'd be taking one hell of a chance,' I said.

'We have surprise. They not expect us. Delta and me, we put on uniforms, go with Sanya, take car. Meet two of you on road to strip. You fly plane. We be in Thailand by sunrise.'

'I'd much rather do that than try to make it through the jungle,' Jillion said.

'Either way big risk, *Lŏk*. This way quick.'

I rubbed the sweat from my face. My hands were filthy. The others watched me, hunched under the low ceiling of the crawl space, waiting for me to make a decision I didn't want to make. Then Sanya screamed again, louder than before, and I thought I heard laughter from the roof.

'All right,' I said.

We made our plans as carefully as we could. Kam would go through the closet and take out the one with Sanya. Delta would back him up. I would cover them through the screen. When it was safe, Jillion and I would join them in the suite below. Then Kam would call the second Chinese in from the corridor.

'I hope to hell he's out there alone,' I said.

'Who's going to carry the pouch and the Polaroid strips?' Jillion asked.

'You,' I said. 'If you've got room in those pockets.'

'I've got plenty of room,' she said. She sounded indignant. I looked at Kam. He had his knife in his teeth.

I inched back to the screen. The man had exchanged his uniform for a heavy silk robe. Black dragons with claws extended and nostrils breathing fire coiled across a yellow field. He was directly below me. He stood over Sanya, whom he had bound with velvet ropes to a straightbacked chair. Her blue gown was zippered, and he had unzipped it until she was naked to her waist. He spoke to her. She did not reply. Her skin was the colour of copper, and her breasts were small. They glistened in the heat of the room. Her eyes were blue. Her head was at the level of his waist. He spoke to her again. She leaned forward and began to undo the sash of his gown with her teeth. He watched her. I could see the rolls of fat on the back of his neck.

I crouched over the screen, holding the automatic in both hands, aiming down. Kam and Delta had finally gotten the closet panel away. I watched them slip like shadows through the opening. Jillion started to come towards me. I shook my head. She stopped, poised on her hands and knees. I could hear the footsteps of a guard pacing the roof over my head. Bits of dust sifted through the rays of light from the louvers. The crawl space was an oven. Drops of sweat rolled down my face. Sanya was still working on the sash. The man was speaking impatiently to her. Then suddenly he put his hand on his neck and looked up.

He looked directly up at the screen, and it seemed to me he looked directly through it and into my eyes. I slipped the safety off the automatic. He slapped at his forehead as if to kill a mosquito, said something in Chinese, and it was only then that I realized drops of my perspiration were falling into the room.

He went for his gun. It was in a holster on his Sam Browne belt. He had draped the belt over the back of

Sanya's chair. The gun was a clumsy-looking revolver. He cocked it and pointed it at the screen. He was shouting now. I saw Kam appear in the doorway across the room. His arm went up and then flashed forward. There was a glint of light. The fat man stopped in mid-shout, the Morseth through his neck. He clutched at it and went down. I heard the revolver go off, heard Sanya scream, heard shouts from the corridor outside the suite.

'Jesus,' Jillion breathed.

'We're in for it now,' I said.

Scrambling past her, I dropped into the closet. I could hear Kam shouting in Chinese. By the time I got to the room, he was unbolting the door to the outside. Delta stood behind it. Two men came in. One was the second Chinese officer. Delta took him silently with his K-bar. The other was a uniformed Khmer Rouge with an olive-drab pith helmet. He had an AK rifle, which he started to level at me. I took him with the automatic, firing once. The slug drove him back against the wall, and he crumpled there, teeth bared, under a fountain of arterial blood. The sound of the pistol had been deafening.

'Other guards come quick,' Kam said. 'Hear shots.'

'Bolt the door,' I said. 'Cut Sanya loose.'

Delta and I dragged the bodies of the three dead men into the next room. We could hear the sounds of voices and rushing feet in the corridor. Kam brought Sanya to me. She looked stunned. I helped her with her dress.

'Do you remember me?' I said.

'Yes. You were with the embassy.'

'Did you come to Kampong Som by plane?'

'Yes. They often bring me here. They are billeted in Phnom Penh . . .'

The guards outside were banging on the door. Kam was shouting at them in Chinese. Sanya glanced that way, obviously frightened.

'We need your help,' I said. 'We need you to convince those Khmer Rouge everything is all right in here.' I was prepared to threaten her if I had to. As it turned out, there was no need.

'If I agree to help you,' she said, 'you will take me with you from this country?'

'Yes.'

'Then I will do it,' she said.

She loosened her gown. Kam put on the dragon robe of the dead Chinese. He lay on the couch in the master bedroom, revolver in one hand, bottle of rice wine in the other. Sanya went to the door and spoke through it, softly at first, then angrily. Delta and I watched from the bath. I held the automatic. He held the AK.

It seemed to go on forever. The guards shouted at Sanya. Sanya shouted at the guards. Now and then Kam would join in. Once, he fired the revolver into the wall. Finally Sanya opened the door. She was clutching her dress with one hand, not quite managing to keep it up. Three guards started to press past her into the room. They each held an AK. Then Kam fired the revolver again, this time into the ceiling. He tipped the bottle over his head and took a bath in the wine. Then he began to laugh. The light was soft in the room. His back was to the men. They looked at him, then looked at Sanya. One of them spoke sharply to her. He was asking the whereabouts of the other officer. I heard Delta shout something in Chinese just behind my ear. Then he reached past me and turned on the shower. One of the Khmer Rouge started to come our way. Sanya flew at him. By the time she had finished screeching, he was backing out the door of the main room with his hands over his ears.

Then they were gone. They had not searched the bedroom where the bodies were. They had not made inquiries about the missing guard. Our ruse with Sanya and Kam had worked.

'We wait maybe half-hour,' Kam said. 'Then three of us, we go down and get car. Meet you and Jillion where road curves by beach towards Kampong Som.'

I looked at Jillion. She had come down from the crawl space after the guards had left. She looked hot and tired and more than a little afraid.

I took her hand. 'Let's go,' I said. 'We're almost home.'

# 30

We slipped out of the hotel the same way we had slipped in. Down six flights of stairs. Through the ballroom. Across the rear lawn to the wall. Our rope was where we had left it, knotted to a clot of vines. I went down hand over hand. Jillion did a body-wrap rappel, moving gracefully where I had been awkward. Then we sprinted in the shadow of the sea wall across the beach to the bend in the road where the others would meet us. We lay concealed in a thicket of bamboo. Behind us, combers rolled on the beach. The air was dank, almost cool. It smelled like mushrooms gone to rot.

'I'm trying to remember how far the airstrip is,' Jillion panted.

'Mile and a half. Maybe two miles.'

'Will it be guarded?'

'I don't know. The Khmer Rouge probably wouldn't bother with it. The Chinese might have left somebody with the plane.'

'What do we do if Kam and the others get caught?'

'Make a run for it.'

'I'm beginning to think they should have come with us.'

'It'll help a lot having that car. Be much safer than trying to walk the road.'

A Jeep rumbled by on its way to the hotel. Its lights flashed brightly through the bamboo. We pressed ourselves flat to the ground.

'There are foot patrols too,' I said. 'We better keep our voices down.'

'What are you going to do first when we get back?' Jillion said. She was so close to me I could feel her breath on my ear.

'Sit in a hot tub,' I said. 'Eat, drink, and make love.'

'God,' she said, 'wouldn't that be great.'

Fifteen minutes later, the staff car showed up. Its widely spaced lights were unmistakable. Fog lamps gleamed yellow from its bumper. It weaved towards us. I knew the guards on the roof of the hotel had a clear view of the road. Kam knew it too. He played his part well. I could see him now as he swerved towards the thicket and brought the car to a stop. He had on one of the Chinese uniforms. So did Delta. Sanya Tohmi sat between them on the front seat.

Jillion and I had already started forward when more lights appeared on the road from the hotel. We ducked down. Kam got out of the staff car and began urinating drunkenly against one of its fenders. A Khmer Rouge Jeep slowed, then rattled by, sounding a klaxon horn.

'Hurry *Lōk!*' Kam called. 'They find out pretty soon what happened at hotel.'

'We're in,' I said. 'Let's go!'

We sped down the road. Ahead, I could see the taillights of the Jeep that had passed us. Then there was another set of lights behind us, coming at high speed.

'There's the turnoff for the strip,' I said. 'That first Jeep went by. Break left.'

We skidded into a narrow road with jungle tight to either side and a faint glimmer of light in the distance.

'Have we got that other Jeep behind us?' I asked.

'No,' Jillion said, peering back. 'Yes, yes, they just made the turn.'

'Can't outrun,' Kam said. 'Have to block road.'

'Get closer to the strip,' I said. 'Get as close as you can.'

I could see it now, fifteen hundred feet of linked PSP

about fifty feet wide. The plane was parked at the close end. It was a U-10. Next to it I could see lantern light gleaming through the windows of a guard shack.

'Sanya and Jillion will go straight for the plane,' I said. 'You and Delta take the guards. Leave the AK with me.'

Kam was fishtailing the car. 'Got to block road now,' he said.

'Okay,' I said. 'Do it.'

He cut the wheel, hit the brakes. I felt myself slam against the door, thought for an instant we were going to tip over. Then we were out, the four of them running towards the strip, me crouched behind the hood with the AK. The pursuing Jeep had closed to two hundred feet. I fired full automatic, letting the muzzle climb from radiator to windshield. The Jeep swerved, pitching into the undergrowth. Then there was another Jeep squealing to a stop behind the first and I could feel bullets begin to thud into the staff car and I felt the windshield shatter and then after what seemed a long while Kam and Delta were at my side, each now with an AK, firing steadily up the road.

'Guards think we okay Chinese,' Kam said. 'Not realize until too late. You go fly plane now, *Lōk*.'

I sprinted a hundred yards down the road and across the runway. The US markings had been painted out on the U-10. There was a red star and bar high on the rudder. Jillion and Sanya were already on board. I kicked away the chocks and climbed up the left strut to the pilot's position. Jillion was in the front passenger seat. Sanya sat behind her. The inside of the aeroplane was like that of a four-door passenger car except there was no door behind the pilot's bucket on the left side.

'Pull the hinge pins on that right-rear door,' I shouted. 'Get it out of the way for Delta and Kam.' Sanya moved to do that. The sound of rifle fire was steady from the road. Unlike Coyle's 727, the cockpit of the U-10 was

familiar to me. There wasn't going to be any time to warm up. I prayed the magnetos could handle the load.

I cracked the throttle with my right hand, slammed mixture and pitch control full forward, flipped on the master switch, turned on the boost pumps. With my left I moved the controls in all positions to make sure there were no locks, opened the cowl flap, reached overhead and cranked the wing flaps down, checked the trim neutral. I did these things simultaneously, both hands working. Nav and panel lights were off. I left them that way.

'Hurry,' Jillion said.

'I am, goddammit!'

I punched the starting button, let the three blades of the big Hartzell prop crank over, turned on the magneto switch. Nothing happened. Bullets had begun to whiffle the air around the plane. As far as I knew, we hadn't taken any hits. Jillion had been looking up the road to her right. Kam and Delta still hadn't appeared. Now she looked at me. 'What's wrong?'

'I don't know!'

'Can I help?'

'The son of a bitch won't fire!'

'It *sounds* like it's not getting any gas!'

I kept the engine cranking, left the mag switch on, opened the fuel valve. Jillion looked at me.

'All right!' I said. 'I forgot the fucking valve!'

Now we had to wait until the pumps pushed fuel to the cylinders. Bullets were skipping around the plane. I couldn't tell if the bad guys were aiming at us or if these were just strays from the firefight they were having with Delta and Kam. The engine coughed. The inertia whine of the starting motor was decreasing noticeably as the battery weakened under the long drain of current.

It seemed an age before the cylinders finally took hold, one after another, and the big prop began to spin faster. I eased the throttle full forward as quickly as I dared. The

engine backfired once and flame shot out from under the cowling. Then it settled into a steady wind-beating roar at 3100 rpm's.

'Here they come,' Jillion said.

I looked past her. Delta was limping across the runway towards the open door of the plane. Kam was kneeling and firing back towards the road, spent cartridges ejecting in a stream. I had the control column full back in my lap and the brakes pressed tight. The tail was bouncing up and down as the prop blast fought the control surfaces. Delta was battered by the wash as he climbed aboard, Sanya helping him in.

'Come on, brother!' I shouted to Kam. 'Let's roll!'

He was up and sprinting towards us, running in a zigzag pattern, and then seemed to hang motionless as if in stop time, and then he was throwing his AK to Delta and pulling himself up and in, as I released the brakes.

Under full power, the aeroplane shot forward. I tapped the right brake to counteract torque. We had a minimum power-on stall speed of twenty-six knots. I intended to be airborne at twenty-seven. Without lights, I had to go by feel. The second Jeep had made it around the staff car now. I could see the headlights racing towards us, and the muzzle flashes from an automatic rifle. Kam sat in our open doorway, feet braced against a strut, firing back as we gained speed.

Jillion shouted something. I couldn't hear what it was over the howl of the engine. She pointed to her right. I glimpsed the Jeep paralleling our takeoff run, a gunner crouched in the rear. Kam blew him away. The driver dropped back and swerved behind us. Then he was at my left, banging away with his sidearm. The Plexiglas shattered in front of me and the vision through my left eye was lost in a blur of blood.

Instinctively I pulled back on the controls. The aeroplane skipped once and we were airborne, but barely. A thousand feet ahead, more Jeeps had pulled on

to the runway. I could see their lights. I levelled off at ten feet to try to gain maneuvering speed. We were trapped in a canyon of palm trees sixty and seventy feet high.

'Pull up!' Jillion shouted. 'Pull up!'

One of the Jeeps at the far end opened up with tracers from a heavy machine gun. They looked like glowing red balls that seemed at the last moment to speed up and bend away to one side or above or below the plane. In seconds they would be in effective range.

'Jesus!' Jillion shouted.

'I need more air speed!' I yelled.

Then it felt right. I pulled back on the controls, rolled left, and chandelled away from the Jeeps, up and over the palms. It was a climbing left turn that took us out of the canyon and out of sight and range of the gunners below. I flattened out, all but brushing the trees, headed away from the strip. The last of the tracers arced harmlessly overhead.

'Is everybody okay back there?' I shouted. The wind was ripping my bad eye. The noise of the engine was terrific.

Kam stuck his head between Jillion's and mine. Even that close he had to raise his voice over the blast through the open door and shattered windscreen. 'Sanya okay!' he said. 'Delta, he take bullet through leg, be okay too!'

'Good!' I said. 'We'll have to head east for a while, then swing northwest. The seaport is loaded with antiaircraft.'

'What about fighters?' Jillion said.

'They don't have any,' I said. 'At least, I don't think they do.'

'Let's hope to bloody hell you're right!' she said.

'Roger that!' I said.

We skimmed low over outlying villages and a black hole of jungle until I figured it was okay to do so, and

226

then I turned towards the north and started to climb. I had the instrument lights on now. When we reached eight thousand, I levelled, put us on a heading of three-three-zero, and checked the gauges. The cylinder-head temperature was high, the right fuel tank low. I hadn't had time to check if the left and right tanks were balanced before we took off.

'Hand me the Aldis,' I said to Jillion. She gave me the lamp, and I shone it out my side of the aeroplane to look up under the wing. There were several holes in the flap panel, but no apparent fuel leaks.

'Anything wrong?' Jillion asked.

'I don't know,' I said. 'Try shining the light under the wing on your side.'

She did that, and even from where I sat the bright beam of the Aldis made the fuel spray from the holes in that wing look like escaping steam – a lot of steam, blowing back under the wing.

I checked the fuel gauges again. The needle on the right side gauge was close to zero.

Jillion was watching me. 'How much do we have?' she asked.

'Enough in the left-wing tank to make it,' I said. 'The right one will drain out. When it does, we'll be left-wing-heavy.' I checked the fuel-selector valve on 'Left,' pushed the mixture to full rich, and brought the throttle back in an attempt to lower the cylinder-head temperature. No dice. The temperature stayed up, and now the oil pressure was dropping.

'We must have taken a hit in the oil line too,' I said.

'Bad?'

'I don't know. If we lose it all, the engine's going to freeze up.'

'Can't you do something?'

'Sure,' I said. 'I can pray for some luck.'

I had the choice of throttling back and opening the cowl flaps to keep the temperature down or pushing to

max power in order to get as much distance and altitude as I could before the engine seized. Since the oil leak was a function of time, I chose the latter. I thought we should be over Adune's ranch in about thirty minutes. I pushed the throttle and pitch to maximum. We started to climb.

'Where do we land?' Jillion asked. Her hair was a damp tangle, her face so smudged with dirt I could barely make out her features in the soft light from the instrument panel. Behind me, Kam and Sanya were talking in Khmer.

'The closest place I know is the main strip at the Adune plantation,' I said. 'We'll radio in, once we're clear of Cambodia. Adune will have to have the Thai interceptors called off.'

Jillion smiled. Her teeth were white. 'There's no way you can keep *this* story off the wire,' she said.

'Don't forget our deal,' I said.

'That ambush at Trat and your little skirmish at sea will have been banner heads yesterday morning. If you think I'm going to get scooped on the rest, you're crackers!'

'You'll have to clear it with Campbell,' I said.

'You seem to forget,' she said, patting the pockets of her combat blouse. 'I'm holding all the cards. I've got the diamonds, *and* the pictures, *and* the pouch . . .'

'Better keep it quiet,' I said.

'Nuts to you,' she said. 'I'm going to write a book.'

'My eye's bleeding,' I said.

'Don't change the subject.'

'Take a look at it, will you?'

She picked up the Aldis lamp, switched it on. Her face gleamed like a jack-o'-lantern in its light.

'You've got some Plexiglas splinters,' she said. 'Want me to yank them out?'

'Yes.'

She began to pluck at my brow. Each time she did, it felt like a needle being drawn through the skin. My eye

228

blinked involuntarily and began to pour tears. I wiped the corner with my wrist. Blurry images swam into view. The blood had congealed in the wind.

'How about this for starters?' she said, her voice raised over the chaos of sound around us. '"According to unusually reliable sources, a clandestine raid on Cambodia last night was carried out ..."'

'Not unless you clear it with Campbell,' I said.

'Is he coming to Bangkok?'

'Five will get you ten he's already there,' I said.

We continued to fly through a smooth, clear night. Cylinder-head temperature in the red. Oil pressure dropping. Left wing heavy. As soon as we were out of Cambodia's air space, I made radio contact with Khao Wah, told them we were inbound with one wounded and some aircraft problems. They contacted the Adune plantation by land line and relayed that the strip by the main house would be lit up for us. Adune himself was going to alert the Thai air-defence command of our approximate position and flight path to Trat. He would tell them we were friendly and to keep their interceptors off. If anyone was wondering where we had picked up the plane, they didn't ask. When I had finished with the radio, I took the Aldis from Jillion again, tried to see if our tires had been punctured. I couldn't tell. Jillion sat now with her hands in her lap. No one was talking in the backseat.

There weren't many lights at Trat, but the curve of the harbour was unmistakable. North of the village, I could see Adune's strip, fully illuminated, like two small strings of diamonds laid side by side. I breathed a sigh of relief, gave myself an A in navigation, prepared to descend. I pulled the throttle back. The engine roar decreased by half, then there was a very loud double-banging sound, and the prop stopped dead. Cylinder temp pegged. Oil pressure zero.

I heard Jillion catch her breath. Kam was peering over my shoulder.

'It's okay,' I said. 'We're still over ten thousand feet. The runway is close. I can spiral down and dead-stick it in. We'll have to land a little faster than usual to offset the prop drag. But it shouldn't be any big sweat.'

'I tell others not to worry,' Kam said. 'We maybe sing song now.'

I let down at seventy knots, directly over the airfield in a descending left-hand turn. Wind noise through the struts and around the aeroplane hummed and whistled. The smell of burnt oil, which had been strong for a while, was cleared by the air rushing in the windscreen and out the open door. I told my backseaters to check their belts. Jillion told them to put their heads down on their knees and protect themselves with their arms just before we touched down. Nobody was singing any songs.

I turned to the right several times to get the feel of the heavy left wing, made one last turn directly over the middle of the strip, and entered my descending landing pattern.

'Geronimo,' I said.

'If God had meant for us to fly ...' Jillion said, sounding grim.

I rolled out on final at about three hundred feet, a half-mile from the runway, held my glide at sixty knots. I checked the ignition, fuel, and master battery switches off. I had plenty of altitude and air speed, so I skidded and slipped some to pass over the approach end of the runway at about ten feet. The left wing got heavier as I bled off the air speed. I knew the U-10 was a ground-looping whore who would never stand for a two-wheel landing. It would have to be three-point, with both mains and tail wheel simultaneously, in a full stall.

When we were a foot above the runway, I held it off, bringing the nose up, counteracting the heavy left wing. The air speed bled off quickly. The plane gave a little

sigh, sank the remaining inches, and touched down lightly, tail wheel first.

Perfect, I thought.

And then things turned to shit.

The minute the main gear touched the runway, the plane swerved left like a car in a skid on an icy road. I mashed the right rudder and brake as hard as I could, but it didn't help. The plane pivoted around the left tire. Centrifugal force threw the right wing down.

'Cover up!' I yelled as we skidded across the tarmac, right wing low, tires screeching like a banshee. I heard the right strut snap under the load, dropping the right wing to the ground. Then the plane slid sideways, jolting up and down like a jackhammer.

I heard one final sickening crash.

Then the whole runway seemed to fall on my head, and I was out.

# 31

When I came to, I was lying on my back in a large canopied bed. Jillion was standing beside me.

'God,' I said. 'I feel awful.'

'Drink this,' she said. She handed me a glass of brown liquid from a medical tray beside the bed. The liquid tasted vaguely of iodine. Gradually, things came into focus.

The room I was lying in was large: ten-foot molded ceiling; off-white walls; polished teakwood floors. One end of the room was open to the outdoors, screened by a mesh curtain. A soft, perfumy breeze was moving the curtain. Jillion had sat on the bed now, by my side. I blinked away the last of the fuzz and looked at her.

'Welcome back,' she said.

'Thanks,' I said.

She wore a fresh tiger suit. Her long, tawny hair was clean, her cheeks bright from having been scrubbed.

'You okay?' I said.

'Yes.'

'The others?'

'The others are fine too. Kam's with Delta at the infirmary . . .'

I tried to sit up, got dizzy. She eased me back.

'Take it easy,' she said.

'I need to find Campbell,' I said.

'He's already here. He flew in from Bangkok as soon as Adune called him about the crash. You've been out for a while.'

'Did you give him the pouch?' I asked.

She looked away. I sat up again.

'What happened?' I said.

'It's gone,' she said.

'What do you mean gone?' I said.

'Somebody must have taken it from me after we crashed – the pouch, the Polaroid backings, everything. I told Campbell as soon as he arrived. He's trying to track it down.'

I grabbed a fistful of sheet, felt a rush of impotent rage. 'Goddammit!' I shouted.

Jillion winced. 'Adune's men were all over the plane when it crashed,' she said. 'I had to help them get you out . . .'

'The hell with getting me out!' I said. 'The hell with that! The *pouch* was all that mattered!'

'Well, I *just* didn't happen to see it that way,' she said.

'You damn well should have!'

'Well, I *didn't*.'

I pointed a shaky finger at her. 'And that's *exactly* why they don't send women into combat!' I said. 'They're always sentimental at heart.'

'Oh, *stuff* it!' she said.

'Tell me I'm wrong!'

'I'll tell you what you are,' she said. 'You're an insufferable, egotistical, buggering *prick* of a man!'

I groaned and lay back. She stood by the bedside now, looking murderous, her hands clenched at her sides.

'Where's Campbell?' I said finally.

'I don't know,' she replied, clipping her words as she spoke.

'Sanya?'

'She was around for a while after we crashed. She had some scrapes and bruises. Nothing serious.'

I thought about that, my mind still muzzy.

'She didn't happen to help you get me out of the cockpit, did she?' I asked.

'Yes. She seemed even more worried about you than I was. I can't imagine why.'

'Swell,' I said.

'What do you mean, swell?' Jillion said.

'I mean I'll make book it was our Pearl of the Orient who walked off with that pouch.'

Jillion's eyes darkened towards a deeper brown. 'Damn!' she said.

'Sanya's a professional pickpocket, among other things,' I said. 'It was part of her act at the casino.'

'And she could easily have heard me blabbing to you about the pouch and the diamonds on the flight from Kampong Som. She was sitting right behind us . . .' Jillion trailed off, walked over to the mesh drapes, stared out at the night. 'I did muck things up, didn't I?' she said.

Campbell came in just then, his angular figure clothed in slacks and a safari shirt, his face drawn with fatigue, blue eyes intense. 'Good to see you, Matt,' he said. 'You've been through a rough time. Some of the reports I was getting had you written off.'

I shook his hand. 'We've all had a rough time,' I said.

'I checked in once before, but you hadn't come around. Are you feeling all right?'

'I'd feel a lot better if we hadn't lost the pouch,' I said.

'I've searched the U-10,' he said. 'The runway, the bush on either side. I've questioned the men who brought you in, and the servants who helped Jillion wash up. So far, I haven't come up with much.'

I told him my theory about Sanya. He listened carefully. 'You could be right,' he said. 'I know she's been with Adune since the crash. He's been orchestrating something. I can't get a handle on just what it is. I'm on my way to meet with him.'

'I'll go with you,' I said.

He looked at me evenly. 'No,' he said. 'We're in my area now. Your job is over.'

'Like hell it is. Not for as long as that pouch is missing.'

'I'm not asking you, Matt. I'm telling you. Until you hear otherwise from either me or Adune, *stay here.*'

And with that my father-in-law turned on his heel and went out the door.

'What do you make of it?' Jillion asked.

'I don't know,' I said.

'He was harsh. I've never heard him that way. Are you going to do what he says?'

'I don't know that either,' I said. 'Right now I'd like a shower and some clean clothes.'

'One of Adune's men brought some by for you: polo shirt, slacks, and a pair of sandals. I was going to tell you about them before you got nasty.'

She offered to help peel me out of my black pajamas. I told her I didn't need any help, but when I stood up, I started to wobble and had to hold on to her to keep from falling.

'I think I'm going to enjoy this,' she said.

'You would,' I said.

'I've never been this close to such an *evil*-smelling brute,' she said. 'I hope there's a wire brush in the bath.'

'Ouch,' I said.

The bath was the size of a country kitchen. The walls of the shower were made of a wood that smelled sweeter and sweeter the wetter it got. There were five adjustable nozzles. I stood under them, letting the steamy spray wash away my grease, burnt cork, sweat and grime. Jillion did most of the soaping.

'I'm sorry I got nasty,' I said, once I was dressed and back in the room.

'You're forgiven,' she said. 'Are we going to stay put, the way Campbell wants?'

'Yes. I don't know why he wants it that way, but I trust him. I just hope he doesn't keep us waiting too long.'

Forty minutes later, we were summoned by a servant to the private study of Mr Adune.

# 32

The study was located at the rear of the plantation house. The servant took us there. Two Thais, each armed with an automatic rifle, stood guard at the door. I had seen other guards patrolling the halls, more than seemed necessary for the occasion.

The room smelled of incense and was softly lighted. It took a minute for my eyes to adjust. A number of wing chairs had been placed in a semicircle facing a large teak minister's desk. The wing chairs were framed with mahogany and upholstered in gold velour. The desk had ivory inlays. Small oil lamps burned at each of its front corners.

Sanya Tohmi sat in one of the chairs closest to the desk. Mr Adune, wearing a vested grey suit, stood by her side as if to comfort her. Sanya still wore the blue gown she had worn in Kampong Som. One of the sleeves had been torn in the crash; two strips of fresh plaster covered a cut on her forehead. Her long black hair, roughly combed, gleamed in the lamplight. I thought her eyes looked puffy, as if she had been crying.

Campbell stood just outside the group of chairs. His demeanor had changed. I remembered seeing a UPI photo of him once, taken as he came out of the House of Representatives during the congressional hearings regarding the Allende affair in '73. His expression, then and now, was that of a man who has come to the end of a precarious negotiation. He acknowledged our presence with a brief nod.

'It is my pleasure to welcome you to this house,'

Adune said. 'I trust the hours you have spent here have been tranquil, and have afforded you an opportunity for meditation.' He motioned to the empty chairs, asked us to please sit down. His voice was soft and soothing. Here, in this dimly lighted room, he radiated a spirituality that reminded me of the first time I had seen him, aboard his boat on the Chao Phya, dressed in his saffron robes. Once we were seated, he took his own place behind his desk.

'During the hours since you have returned,' he said, 'I have spoken at length with Sanya Tohmi. As a result of our conversation, she has become enlightened, and wishes to follow the eightfold path, serving the servant of the Gautama. She has renounced her former ways.'

I shifted my weight in my chair, heard Campbell clear his throat.

'Sanya, as an emblem of her sincerity,' Adune continued, 'has placed into my hands all of her earthly possessions. These include the diamonds for which you all have risked so much, and the pouch with its variety of papers.'

Sanya bowed her head. It was impossible to tell whether or not her conversion was sincere, but it was easy enough to see why she had stolen the pouch from Jillion and had brought it to Mr Adune. She had landed here without a passport, money, or connections, had burned her bridges behind her. And she must have known that, next to the monarchy, Adune was one of the most powerful men in Thailand. As I thought about this, I heard Jillion, sitting to my right, mutter something that sounded unladylike.

'There is a story that Sanya has related to me, and to your esteemed father-in-law,' Adune concluded. 'And now, at his request and at my bidding, and with great reluctance, she will relate it to you.' He nodded at Sanya. She sat in the lamplight, as if on a small stage, her hands

folded on the lap of her gown. When she began to speak, she spoke softly.

'At the casino,' she said, 'the young German, Horst Von Regen, would come to gamble. In the beginning, he was courteous and gentlemanly. We would play chemin de fer. I would often win and he would often lose, but this seemed not to matter.

'He would come to the casino regularly every three or four months. We would play for a while and then he would invite me to dine with him in the hotel. After dinner, we would dance. He was an elegant dancer. Then we would retire to his room.

'And then two years ago he introduced me to an American, Dennis Capps. He and Capps had become friends through their business dealings at the port. Capps was a heavy drinker. He would arrange parties for the three of us. Horst would only drink when he was with this Capps, but then he would drink a great deal and would become abusive to me in the way of the Chinese.' She paused, hands trembling. I remembered her screams coming through the vent in the crawl space at the Sihanouk hotel.

'And the other man, Capps,' Adune said quietly. 'He would take photographs of this evil?'

'Yes. With a camera that would print its own film. It seemed to flatter Horst that Dennis would do this. When we were through, Horst would arrange the pictures on a table and would study them for a long time, and would require me to study them as well. Then he would destroy them by burning. He was always careful to do that, even when he was very drunk.'

'But one night, in his carelessness,' Adune said, 'he forgot to destroy the backings as well?'

'Yes. Dennis Capps picked these up and took them to his room. It was while Kampong Som was under siege. Horst, realizing now what had happened, demanded to have the backings returned. He was drunk, and terribly

239

afraid of the Khmer Rouge. He made a search of Dennis'
room. Dennis stood by. He was smiling. He said his
employer, Mr Coyle, would be pleased to have such
pictures of Horst. He said Horst had tried to cheat him
in their dealings with the brass, that certain percentages
of the shells had been omitted from the ships' manifests.
He said Horst had been a fool to try to deceive him.

'Horst became furious. He threatened Dennis with a
pistol. He ordered him to produce the backings at once.
Dennis refused. There was a burst of gunfire from
somewhere near the hotel. Horst seemed to become
crazed by the sound of it. He pointed the pistol at Dennis
and fired once. Then he ran from the room.'

Adune asked her if the shot had killed Capps.

'Yes,' she said. 'He died in my arms. It was later
thought he had been killed by the Khmer Rouge. I
believe I was spared by Horst only because of his panic
to leave the hotel.'

Things got quiet in the room once Sanya had finished
her story, so much so I thought I could hear the oil lamps
burning.

Finally Adune fixed his gaze on Jillion and me. 'As you
are aware,' he said, 'I have interests that are of long
standing with Mr Coyle and his enterprises. These I must
not jeopardize. Additionally, through my efforts, Thailand has engaged in a significant forestry project with the
Walramian Count Manfred Von Regen. This too I must
not jeopardize. It has been my wish from the start to
adjudicate the matter of the pouch with sensible regard
to these realities, and to the enlightened truths of the
Gautama.

'When Sanya described to me what the Polaroid
backings will reveal when printed, I knew they were an
abomination and felt it was my duty as a holy man to
destroy them. But your esteemed father-in-law, through
a long and patient dialogue, has persuaded me that were
I to destroy this lesser evil, I would allow a larger evil

240

to go unchecked: specifically, the impending election of Horst Von Regen to the post as chancellor of his country.

'This must not and will not happen. The count has been informed, and the count has agreed. I have assured him I will keep the photographs in one of my most secure vaults in Bangkok, where, I am confident, there will be no need for them ever again to see the light of the sun. I have also assured the count of Sanya's discretion. She is now a dedicated servant of the servant of Buddha, and will carry out this life according to the precepts of the Sermon of the Turning of the Wheel of the Law.'

Adune opened the centre drawer of his desk and took out the four velvet sacks of diamonds that had been in the pouch. As he placed them in front of him, I could hear the lush clicking sounds they made.

'As for this treasure,' he said, looking at me, 'I am happy to return it to you, so you may return it to your employer, Mr Coyle.'

'Thank you,' I said. 'My father-in-law will take care of that. He'll know how to handle the details of getting the diamonds into the country.'

Adune bowed slightly. Then his voice took on a crispness as he looked at Jillion. 'The story you file with your wire service must contain no names except for mine,' he said. 'You will report that mercenaries raided my property out of revenge for the efforts I have made to end their drug trafficking in the Thai segment of the Golden Triangle. You will say they escaped by stealing one of my boats, which was later intercepted and blown up by a Khmer maritime patrol.'

Jillion had raised her brows. 'With all respect to you,' she said, 'I am a reporter. I have an obligation to tell the truth.'

'You also have an obligation to Campbell,' I reminded her.

'All right,' she said, looking his way. 'Let him set the rules.'

He got up from his seat and towered over us. 'If anything goes on the wire service,' he replied, 'it goes exactly the way Mr Adune has said.'

When the meeting was over and the three of us were walking down the corridor to my room, Jillion began to press Campbell about his decision to clamp a lid on her story.

'What's Adune trying to do?' she said. 'Protect Von Regen?'

'As he told you,' Campbell said, 'he has legitimate dealings with the count.'

'Then how do we know for sure—?'

'Leave it alone,' Campbell snapped. 'Just leave it alone.'

# 33

An hour later I sat in the radio room at the big house on Adune's plantation. The room was small but well-equipped. One of Adune's men was working a Collins KWM-2A high-frequency voice transceiver. He had the switch in the upper sideband mode. Connected to it was a D-11 scramble box.

'I have raised White Oaks,' Adune's man said. 'The scrambler is engaged. You will please call me if there is any problem. I will be just outside.'

The radio hookup was not simultaneous. Coyle and I had to work it back and forth. We sounded as if we were talking in a barrel. Our voices echoed. There were times when he faded away, times when he sounded strong.

'Did you get the package?' he said.

'We got it,' I said.

'No problems?'

I ignored the question. 'You lied to me,' I said.

'Yes. About the rubber. It was a policy decision, nothing more. I was afraid if I told you about the brass, your scruples might interfere. Believe me when I say that was all there was to it. There was nothing personal.'

'I want some more money for Kam,' I said. 'He's earned it.'

'Of course.'

'He might decide he wants to stay here. He's not that hot for Texas. If he does, I want you to put in a word for him with Adune. He'll need a job.'

'I'll see to it.'

I could hear the impatience in Coyle's voice. I knew

he didn't want to talk about Kam or anything else, except for the pouch and its incriminating papers.

So I strung him along. 'I had to leave a Chinese boy tied up in a closet at the Dusithani,' I said. 'Your man Jassick had hired him to tail us from the airport.'

'We've already dealt with that matter. Jassick was here on a false passport. He's been picked up for that, and arraigned on wiretap charges. I'd like to hear you tell me about the diamonds,' he said.

'Campbell's got them,' I said. 'He'll take care of the delivery.'

'And the papers?'

'Mr Adune's going to squirrel those away,' I said. 'In a place where they should never see the light of the sun.'

From the other end of the scramble line there was a prolonged silence.

'He's one smart Thai,' I said. 'If I were you, I'd follow his example: take a good long hike on the eightfold path.'

When I had finished with Coyle, I called the Franki Clinic and finally got Whiskey on the phone.

'You get out okay?' she said.

'Yes,' I said. 'I got out fine.'

'The kid's doing great,' she said. 'We got some hand response today.'

'God,' I said. 'That's outstanding.'

'Dr Franki's with him now.'

'Does he think ... I mean, does he think ...?'

'Yeah,' she said happily. 'He does.'

By the time I was able to respond to that, Whiskey had turned the phone over to Maul. 'Eberhart?' he growled.

'Right here,' I said.

'As soon as you get your butt over here, me and that

nurse are going to spring for some schnitzel at the local rat cellar.'

I laughed.

'I'll buy the beer,' I said.

'Negative,' Maul said.


Later, I sat on the veranda of the big house with Campbell and Jillion and Kam. The night was warm, starry. Campbell and Jillion and I were sipping cognac. Kam was drinking tea.

'I see Charlie in infirmary,' Kam said. 'He say tapeworm gone, okay now.'

'Good,' I said.

'We have big party tomorrow.' Kam said. 'Too much tired now. Delta already sleeps.'

'As for the rest of us,' Jillion said, 'we never say die.' She raised her glass. I touched it with mine. Kam raised his mug of tea.

Campbell did not join our toast. He seemed preoccupied. Beyond a grove of palms behind the house, we could hear the muted, well-muffled cough of an aircraft's engines purring into life. I could tell by the sound as they revved up it wasn't Adune's Islander, but some other light, powerful twin.

'We should pick it up,' I said. 'Once it clears the trees.'

Campbell was silent. When the plane appeared, climbing fast into the northwest, its navigation lights winking red and green, I heard him swear softly, once, under his breath.

'He was here, wasn't he?' I said.

'Yes,' Campbell said.

Jillion looked at him.

'The count?' she said.

'Yes.'

'And you let him get away?'

Campbell stood up abruptly and stared down at her.

245

'My dear lady,' he said, 'there was nothing I could do. It was Adune's show. The count was a guest in Adune's house. He had come yesterday to try to persuade Adune to intervene on his behalf once you arrived with the pouch.'

I felt my jaws get tight. 'If I'd known he was here,' I said, 'I'd have damn well done something.'

'And that's exactly why I couldn't let you know,' Campbell said. 'It was delicate, right to the end. I've been in this business most of my life. Things seldom work out in black or white. There's usually a lot of grey.'

He bade us good night then and walked away. We were silent for a long time after he left.

'Well,' I said finally. 'Let's drink to the grey areas.'

Jillion cocked her head, then raised her glass.

Kam watched us. I don't know how much of our conversation he had understood. His eyes were darker than the night surrounding us.

'I will have cognac now,' he said. 'I do believe.'

# THE RED DOVE

## Derek Lambert

As the Soviet space-shuttle *Dove* orbits 150 miles above the earth on its maiden flight, Warsaw Pact troops crash into Poland. What is the deadly connection between the soaring bird and the shattering fist?

The seventy-two-year-old President of America wants to be re-elected, and for that he needs a spectacular. He needs to win the first stage of the war in space: he needs to capture the Soviet space shuttle. But as the President plans his coup a nuclear-armed shuttle speeds towards target America — and only defection in space can stop it!

ADVENTURE THRILLER   0 7221 5348 1   £1.95

Also by Derek Lambert:
I, SAID THE SPY
TRANCE
available in Sphere paperback.

# Tiger Hunt!
# JADE TIGER
## Craig Thomas

The bait: a defecting Chinese agent selling secrets.
The trail: every bolt-hole and hide-out from Hong
Kong to Berlin.
The quarry: JADE TIGER
JADE TIGER, the thrilling new masterpiece from
Craig Thomas, finds espionage veteran Kenneth
Aubrey facing his toughest assignment yet. In six
months he could crack the Chinese defector. But he
doesn't have months, he has weeks. Two weeks
before the Berlin Wall is bulldozed into history. Two
weeks to discover the truth behind the network of
misinformation coming his way . . .
JADE TIGER is the story of a race against time, a
chase across three continents. Ranging from the
heart of Communist China to the Australian
Outback. JADE TIGER is classic thriller writing of
the highest order.

**ADVENTURE/THRILLER**      0 7221 8451 4      £2.25

Don't miss Craig Thomas' other bestsellers:
FIREFOX
SNOW FALCON
RAT TRAP
WOLFSBANE
SEA LEOPARD
also available in Sphere books.

# CLIVE CUSSLER

# PACIFIC VORTEX!

Fully armed and with all hands on board, the nuclear submarine *Starbuck* sailed into the calm Pacific Ocean for sea trials — and vanished. No wreckage, no signals, no survivors — nothing, until ace maritime troubleshooter Dirk Pitt finds a single, chilling clue in the shark-torn surf off Hawaii — the log of the *Starbuck*. 'Do not search for us, it can only end in vain . . .' A crazed journal of madness and death is all that remains.

The search for the *Starbuck* plunges Dirk Pitt into his most shattering assignment yet — a whirlpool of deep-sea mystery and terror.

ADVENTURE/THRILLER          0 7221 2753 7          £1.95

And, don't miss Clive Cussler's other thrillers, also available in Sphere paperback:

**MAYDAY!**
**NIGHT PROBE!**
**VIXEN 03**
**ICEBERG**
**RAISE THE TITANIC!**

A selection of bestsellers from SPHERE

**FICTION**

| | | |
|---|---|---|
| THE RED DOVE | Derek Lambert | £1.95 ☐ |
| DOMINA | Barbara Wood | £2.50 ☐ |
| A PERFECT STRANGER | Danielle Steel | £1.75 ☐ |
| MISSING PERSONS | C. Terry Cline Jr. | £1.95 ☐ |
| BAD BET | Roger Longrigg | £1.95 ☐ |

**FILM & TV TIE-INS**

| | | |
|---|---|---|
| BY THE SWORD DIVIDED | Mollie Hardwick | £1.75 ☐ |
| YELLOWBEARD | Graham Chapman and David Sherlock | £2.50 ☐ |
| STAR WARS | George Lucas | £1.75 ☐ |
| THE YEAR OF LIVING DANGEROUSLY | C. J. Koch | £1.75 ☐ |

**NON-FICTION**

| | | |
|---|---|---|
| THE FINAL DECADE | Christopher Lee | £2.50 ☐ |
| THE DOCTOR WHO TECHNICAL MANUAL | Mark Harris | £2.50 ☐ |
| A QUESTION OF BALANCE | H.R.H. The Duke of Edinburgh | £1.50 ☐ |
| SUSAN'S STORY | Susan Hampshire | £1.75 ☐ |

*All Sphere books are available at your local bookshop or newsagent, or can be ordered direct from the publisher. Just tick the titles you want and fill in the form below.*

Name _____

Address _____

_____

Write to Sphere Books, Cash Sales Department, P.O. Box 11, Falmouth, Cornwall TR10 9EN

Please enclose a cheque or postal order to the value of the cover price plus:

UK: 45p for the first book, 20p for the second book and 14p for each additional book ordered to a maximum charge of £1.63.

OVERSEAS: 75p for the first book and 21p per copy for each additional book.

BFPO & EIRE: 45p for the first book, 20p for the second book plus 14p per copy for the next 7 books, thereafter 8p per book.

*Sphere Books reserve the right to show new retail prices on covers which may differ from those previously advertised in the text or elsewhere, and to increase postal rates in accordance with the PO.*